THE FIVE BARRED GATE II

also by

Jeff S. Bray

The Little Reminders Series
Little Reminders of Who I Am
Little Reminders of Who I Was
Littler Reminders of Who I Will Become

The Five Barred Gate Series
The Five Barred Gate
The Five Barred Gate II

The Transference

THE FIVE BARRED GATE

JEFF S. BRAY

WordCrafts Press

The Five Barred Gate II
Copyright © 2025
Jeff S. Bray

Hardback ISBN: 978-1-962218-94-8
Paperback ISBN: 978-1-962218-95-5

Cover concept & design by David Warren

Published by WordCrafts Press
Cody, Wyoming 82414
www.wordcrafts.net

Dedication

To those who want to be the change and stand strong in
whatever adversity they face.
God bless!

| |

"Can you say that again?" Michael said, almost dropping the phone.

The monotone voice on the line was unmistakable. He never believed he'd be on the receiving end of one of these calls. It was a courthouse liaison known for making these types of notifications.

"Again, Mr. Andrews, we have your wife, Rachel Elise Andrews, aka Rachel Elise Dunham, in custody."

"On what charge?"

"She was arrested by Official Jaspar Aachen on the charge of solicitation. A violation of Subsection 12 of JSI2399 of the Federal Speech Act."

"Federal Speech A— What was she doing?" Michael asked. Rachel had gone to the grocery store, not to a political rally.

"I am not at liberty to say, Mr. Andrews. She is being processed as we speak. This phone call is a courtesy as required by law. You have the option to seek outside representation or to have the court appoint your spouse an attorney. Mrs. Andrews has also been advised of her rights. Do you have any questions for me?"

"When can I see her?"

"As I stated, she is being processed as we speak. She will then be taken to the courthouse, where she will be given an opportunity to plead. Those proceedings are closed door. She will be given the option of a court-appointed attorney or to notify the judge of representation. This is part of the point of my call. To inquire if she has representation. I can then pass this information to our judge, and we can proceed from there."

"Yes, I will have an attorney for her. When can I see her?" Michael asked again, more firmly.

"If you retain a licensed attorney meeting JSI-2399 standards, he will need to submit his request to the court at the hearing. If the judge approves, he will be permitted to represent your wife."

"And if not?"

"Then she will be appointed one by the state at your cost," the stern voice informed him.

"And until then?"

"Your wife will remain in county custody until the hearing tomorrow."

"Can I see her?"

"After the hearing in the morning, sir."

"Can I call someone to speak to her at least?"

"Again, Mr. Andrews, after the hearing in the morning," the voice did not break the monotone cadence. There was no remorse or concern. There would be no getting through.

"Do you have information on what time her hearing will be?"

"The courthouse opens at 8:30 AM. The docket will be printed and on display. Understand that no firearms, drug paraphernalia, or recording devices, including cellphones, are allowed within the courtrooms."

Michael rolled his eyes, "Yes, thank you. I will leave my arsenal at home." He hung up the phone and sat in his recliner. He could feel his heart beating between his ears. *What in the world is going on?* It was a good thing that...

Michael pulled out his phone, flipped a couple of screens, and pressed on the face of a smiling older gentleman. The phone rang three times, and the voice associated with the face answered.

"Michael, what can I do for you, son? These kiddos are giving their grandad a run for his money."

"I bet they are, Frank. One just feeds off of the other. It's like they have it all planned out."

"I'm sure they do. Rachel should be here before long. You lookin' for her?"

"Actually. No. She is the reason why I'm calling."

"What's happened?" Frank's tone changed. Michael could hear him shooing kids away in the background.

"I was hoping you knew. All I got was a notification from the county booking office. Rachel has been arrested."

"On what charges," Frank Dunham said with the same questioning tone he had given the clerk.

"They said something about soliciting and violating Federal Speech Act laws."

"That usually means she was saying things she oughtn't."

"Saying things? Like what?" Michael asked. He couldn't think of what Rachel could say that would get her arrested. Much less at the grocery store. Was she complaining about the price of cereal or that the tomatoes weren't red enough?

"Dunno. The only real things that could get someone in that much trouble would be speaking against someone in office or talking about God, and the person hearin' it didn't like it. All it takes is a phone call now, or an Official heard it firsthand, and that'd do her in."

"I don't know. I don't see Rachel doing that," Michael said, shaking his head. He never knew his wife to be outspoken when it came to politics or religion.

"Just givin' ya reasons," Frank said. "But we would both agree that she didn't go pickin' a fight."

"Agreed. That isn't Rachel."

"Not my granddaughter in the least," Frank said with an exhalation. "Let me call a buddy or two and see what I can find out. I'll get back to you if I find out anything."

"Thanks, Frank," Michael said. He knew Rachel's grandfather was connected with law enforcement and would call up the chain to find out what exactly happened. He made arrangements to pick up the kids and ended the call.

Michael sat and ran his fingers through his hair. He looked up at the clock, giving himself an hour to get ready to pick up Angie and Aiden. Not that they would mind him being a bit late. They enjoyed being at the ranch. Running around with chickens and horses was every four-year-old's dream, and Great-Grandpa was never far behind, even in his eighties.

Frank Dunham had lost his first wife, Eleanore, before Michael was born. Michael remembers growing up with Margaret, his second wife, but everyone called her Maggie. She was a waitress at the local diner. She, too, had lost her spouse. Michael's dad had conducted the funeral. That service was one of his first memories when he was four.

Frank had been instrumental in comforting Maggie through her loss. Then, as they put it, 'God had plans' for them—they were married a year later. Rachel had been the flower girl. She, too, had shared in the pleasure of running around the Dunham farm. Now, *their* kids, Frank's great-grandkids, were experiencing that same joy.

After a quick shower, Michael called his grandfather-in-law back, but he had yet to hear anything from anyone. With how Officials held everything tight to the vest, it was doubtful they would get any information until the hearing; it had always been that way. Frank's contact had been retired for twelve years, but he still had pull. He even said there was a required separation of branches between Official and local Law Enforcement. No one could explain the reason; it just existed.

"Well, thanks for trying," Michael said, looking at his watch, hoping that Rachel would be given something to eat. "I am headed your way now for the kids. I just have one phone call to make."

"We'll have supper waiting," Frank said.

Michael searched his through his junk drawer for a card that he knew was there. He had pushed it aside a thousand times. One of those items he could never bring himself to toss. He finally found it under a book of matches that was so old the would probably never strike.

Johnathan Clarke – Attorney at Law

He dialed the number, and a humbled voice answered on the second ring.

"Good afternoon, this is Johnathan Clarke. How can I help you?"

"Mr. Clarke. This is Michael Andrews. Jacob's son."

"Yes, Michael. I remember you. How are you? How are Rachel and the kids?"

"Not good, Mr. Clarke. I need your help. Rachael has been arrested."

✝✝✝

Neither Angie nor Aiden asked about Mommy when Michael arrived or during suppertime. They ate as a family and talked about feeding lambs and that Aiden could run faster than one of the chickens. The questions came when they loaded into the Suburban, and the lingering smell of Mom's perfume hit the three of them.

"Where's Mommy, Daddy?" Angie asked first. "She said she was gonna pick us up."

"Yeah, she said she would have a surprise," Aiden followed.

"Mommy has a few things she needs to do before she comes home. She asked me to pick you up and take you home." He hated to lie, but what could he do?

"Can we get some ice cream?" Aiden asked, the surprise still in the forefront of his mind. Angie echoed the sentiment. It was for the best. He should be grateful that children are often unaware of how complex life can be. It took him back to the stories of when he was young. He was told that his parents nearly divorced when he was two years old, but that certain life events brought them back together. He had no memories of the incidents that surrounded that timeframe. He now wished he had asked his dad about it.

His little ones will soon not settle for, *Mom is doing a few things.*

"Sure, why not? Double scoops for everyone," Michael said, turning down the road leading to the ice cream parlor.

"Make mine a triple," said Aiden. "I am almost five. I can take it now."

"Hey," Angie reached across the back seat and whacked her brother, "I'm almost five too, silly-head."

"Dad! Angie hit me."

"Oh, come on now, you two. She was just playing, Aiden. And Angela, you don't need to be hitting your brother."

A duet of *okays* sang from the backseat.

Michael pulled into the Dairy Queen, and the family went inside and ordered, settling on double scoops all around.

"Should we order for Mommy?" Angie asked.

"No, Mommy won't be here with us. We'll see her later," Michael answered, feeling the stress in his voice becoming more evident. He knew he had to come up with something because soon, the children would realize that Rachel wasn't coming home tonight. He had to buy some time because he already knew it would be at least until the morning.

Angie accepted his answer and scooped into her double chocolate bowl with whipped cream, syrup, and two cherries. Aiden's was strawberry and vanilla ice cream with a strawberry topping and whipped cream. Forgotten was the punch in the car, and it was replaced with a *taste mine* challenge. They both agreed the other's was good but still felt they had the better deal. Even Dad got to sample each on top of his chocolate-strawberry combo with chocolate syrup and whipped cream, taking bites in between glances at his phone.

By the time the bowls were empty, and both faces and clothing were chocolate-covered, Michael had come up with a plan. Get the kids home, and when Mom wasn't there waiting for them, he'd call Frank for a check-in. He would then tell the kids that she went over there, forgetting that she had asked Daddy to pick them up. Then they invited her to eat dinner. After she ate, she got so sleepy that she didn't want to drive anymore and decided to have a sleepover at Grandpa Frank's house.

Later, when Michael had the kids home and was helping them clean up, he told the kids his well-laid-out plan.

"Oooohh," Angie said. "Can we go have a sleepover with Mommy?"

Michael could only laugh, "No, sweetie. We need to stay here. It's bedtime, and Mommy is already asleep. She was tired."

"Ohh, alright," she said, pulling her pajama top over her head. Michael kissed her on her now clean forehead, tucked her into bed, and headed to Aiden's room.

"You okay, buddy?" Aiden was already in bed.

"Yep," Aiden said, then sat up. "Daddy? Can we pray for Mommy?"

Michael was startled the request came from his four-year-old son. He was a bit nervous because he wasn't sure what he would say. He hadn't prayed in quite a long time.

"Sure, Aiden. We can pray for Mom," Michael said, sitting on the side of his bed.

The second Michael's eyes were closed, Aiden began to pray, "Dear Jesus, please be with Mommy right now. Please help her to sleep good and don't let her be sad. Amen."

After his *Amen*, Aiden laid back down in his bed, "Thank you, Daddy. I feel better now. Good night."

Michael turned his son's light out. He wasn't sure where the prayer came from. He knew it wasn't from anything he had taught him. He didn't pray. Was it something Rachel had been teaching the kids? Whatever it was, it had helped comfort the boy.

And to be honest, he felt much better, too.

‖

"Next case on the docket, County vs. Andrews. Two counts of soliciting an undercover Official, agent of the state. One count of violating subsection 12 of JSI2399 and one count of violating ADA Title VI."

"Thank you, bailiff," the judge said. Then, reviewing her notes, "These charges state you were openly attempting to coerce an innocent bystander to acquiesce to your religious views. Is this accurate, Mrs. Andrews?"

"Pardon me, your honor. Sorry, Johnathan Clarke, for the defense." Rachel Andrews' attorney stood as he answered. He lifted a file folder toward the bailiff, who approached him, delivering it to the judge. "I am submitting my qualifications as stipulated. You should find my standing above reproach. I am here to represent Mrs. Andrews in this case."

The judge flipped through the folder handed to her. She nodded with an approving pout. "You have excellent credentials, Counselor. I will grant your motion. You may represent Mrs. Andrews."

"Thank you, Your Honor," Clarke said with a nod to Rachel. "I would like to begin with a formal request to dismiss this case. "

"And your reasons," the judge countered.

"This is Mrs. Andrews' first offense. She is a model citizen, and these laws are vague when they concern the matter of faith. The discussion she engaged in was a mutual, private conversation. If anything, *we* should be filing charges against the filing party for invasion of privacy."

"Counselor. If you examine the documents closely, you will find that the charges are filed *by* the party she was having the discussion with."

"Pardon?" the attorney reexamined the documents he had. The names were there, but it did not mention who filed the complaint by name.

"Page twelve. Paragraph four, Mr. Clarke."

Clarke thumbed through his file. "Nine, ten, eleven… Your Honor, my documents do not contain a page twelve."

"I am not sure what to tell you. Your office must be lacking in its ability to file correctly. Are you sure you can handle your client's defense, Counselor?"

"I'm quite sure, Madame Judge. I am not in the habit of losing critical documentation," the attorney said in a firm but respectful tone.

The judge exchanged glances with him and his client. "It doesn't change the facts. This case was brought against Mrs. Andrews by the party she was harassing. The charges will stand, and she will face her accuser. As for the law and its ambiguity, that is a matter for trial. You can argue your case, and the jury can make that decision."

"A jury trial, Your Honor? For two counts of solicitation?"

"You are forgetting the count regarding the Anti-Dehumanization Act of 2015. Dr. Houston's rights were violated when Mrs. Andrews approached her and verbally berated her. It is within her rights to request a trial by jury. And so, she has requested." The judge turned her attention toward Rachel. "Mrs. Andrews. Did you or did you not ask Dr. Houston if she was a Christian?"

Johnathan answered quickly, placing his hand on Rachel's shoulder, "Don't answer that, Rachel. It's a trap."

Rachel had been sitting quietly. She looked up at Johnathan, who shook his head, "Don't say a word," he said in a near whisper. "We'll talk later."

He turned back to the judge. "Your Honor. We are not at trial.

This is only the representation phase to show Mrs. Andrews has an attorney on record and to present the charges against her. Just as you will not allow me to question her accuser, I ask that you do not question my client until trial. I can now see we have no other option but to proceed to trial."

The judge glared at the attorney who dared challenge her in her courtroom. But Johnathan knew he was in the right. And he knew she could do nothing because just as any foul-up he made could get him thrown off the case, any chance of her showing prosecutor favoritism would give him grounds for a mistrial.

"Counselor. How long will you need to prepare for trial?" the judge's tone floated on air.

"Since I have a weekend to prepare, I can be ready Monday morning, Your Honor."

"We will commence with this case Monday morning at nine AM. Be ready, Counselor." The judge slammed her gavel with a force that resonated through Johnathan's spine and made Rachel jump. The judge rose and exited to her chambers.

Johnathan turned to Rachel, still in a whisper, "You, okay?"

"I'm not sure. I guess I'm still a bit in shock."

"I will meet you in the back office so we can talk more," Johnathan said, placing his paperwork in his leather briefcase and standing. The bailiff took Rachel by the elbow, leading her through a side door and out of sight.

✝✝✝

Michael saw Johnathan push through the swinging doors of the courtroom. He had been sitting on a bench, his head between his knees, waiting for news about his wife. The break in the silence startled him. He was at the attorney's side after a couple of steps.

"What happened in there?"

"Nothing, Mr. Andrews. As I said before I went in, this was just a preliminary hearing. The charges were brought against her, and a trial date was set."

"Her trial? I thought you—"

"Mr. Andrews," the attorney began, "believe me, I tried. But the prosecutor already explained his client wants to go to trial. The charges against your wife pretty much state it will go to a jury trial anyhow. It's gray, but to argue would've been futile. The laws that exist now side with the faulted party—you, above everyone, should understand this."

Michael shook his head. Anytime federal laws were mentioned, everyone seemed to remind him of what his family has been through. Even after more than twenty years, it was still a weight he had to bear—although he was only two years old when the events that created that weight occurred, and he had no memory of what transpired. How was he supposed to deal with that?

"Did they say anything about the charges? What was she arrested for?"

The attorney stopped walking; his head cocked to the side. "They didn't mention the details of what happened, but the judge did question Rachel about asking someone about God."

"Asking someone about God? Are you serious?"

"That's what the judge said, or rather asked Rachel. I told her not to answer. The judge isn't supposed to ask those types of questions at a preliminary hearing. His job is just to determine if there is enough evidence to move forward with the charges. Another reason why I felt it was best to go straight to trial. It just didn't feel right in there."

"Where are you going now?" Michael asked.

"To see Rachel. You can join me if you behave yourself." Johnathan eyed Michael. "They have rules, Mr. Andrews. You are to stay ten feet away from her—no hugs or kisses; no touching. You cannot pass her anything, not even a glance or blink—no coded messages. If you violate these rules, they will ban you from future visits, or worse, I could be removed from representing her. So don't break the rules, got it?"

"Got it," Michael said as they rounded a corner.

Johnathan knocked on the door, and a man in uniform answered and gave both of them a once-over. When he seemed satisfied, he let them through the door.

"I'll need to frisk both of you," he said.

Michael and Johnathan submitted to the search, and after a couple of minor personal space violations, the bailiff grunted his approval. "Mrs. Andrews will be brought to you shortly," he said, then turned to Michael. "You know the rules about fraternization, correct? You can look but don't touch. Ten feet, or you're out of here."

"Understood," Michael said with raised hands.

"Alright. I will be back with the accused," he said and left the room.

"Did he have to say it like that? *The accused?*" Michael snapped under his breath.

"Relax. He's just trying to get under your skin. They all are," Johnathan answered. "Sit back and say as little as possible. Remember, remain seated when he brings her in. Even if she approaches you, don't react if he restrains her. Overreaction will get you kicked out of here fast."

"Why are you telling me all of this?" Michael asked.

"Because I don't want you to get barred from seeing your wife. I've seen it too many times. One slip-up and you're done. So please listen to me. You'll thank me later."

"Okay. I just hope they are giving her the same lecture. Because I'm sure she will wonder why I won't hold her."

"You can explain. Or I can if you'd like me to, if that's easier. We'll play it by ear when she arrives. Just relax. We'll have this case wrapped up before you know it, and Rachel will be home with you and your kids soon." Johnathan grinned and turned back to his paperwork.

The sound of approaching footfalls tapped then stopped at the door. The knob turned, and Rachel, now in an olive jumpsuit, entered the room, her makeup smeared around her eyes. The bailiff held her by the arm and directed her to a chair across from them.

He rearranged the cuffs from behind her back to a clip attached to the table. Then, he stood at ease in the corner.

Michael wanted to reach out and hold her but remained where he was. "How are you?"

Rachel sniffed, "Okay, I suppose. How are the kids? Are they with Pop?"

"Yeah. Don't worry. They don't have a clue what's going on. I told them you had a sleepover at Grandpa's." Michael tried to laugh a little to ease the tension. Rachel smiled, but that was about all the emotion she showed.

"Thank you," Rachel wiped her eyes. The cuff chain was just long enough to allow her to raise her arms that far. She looked to the ceiling, then back to him. "I'm sorry. I shouldn't have been so careless."

"For what?"

"Talking to people."

Michael nodded.

"That's enough, Rachel," Johnathan said. "If you start acting guilty, they will treat you as guilty. Don't give in to their pressure. Stand firm."

Rachel nodded, wiping her eyes again.

"He's right, Rache. Stay strong. We are here for you. Mr. Andrews is here to see that you are treated fairly and that you get out of here as soon as possible."

Johnathan pulled out a yellow legal pad and a pen from his jacket pocket. "Okay, Rachel. I need you to take me through your day. From the time you woke up until you were brought into the courtroom to see the judge. Don't leave out any details. What did you do? Who did you see? What did you say? What was said to you?"

Rachel recited her account of the day beginning with seeing Michael off to work that morning. She gave Johnathan times and details Michael had forgotten, like the color of the shirt he had been wearing. She mentioned their disagreement about what time he would pick up the kids, which turned Michael a couple of shades of embarrassed pink. She proceeded through her day with various errands and then to the grocery store.

She took a deep breath and slowed her pace. "I don't know what it was. But I kept passing a woman in the store. Nearly every aisle we would cross paths."

"Wouldn't that be a common occurrence in a grocery store?" Johnathan said. "When I'm grocery shopping I frequently see the same people as our patterns match up."

"Yeah, but this was different. It's hard to explain. I began to feel like I should talk to her."

"What made you feel that way? Do you know her? Had you seen her before that gave you some familiarity?"

"No, not at all," Rachel said, shaking her head. "I had never seen her before."

"But you had the urge to speak to her?" Johnathan said, writing on his pad.

Rachel nodded, "An overwhelming urge. I finally figured maybe God wanted me to talk to her or say something to her."

"God *wanted* you to talk to her?"

"Yeah. It was the only reasonable explanation I could think of," Rachel shrugged. "She hadn't given me any reason to believe she was looking to speak to me. I know I didn't know her."

"Are you sure?"

Rachel's eyebrows furrowed. "I don't think so. Why?"

"Just asking," Johnathan wrote. "Continue."

"We crossed paths again in the produce section and made eye contact. That's when she smiled at me. I figured that was my opening. I figured, there is no better place to strike up a conversation with a stranger than in the produce aisle. We were near the onions, and she had placed both sweet yellow and white in her basket. So, I asked her about the difference."

"But you know the difference," Michael said.

"I know that. But she didn't. It was a conversation starter," Rachel explained.

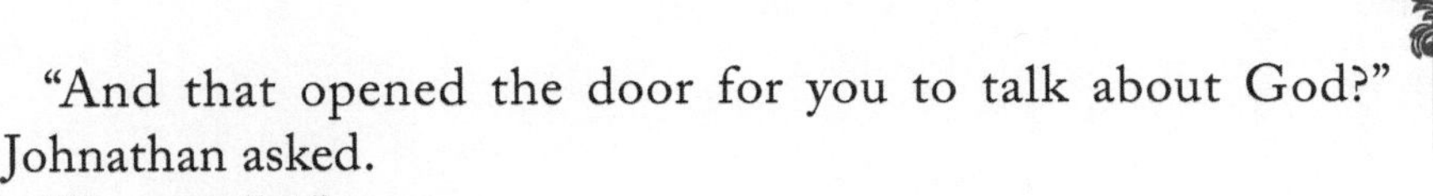

"And that opened the door for you to talk about God?" Johnathan asked.

"Eventually?"

"How did that work?"

"We first talked about food. Then, cooking and cooking times. That led to who for. It turned out she was new to the area. That's when I felt led to ask her if she had been able to find a local church."

"You know that's close to going too far, right?" Johnathan asked. "There are laws."

"I know. But I didn't ask her if she believed in God. I just asked about church. That didn't step over any lines or laws."

"You certainly toed it, though. And if someone were an atheist, they could very well take offense to even the mention of *church*."

"Yeah. I suppose. But the truth is. It's what I felt led to do. And I would do it all over again," Rachel said with a smile, tears nowhere near her face.

"How did she handle you asking her about church?" Johnathan continued.

"She thanked me and said she would consider it. Then we ended our conversation. She went to find tomatoes. I headed for the cashier."

"Mrs. Andrews, did Dr. Houston at any point give you any indication that you upset her with your words? Did she frown, growl, snarl, smirk, squint, throw a turnip, or say anything that would give you the inclination she disapproved of your conversation that day?"

"None whatsoever."

"Hmm," Johnathan scribbled on his pad, then looked up. "We may be in a good position here, Mr. and Mrs. Andrews. I don't see any laws broken. If the encounter went as you say, there shouldn't be any reason we couldn't settle out of court. I will speak with opposing counsel and see if we can work something out."

$$|||$$

"You're joking, right?" prosecuting attorney Xavier Ford said, leaning back in his chair. "A slap on the wrist?"

"Who has she hurt here? What real law has she broken, Xavier?" Johnathan said.

"Federal law, John. You're lucky we are still sitting in County courts."

"For asking a woman to church?"

"Precisely. My client is an atheist. She was offended by your clients' forward remarks."

"She was attempting to be friendly."

"To Mrs. Andrews, maybe. But a clear infringement of Dr. Houston's Dehumanization Act rights to remain free from such abusive language hurled at her."

"Abusive language? I don't see how this discussion can be abusive."

"Did you know Dr. Houston had to leave the market immediately and abandon her purchases? She needed to call her therapist and take a Xanax to calm down. She had been off those meds for nearly two months. Your client set Dr. Houston's mental health progress back months, if not years."

Johnathan didn't have a response. How could he? This was turning into something far more serious than he had imagined. This wasn't going to be settled with a handshake and a slap on the wrist.

"What are you suggesting?"

"We are beyond apologies and simple fines, John. They are seeking time here. *Serious* time. The amount on the table is two million and the full sentence of twenty years."

"All because my client invited her to church?" Johnathan asked, proud of himself that he was able to maintain his composure.

"It seems that way," the opposing lawyer nodded. He pushed a file folder across the table. "I'm afraid this deal is non-negotiable. I'm sorry, Johnathan. The ink was dry even before I touched it."

"Non-negotiable?" Johnathan said.

"The only two who can alter the terms are the client and the judge at sentencing."

Johnathan gave a derisive snorth. He knew how likely either of them was likely to budge—not only in this case but in any case brought to trial. It was the reason cases went to trial, to exact justice. Or rather, the form of justice that fits the day's definition—that, too, was ever-changing.

"Can Mrs. Andrews be released on her own recognizance?"

"I doubt my client will go for that, but I can ask," Xavier shrugged.

Johnathan sat back in his chair and sighed. "You know this was much easier when judges could handle stuff like this. Laws have gotten frustrating."

"For you and me both. JSI2399 and the AD Act took a lot of power away from the system and put it into the offended party's hands. *Heh.* I even have to watch what I say to my client. She's a feisty one. And please don't repeat that, or I will be on that side of the table with you."

"I'm not looking to get anyone in trouble. I'm just trying to get Mrs. Andrews home to her children and husband. Even if it is temporary."

With a sigh, Xavier Ford removed his glasses and placed them in his pocket. "Understandable. But I have my client's best interests to represent, even if they are contrary to my own belief in what's right. I'm sorry, Johnathan—my hands are tied. The only hope your client has is if the judge is in a forgiving mood or my client gets on the judge's bad side. But either way, this goes to trial."

"I get it. But don't think I'll go down without a fight. I will dig into your client's past and uncover anything I can to get this case thrown out. False accusations or a history of abuse of the system."

"She's not a plant, if that is what you are hinting at. Plants don't exist anymore. And don't even try to bring that up. I know about the *Andrews family history*. Jacob Andrews is a well-known name. Don't think we aren't privy to his connection to Rachel."

Johnathan squinted at the mention of Jacob. "Why would you bring Jacob into this? What does his history have to do with Rachel?"

"C'mon, John. Do you think I am stupid? Everyone knows about what happened in this town twenty some-odd years ago between the Andrews family, that pastor, and Official Nathan Edwards."

"I'm afraid you've lost me," Johnathan said. He had heard the stories but was vague about the connection.

"You think there are plants out there and that Rachel was targeted by one of them. Mind you, perhaps not because she is an Andrews, but because she was forced into a situation she was unprepared for."

"That's insane. I thought no such thing. I'm trying to defend my client from an outrageous law that shouldn't be on the books to begin with."

Xavier looked at him with piercing eyes, then shook his head. "Perhaps you are. But be careful, Counselor. If you start to rattle cages, her being an Andrews may make more of a difference than you bargain for."

"It's been forever ago. Why would a case from a quarter century ago matter now?

"Some folks have longer memories than others is all I am saying. You never know who is watching." Xavier closed his briefcase and stood, indicating their meeting was at an end.

"All that matters to me at this moment is defending *Mrs. Andrews* to the best of my ability and seeing she gets home to her family."

"You're in for a battle then. Dr. Houston isn't going away. As I said, she even has *me* scared." Xavier extended his hand. "For what it's worth, I am glad Mrs. Andrews has you to defend her."

Johnathan accepted his hand, rolling his eyes. "Thanks."

"So, I'll see you in court, Counselor," Xavier said and exited the office.

Johnathan looked over his notes and the documents he had been handed. He felt something was amiss. A crucial document short going into trial? And the page numbering was off; the numbering for page five in the lower right corner was a stick figure. That didn't make sense to him. Why just one-page number? That was the least of his concerns. He had a client to defend. A court clerical error was the least of his worries.

The laws were clear, and Rachel had indeed violated them. He needed to find a loophole that would get her exonerated. Xavier did make a mistake. Johnathan hadn't considered the possibility of Dr. Houston being a plant. What were the chances? He had only heard the term used a few times, but he knew what they were. This possibility gave him hope and a new avenue to investigate.

✝✝✝

Michael paced the room. He could tell he was making Johnathan nervous from his paperwork shuffling and pen clicking. Even he seemed lost.

"I've looked at this every way I can, Michael," Johnathan said. "I don't believe there is anything I can do, unless this judge is sympathetic to your situation."

"So, what happened in your meeting with the prosecutor?" Michael asked, finally picking a spot to stand.

Johnathan shook his head, "It started off fine, but then the prosecution dropped the hammer," he pulled out the file Xavier had given him and set it on the table. "Maybe you better sit down."

Michael didn't like the sound of those words. The look on Johnathan's face made it worse. He sat next to his attorney and read over the complaint and stipulations. He wanted to vomit when he read all the zeros. They didn't even extend the courtesy of abbreviating it. Michael closed his eyes and did the math; the kids would be entering grad school when she got out.

"Do you need a moment?" Michael could hear his attorney say. He opened his eyes and looked over at him. His eyes were filled with genuine concern.

"No. I'll be fine," Michael ran his fingers through his hair. "So, what do we do?"

"As I said, pray for a kind judge who will allow your wife to go home during the trial. That's about it. There is nothing I can do at this point; she will see a judge and jury."

"Because you think she's guilty."

"Michael, if she was talking to a person beside her and said 'Jesus,' and this woman walked beside them and overheard her, she can be considered guilty. The fact that she spoke to her directly and admitted that she invited her to church? Yeah, she *is* guilty, according to the laws as they are written. And those laws will be spelled out in that courtroom," Johnathan said, pointing toward the wall.

Michael released an exhausted sigh. "What's next?"

"I'm heading in there and fighting for your wife, that's what," Johnathan said, meeting his stare. His dark grey eyes didn't flinch. The wrinkles that creased his face lent gravitas to his determination. "I have been on the sidelines for far too long. Our common friends knew what was going on way before I did. But, according to Xavier, this is not like the situation that your family went through."

Johnathan stroked his chin, "What strikes me is that I didn't mention Frank or your father, nor had it crossed my mind. Which makes me wonder whether that is where I am supposed to look or if it is an attempted red herring to keep me occupied."

"What can I do to help?"

"How close were your dad and Frank Dunham?"

"Close. They worked together at the church before it closed a few years ago."

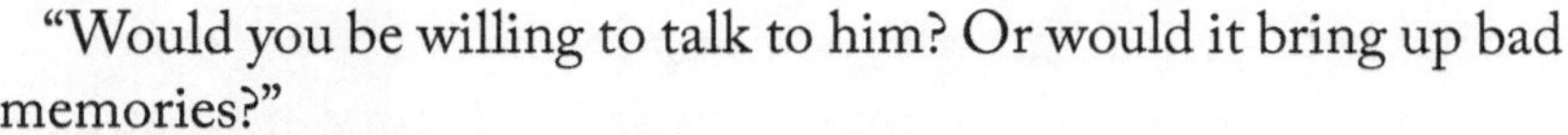

"Would you be willing to talk to him? Or would it bring up bad memories?"

"What do you need to know?"

"How plants were used against him. Xavier says they haven't been used in years. But if we want to do anything about getting Rachel out, we need to explore all our options, including the possibility of Dr. Houston being a plant."

"I am still trying to understand the whole idea of *a plant*."

"From what I understand, the government used to place paid individuals within communities to ensure the Federal Speech Act was being enforced. They would sneak into places to listen to people's conversations, teachers' lectures, and pastors' sermons to ensure they were not breaking JSI2399 laws. Then, all it took was one phone call, and they could arrest the speaker. Like an Official, a plant's word was above reproach. And if they could find a single witness, a conviction was guaranteed."

"Do they have a witness?"

"Their witness list is blank at this point," Johnathan said, shaking his head. "But that doesn't mean much, given that she is a doctor. Her title *is* their witness list. It places her in a higher category than a common citizen."

"And you believe she is a plant sent to trap my wife?"

"Not your wife, per se. It could've been simply the wrong place at the wrong time; could have been her job at the county office…" Johnathan's eyes diverted to the door.

"What?"

"I don't want to bring it up because its connection is minute, but it could be concerning what happened around twenty years ago."

"What are you talking about? My dad and his friends?"

Johnathan held up his hands. "I'm just tossing out possibilities. I don't want to leave any stone unturned. This is your wife we're talking about, remember?"

"Why would someone want to retaliate against something that happened over twenty years ago on someone who wasn't even born?"

"*You* were," Johnathan said, pointing at him.

"I was two. And I don't even know the full story of what happened," Michael exhaled and sat. "All I know is that my dad lost a friend because of what happened, and my parents got back together. Then they led the church of the friend that died. There was something in there about a corrupt cop."

"An Official. Yes. They were the ones who were in charge of placing plants to catch people breaking laws."

"Oh. I didn't know that. And you think this has something to do with Rachel?"

"I didn't say that. But with the warning I received from Xavier, we have to keep all options on the table. Nothing is impossible. I will say, up until today, I didn't believe plants existed anymore. But it has been a long time. The old ways have a habit of resurfacing when new ways become lax and unfocused."

Michael shook his head. "I don't know what to think. I just want Rachel out of here."

"I will do my best. But don't be surprised if she is held indefinitely."

Michael began to pace again, and Johnathan went back to clicking his pen and reading over the documents Xavier handed him. Michael knew he had to get home to the kids. It would be suppertime soon, and he had already put enough on his in-laws. Even though they never made a fuss, Michael never felt comfortable pushing responsibilities onto others. He and Rachel agreed early on to do their best to rely on each other and make the best of every situation. Then the twins happened. Help became a common word, and it was something Michael desperately needed now.

I t was Michael's first day home alone with the kids in a long time. Rachel usually woke up early to prepare breakfast. He'd be lucky even to remember what they liked. *Kids still ate waffles, right?* He trekked to the kitchen to search the fridge for a simple option that wouldn't make too much of a mess and would excite the kids enough to take their minds off the fact that Mommy still wasn't home.

The sleepover excuse worked for Wednesday, but their buying it for Thursday night took more convincing than just a bowl of ice cream. He eventually told them she had a bad cold and didn't want them to get her icky germs. A downright lie, but he didn't know what else to do. He knew he would have to find a way for them to at least speak to her by the end of the day.

"Hey, Pop," Michael said into his phone as he set the toast feature and timer on the air fryer. "I'm going to call my parents today for the kids. I need to head into the shop to check on the guys. Mr. Clarke says we can't do much today with the hearing not scheduled until Monday. We put in a request yesterday for the judge to hear her case but haven't heard back yet."

"Sounds good," Frank said. "The missus and I will be praying. Let us know if you need anything. Tell Jacob and Renae hello for us."

"Will do," Michael replied. "Talk to you later."

The aroma of blueberry wafted through the kitchen. It must've been driven much further because a dark-haired angel was soon clinging to his side.

"Smells yummy, Daddy," Aiden said.

"It's almost ready, buddy. Where's your sister?"

"She's coming. She's checking to see if Mommy's here."

Michael closed his eyes and took a breath, "No, sorry, Aiden, Mommy's still at Grandpa and Grandma's house. She doesn't want to give you her tummy ache."

"Alright," Aiden said in a disheartened tone.

Michael buttered the waffles and walked Aiden's plate to the table, "Now, is it you or your sister who doesn't like syrup? I can never remember."

"I love syrup. It's Angie who's the weird one," Aiden said with a twisted nose.

Michael laughed, watching Aiden douse his waffle with an unhealthy amount of syrup.

"Angela!" Michael called into the hallway. "Your waffles are ready."

"No syrup!" came a sharp reminder from the other room.

"See, told ya," Aiden said.

Angela entered the kitchen wrapped in a blanket and carrying her favorite doll. While he may not have remembered she didn't like syrup, he did know that if she was wrapped in her blanket, it meant she wasn't happy. It was one of her tells, and although sad, Michael was grateful for it.

"You okay, sweetie?" Michael squeezed her shoulder, knowing he needed to ask.

Angela didn't respond but plopped in her chair, resting her chin on her hands that were folded on the table.

"Do you want butter?"

"I'm not hungry. I want Mommy," the sad but firm voice explained.

Michael was getting tired of lying to his kids. "Mommy will be home soon. And she would be sad if you didn't eat your breakfast. So, will you eat it? For her?"

Michael set the plate in front of his daughter. She stared at it for a moment. He was sure a battle of stubbornness was waging. Blueberry was her favorite, another fact he was sure of. He saw the fight in her eyes beneath the curls that almost hid them. He let it go for a few seconds, then sighed.

"Well, if you don't want it…" he feigned, reaching for her plate.

"I want it, Daddy," Angie said, grabbing the plate and fork beside it.

"I figured you did," her dad laughed. "Milk?"

"Yes, please," she said through a mouthful.

Michael watched his children finish their breakfast and was grateful for the momentary reprieve. But he knew that it was just that. Both would soon ask again about their mom's whereabouts and wonder when she'd be home. He could only hide it a little while longer. He would have to return to the courthouse on Monday, and by then, they would know something was wrong.

It was more than talking to the kids; Michael was nervous about talking to his dad. It wasn't that they didn't get along, but every time he mentioned a problem, his response would be to *trust in God* or that *it was in God's hands*. He never felt listened to when he brought a problem to him. It wasn't that he didn't believe in God; it was more that he was tired of hearing about Him. He was there in the church, there in the home. It became overwhelming, and Michael needed a break. That break turned into a few years of separation. Lately, he had been closer to Frank Dunham than his own flesh and blood.

After breakfast, Michael washed dishes, wiped down the table, cleaned up two gooey toddlers, and then got ready to head to his parent's house. They still lived in the same house he grew up in. It was one of the comforts he enjoyed about returning home. He and Rachel had found land just outside of Polk to build a new home. It was an investment Frank Dunham was proud to be part of. His restaurant, Dunham's, had expanded into a new location, and the growth had been, as Frank put it, "a blessing from the Lord and his commitment to Him." His wedding gift was the finances to build on the land. His parents added to it, and through everyone's generosity, they had enough to create the modest home of their dreams.

The second investment Frank and his parents devoted their time and money was Our Savior's Cross. While Michael was a toddler, he did recall bits and pieces of the musty band hall they used to meet in. He was almost five when they graduated from the school and moved into the new facility under the guise of a concert hall. At least, that's what it was on paper. And despite all that had happened in Carrolton when he was little, no one paid much attention to them and their *band of believers*, as his dad called them. The laws didn't get crazy until about a year after the church was built—*another blessing*, as Pop called it.

The first round of laws enacted didn't have much to do with what happened in their area. The second round did. The federal authorities discovered what had happened in Carrolton when he was a child and used it as precedent. It set the ground rules for the behavior and authority of Officials so that another Nathan Edwards could not ascend to power. It sounded good on paper, but the spotlight was now on Carrolton, and with the subsection additions to the Federal Speech Act it only strengthened Edwards' position, making the situation worse for the town.

Then there was no need for plants. Authorities could spy on you out in the open. The laws had not extended far enough to outlaw Christianity, but it was insinuated. Public speakers were required to submit speeches for scrutiny before they were delivered to prevent offensive speech. This affected churches the most. Pastors were required to submit their sermons to ensure they did not break the law. Some obliged. Many more preached while going off script *as the Spirit led them*. His father was one who was reluctant to turn over his sermon outlines. The doors to Our Savior's Cross as a church was more of a forced closure than a peaceful one. It was the price you paid. Don't submit to the law; you lose your permit to hold services.

It was yet another division between him and his father. Michael couldn't see the harm in turning in a falsified sermon. Everyone else was doing it. *As long as God's word was being preached* was the reason other pastors were giving for their falsification. But his dad wouldn't even go that far.

"A lie is a lie, son. Even if there are good intentions behind it, I don't feel God would be pleased."

Michael would shake his head and constantly worry about if this was the week his dad was going to be arrested. With the doors now closed, he no longer had to worry, but if it got out that his dad was holding services secretly, that could pose a new problem.

Michael sighed as he gathered the remaining items for the go-bags for the kids—the miscellaneous things he figured the kids could not live without. Angie's blanket and doll he knew she slept with. If a nap came around, she would not lay down without them. Aiden needed two or three ballcaps because he could never decide which he wanted to wear. He already knew his parents had an endless pantry of snacks; the kids would squeal about it every visit, wondering why they didn't have such a treasure trove.

Michael buckled a wild-legged Aiden into his seat while Angela took care of business herself. "I got it, Daddy." She told him. She fussed with the buckle a bit but eventually got the three-point harness connected. *Girls definitely advanced faster than boys,* as his wife would always kid with him each time Angela hit a benchmark before Aiden. The theory that twins were molded together was a myth, at least for these two. Even their heads mismatched. Angela's hair was full of red curls, and Aiden's was straight as straw and brown.

"Hey, Daddy? What's that?" Angela asked, pointing at the garage door.

Michael looked up. At first he couldn't see what she was pointing at, but after staring for a moment, it was clear as day.

"I don't know, sweetie."

On the garage door, it appeared that someone had etched four lines with a diagonal crossbar connecting them.

"Why did somebody scratch our house?"

Michael was silent. Not sure what to say.

"What does that mean, Daddy?" Aiden asked.

"Well, it means five. It is usually used to count. Four lines, and you cross them to mean five," Michael said, drawing in the air. "But I don't know why someone would do that."

Michael unbuckled his seatbelt. "I'll be right back. You two stay buckled."

Michael went to the garage door and ran his finger over the scar. It looked fresh. The etching was bright and not dampened by the dew. Michael spun around and looked for anyone on the street, but the only thing he saw was his neighbor's vehicles parked in their usual spots. He took a breath and walked back to his truck.

After buckling in, Michael looked into his rearview mirror to double-check the tots when his phone rang. The half-smile of a preacher man stared at him, and he answered. "Hey, Dad. What's up?"

"Hey, Michael. Change of plans. Don't worry. We're still able to watch the angels. I just need you to drop them off at the Rec Center instead of the house. I have to take care of a few things this morning."

The Rec Center was code for the church. It had been since they disbanded five years ago. And with the building funds originally coded for a civic center, it only made sense to call the location a recreational center. His dad was always careful about coding his communication. Michael supposed it had become second nature to him. He wasn't even sure if his dad realized he was doing it. In any case, he didn't like leaving his kids there for too long, especially with him going against a federal mandate.

"How long are you planning on being there?"

"Not too long. Just wrapping up a few things. Should be no more than a couple of hours."

Michael growled under his breath but relented. He needed to get to the courthouse to see if they would allow him to visit Rachel today.

"I'll be there in about fifteen minutes," he said and hung up. He knew he shouldn't have been upset. His dad was doing him a favor, not that spending time with family should ever be considered a favor. But when it came to his father, it sure felt like it.

When he pulled up to the rec center, aka church, several vehicles were out front. He did have to admit that the facility his father chose gave the impression that it was a fitness center. There were silhouettes of musclebound men in the windows. What many failed to notice was that their arms and hands are in a prayer pose at their chest, signaling the power of prayer.

Your strength comes from within you, was written beneath one.

Never doubt your inner strength, was beneath another.

In reality, there was a full gym inside. There was workout equipment and treadmills—the church's idea to keep the front should they be audited or visited by their past. It was utter nonsense to Michael. He knew the façade and was embarrassed by the lies. He had little respect for the man who hid behind a façade. At least his grandfather-in-law knew how to run a successful business. He knew when to give up and let things go. He let what happened in the past rest and moved into the future. It was why his business had grown into two restaurants. His dad? His church was gone now; he lost. Now he was in hiding.

Michael found a spot and parked. Once the kids saw where they were, their excitement exploded.

"Grandpa!" Angie gushed.

"Yay!" Aiden started kicking in his seat.

Although Michael wasn't excited, he was glad they were happy. Their feelings could've been his, and he would feel even worse for leaving them with him. And he knew their excitement was also his father's. So much so that even before he clicked the door lock key on his fob, his father approached them, and two child-like streaks were beelining toward him.

"Grandpa!" his two kids holler in unison.

Jacob laughed as he knelt to grab both necks in a hug.

"So, how are my two little munchkins?" Jacob asked, kissing Angela on the cheek and giving Aiden a head rub.

Both kids gave him their story of the past couple of nights of missing Mommy in unison, with his dad's head dancing back and forth, nodding in concern and chuckling over their concern at Mommy's inconveniently-timed illness. His way of comforting the children was admirable.

Michael was glad about it. His dad took the kids in his arms when they seemed to get finished with their stories, then Jacob looked up at Michael, his smile vanishing.

"Come on inside. We need to talk."

"A Denali," Michael said. "Are you sure?" Michael didn't know what to think. Denali's weren't a common make of truck anymore. They practically didn't exist. So his dad's defenses went into overdrive whenever he thought he saw one, even after all this time. Still, Michael wasn't too concerned.

"Positive. Two of them. Dark, brand new with tinted windows. They drove down the highway there." Jacob pointed out the office window where they were sitting. "Not the normal tint to keep the sun out of your eyes either. The kind of tint that keeps people from seeing inside. And these Denalis or whatever they were, drove in formation. There was something off about them."

"Dad," Michael said.

"No," Jacob snapped. "It's not paranoia. This time it was real, Michael. I tell you, they are out there again."

"Then why did you risk me bringing the kids here?"

Jacob shrugged.

Michael could tell that his dad had his own doubts. Looking over your shoulder for so long had its way of playing with your mind. His father had a habit of allowing his past to take over sometimes. He knew Nathan Edwards was a ghost, a memory. And even though the Federal Speech Act remained intact, for a while, they didn't monitor it as they used to. His dad felt freer to preach the way Eric had entrusted him. But with the updated laws, the comfort they once experienced had been shaken, especially in the last couple of years. Now, with the pickup sightings, he was starting to pull back. Even his sermons had been affected.

"The kids comfort me," the older man breathed at last. "Plus, I don't think they would do anything with the kids around."

"So, my children are your shield now?"

"That's not what I meant, Michael."

"Sure sounds like it."

Jacob exhaled, leaning back in his chair. "I just feel safer here, Mikey. And the kids keep my mind occupied."

"Honestly, I think you're seeing things," Michael said, leaning forward and placing his hand on his father's arm. "It's all in your head, Dad. We've been through this before. All of that is in the past. They can't hurt you anymore. *He* can't hurt you anymore."

"Don't patronize me, Michael." Jacob shook Michael's hand from his arm and stood. He paced the floor and ran his hand through his hair. "I know what I saw. And I'm not losing my mind, if that is what you are concerned about. You're fine leaving the kids here today and doing what you need to do. Rachel is more important than this old man's eyes. I just wanted you to be aware of what I saw in case there is more to come. And Son, if I did see what I think I saw—Rachel's arrest could mean a lot more than you could possibly imagine."

"Dad, she just mentioned God to the wrong person—"

"Uh, huh," Jacob nodded furiously. "To a plant."

Michael shook his head. Jacob was the just one more person to suggest the possibility of this being a setup.

"Why does everyone keep on saying that? First, Johnathan—"

"Johnathan thinks this too?"

Michael explained what his attorney told him about his conversation with the plaintiff's attorney regarding this new vocabulary word that should have been extinct long ago that kept popping up.

"You need to be careful, Michael," Jacob warned. "Something isn't right here. Everyone sees it but you. Don't get blindsided.

When you go into that courtroom, be prepared for anything. Talk to Johnathan. I'll talk with Frank, and together we'll get to the bottom of this."

"Frank said he was going talk to his law enforcement buddies to see what he could find out about Rachel," Michael replied.

"Good, maybe he already knows something. We need to talk to him before you meet with your attorney." Jacob picked up his phone and dialed. "What time is your meeting?"

"Ten-thirty," Michael said, looking around his shoulder to the clock that told him he had an hour and a half to get across town to the courthouse. He looked back to his dad.

Jacob's eyes lit up as someone answered his phone call with a muffled greeting. Jacob sat up straight. "Maggs, how are ya this morning? You didn't have to work the restaurant?"

Maggie, Frank's wife, worked both at the diner and Dunham's, splitting her waitressing talents. It being Friday, she would be at Dunham's getting ready for the lunch crowd. After some small talk, she passed the phone to Frank.

"Good morning, sir. I know you're busy. I wanted to see if you had an update for Michael. He's about to head to the courthouse, and I believe there is more to this than a silly misunderstanding."

Jacob paused.

"Yeah, you too, then," Jacob said, nodding.

More nodding and listening.

Michael watched as the two confirmed their past confrontations with Officials and the hidden plants that everyone seemed to know about but that everyone else seemed to insist didn't exist. Jacob repeated his encounter with the two Denalis, which appeared to interest Frank. Michael wasn't sure, but his tone of voice appeared to changed when Jacob mentioned it.

Jacob ended his call and released a long exhale, then swung in his chair to face his son. "Frank says he's seen the two Denalis as well."

"Wait. What?" Michael asked, almost slipping out of his chair.

"Yeah. He said he was at The Original Dunham's about a week

ago. He was closing up and heard the humming of engines. He turned around and saw two pickups sitting in the next lot. They were far away, so he couldn't be sure. He's eighty now, and his eyesight isn't what it used to be. He said they were gone before he could get a better look."

"That's insane."

"No kidding."

Michael sat, considering what his father had been saying. *What if these trucks are real? What if both Dad and Frank have seen them? What if…* "Rachel!" Michael was on his feet.

"Take a deep breath, Michael," Jacob said. "We don't know for sure if they have anything to do with this."

"But you said—"

"All I said was that it was possible." Jacob pointed back to the chairs. "We need to do some research before we jump to conclusions. We just confirmed that Denalis have been seen in multiple location. But that's just the first step."

"We need to do something for Rachel—"

"And we will. But we have to go about this the right way. If we go off half-cocked, more people will get hurt or imprisoned… like Rachel is now. This isn't like before. You can't get off by just saying she's innocent without solid proof. And you can't call out an arresting officer, much less an Official, without repercussions. Trust me, I know." Jacob said, rubbing the scar on his cheek.

Michael exhaled, lowering his shoulders. "So, what's our next step?"

"Go to your meeting. Act none the wiser. Pretend you know nothing. Even if there is more to this, you cannot call them out, not yet. We don't know enough. When you see Rachel, tell her you love her, tell her about the kids and that they miss her. Say you are doing all you can to represent her, but do *not* tell her you think something is wrong. The walls have eyes *and* ears. If she asks, just say you are still looking into it."

"I understand." Michael looked to the ground. "I keep forgetting you were there—where she's at."

"I'm sure she has much nicer accommodations if that is any consolation. Times have changed. And there are laws now because of what Edwards did."

"I know, Dad. Still, I don't like that she is in there."

"She will be fine. You have excellent representation with Johnathan Clarke. Frank trusts him, and I believe he is as good as they come. She is in good hands."

"I hope so. I've only met with him briefly, but he seems okay."

"He is better than okay. After what we've been through, we no longer let many people in our circle. If Frank called him, he's in that circle. You're good."

Michael took a long breath and looked at the clock. It was time to meet the man he was weighing the credibility of.

"I need to get going. Johnathan is expecting me." Michael stood. "Can I at least tell him what we believe is going on?"

Jacob stared into the distance momentarily, then looked up at his son, "Maybe it's best to keep a lid on this for now. Go to this hearing, and we will all talk afterward. I don't think him knowing now will affect Rachel's status."

"Okay, I won't say anything until after the hearing."

"But Michael." Jacob's tone changed. "You must understand that *if* there is more to this, then Rachel most likely won't get out today, even if Johnathan makes a convincing argument. He could even hold unequivocal evidence of her innocence and they still might not accept it. Do not react to it. Don't try to fight it, don't allow a sudden outburst. That's what they want you to do. So remain calm, smile at your wife, and tell her you have it under control."

"Got it," Michael said, but he wasn't so sure he could remain silent. This was his wife he was talking about his wife—the mother of his children; the mom of two young children who were playing in another room right now, who were none the wiser about what is going on. How was he going to go home and explain the situation to them? He had expected to walk into the courtroom and have Rachel released on her own recognizance. The thought that she might be held indefinitely until they could convict her of a crime on trumped up charges that could result in a sentence of up to twenty years was inconceivable.

"Michael, I mean it. No outbursts," Jacob reiterated. He must've noticed the mental wheels turning in Michael's head or the red in his eyes.

"Dad, I got it. No outbursts. No chair-throwing. Keep calm, cool, and collected." Michael managed a weak grin, extending a thumbs up.

"Michael," Jacob said, his tone strengthening.

Michael surrendered his pose, "Okay, Dad. I understand. Believe me, I don't want Rachel in more trouble than she is now. Heck, I don't even know what that means at this point. But I know that blowing up is not the best way to find out. I promise, I will keep my cool."

"Thank you," Jacob said, his shoulders lowering and his hands falling to his sides. "Let me walk you out."

Michael followed Jacob to his truck. Both men kept a watchful eye. Vehicles passed the gym, and a couple of them pulled into the lot. Jacob called each one out by name, and gave Micheal a brief backstory on each person. Michael remembered how much of a people person his father was. He knew people, and not in a superficial way. Jacob Andrews knew individuals. He knew their names, jobs, kids, and stories about their pasts.

I guess that's the pastor in him was shining through, Michael mused. *Still shining through.*

Michael and Johnathan Clarke sat outside the courtroom, waiting for the bailiff to escort those on the docket into the arena. The mumbling of attorney and client-privileged information echoed off the marble walls and tile flooring. The reverberation made the conversations appear to sound louder than they actually were. The posted docket listed Rachel's case as fourth, adding to Michael's anxiety. He just wanted it over with. He felt he'd been lying to Johnathan all morning by not mentioning his talk with his father. But he knew it was for the best.

Michael leaned forward and glanced across the hallway again. His attempt at appearing nonchalant was not as disguised as he hoped.

"Michael, what's wrong?" Johnathan asked, peering at him over his glasses. "That is the third time you've scanned the lobby in the last fifteen minutes."

Michael sat back, releasing his fake stretch. "What? Nothing. I've just been sitting too long. I want to get this hearing over with."

"I do too. But who are you looking for? You keep scanning the room."

"I am not."

"Michael. You forget, I am an ex-P.I. I know the tricks of the trade. You're attempting to, and rather poorly I might add, scan the room. You're looking for something or someone. Now spill it."

Michael exhaled in defeat.

"If there's going to be a surprise in there," Johnathan thumbed to the courtroom, "I need to know about it. The better prepared I am, the better I can defend Rachel. I don't need to be blindsided."

Michael looked both ways and switched seats to the one next to Johnathan. He looked up and around again. "You remember when you mentioned that your attorney friend—"

"Xavier."

"Yeah, well, you mentioned that Xavier had talked about *plants*. And you were surprised he used that word."

"Yes?"

"And we talked about there may be more to this because of that."

"Okay. Continue."

"Well, it goes back to who could be sending these plants. Officials, right?"

"Mm-hmm."

"Well, first, I don't want to get you worried. I promised my dad I wouldn't say anything until after the hearing because he didn't want you to react in the courtroom based on what I'm about to tell you."

"Michael. Just out with it."

Michael exhaled. "My dad thinks Officials are watching him."

"Really?"

"Frank Dunham, too."

"Frank believes this too?"

"Remember, he was there back then. Both of them were. They know what to look for."

"And they've seen Officials watching them?" Johnathan put his file down. Michael had his full attention.

"My dad said so. And I was in the room when Frank admitted as much."

"What did these Officials look like?"

"You know that Officials drive those newer model GMC Denali SUVs?"

"Yeah, you can't miss them. GMC makes them specifically for the unit." Johnathan nodded.

"Well, back in my dad's day, they drove GMC Denalis."

"Yes, so I've heard."

"Both my dad and Frank have seen two Denalis. My dad saw them driving past his gym. Frank saw them across from his restaurant. They were parked in the next lot. They flashed their lights at him before driving off."

"And you are sure about this?"

"If it were one or the other, I'd probably shrug it off. Let's face it, my dad has always been nervous—ah hell, I'll say it, paranoid about these guys coming back. And Frank? Well, he's in his eighties now. He could've been just seeing things. But both? Seeing the same thing?"

"Yes, more than coincidence, I will admit," Johnathan said, stroking his chin, eyes focused in the distance.

"Look, Johnathan. I'm sorry. I didn't want you to go in there with this on your mind. I don't want it to cloud your judgment in front of the judge. For Rachel's sake. For Aiden and Angie's sake. Please."

"No. Don't worry about me. I can be impartial. But now my eyes will be open. I'll be more alert to what is going on."

"But if you *see* something, don't react to it. Please."

Johnathan looked up at Michael; their eyes locked. A knowing look fell over Johnathan's face, and he nodded and patted Michael on the leg. "I get you. I promise not to overreact. We will get the feel of what is happening and develop a strategy."

"Thank you."

"You realize that if something *is* going on, she's not coming home today—or anytime soon."

"I know. My dad said the same thing. I thought about that the entire way over here and have come to grips with it. I just need to decide how I'm going to tell the kids."

The murmurs of the courtroom hall were broken when a bailiff entered and announced that the judge was ready to accept the first four cases into the gallery.

"That means us," Johnathan said, standing and grabbing his briefcase.

Michael again scanned the room, forgetting the cloak and dagger. He was watching to see if anyone was watching him. When no one glanced his way, he stood and followed his attorney into the courtroom.

†††

"All rise. The Honorable Charlene Ellison presiding," the bailiff announced, then stood at ease at the judge's side. The judge thanked the bailiff and inquired about the docket when she was seated.

"First case is David Allan Jenkins. Loitering and Possession. Second Strike. Gamboa, Thames, and Richter are representing," the bailiff introduced, handing her the case file.

"Mr. Jenkins. Here we are again. I thought we had this taken care of the last time we met, sir?"

"Your Honor," Mr. Jenkins' attorney stood and spoke before his client could respond, "Sorry. Everett Richter for the defense."

"What do you have to say for your client, Mr. Richter?"

"Mr. Jenkins was simply crossing the park when the park police stopped him. They conducted an unwarranted search of his person and found a hair above the legal limit of his allowance for his marijuana card."

The prosecuting attorney snickered.

"Something amusing, Counselor?" Judge Ellison asked.

"Yes, Your Honor. The amount found on Mr. Jenkins was four ounces. That is four times the amount his card allows him to carry. Even if he was simply transporting the three bags of pre-rolled joints from one location to another, he was well beyond his carry limits. And him being in Douvett Park placed him in an area known for drug activity. His home is fifteen miles from the park."

"Your Honor," Mr. Richter said, "Mr. Jenkins was visiting a friend in the area and was on his way to the bus stop when Park Police stopped him. You can verify with the friend. Her information is on record."

"Yes," the prosecuting attorney continued, "a woman of ill repute who has a couple of strikes and has probably been in this courtroom herself. Such a reliable witness."

"Is this true?" the judge asked, looking over her thin-rimmed glasses.

"Her record makes little difference. She will testify under oath he was only visiting. Yes, she may have a record, but it doesn't change the fact he was on his way from her residence and not up to the business he is being accused of."

"But four ounces, Mr. Richter?" the judge questioned. "Can you explain, Mr. Jenkins? If it was just for medicinal purposes, why were you carrying four ounces in a park known for drug activity?"

David Jenkins and his attorney exchanged glances. His attorney shrugged, and Mr. Jenkins cleared his throat. "She was teaching me to roll a better joint, Your Honor," he said.

The courtroom was filled with soft laughter and murmuring. The judge tapped her gavel. "Is that so, Mr. Jenkins? You have been known for narcotics and don't know how to roll a simple marijuana cigarette?"

"No, ma'am, er, Your Honor," Mr. Jenkins admitted, then looked down at the table.

Judge Ellison smiled, then cleared her throat. "Counselor."

"Yes, your honor?"

"Was there any cash or other form of currency found on Mr. Jenkins?"

"About forty dollars in his wallet."

"Large or small bills?"

"Two twenties."

"Would that be a denomination and amount someone distributing carry on their person?"

The prosecuting attorney sat speechless, "I suppose they would carry more than that and smaller bills. Still, the quantity of Mary Jane he was carrying was well over the limit."

"I understand your concern regarding Mr. Jenkins' excess, but

I see no intent to distribute. He does need to second think the company he keeps, but I think a fine regarding the excess of his limit and ten days incarceration should suffice."

"Ten days?" both attorneys say in unison.

"Do I need to change my mind here, gentlemen?" the judge raised both hands, the gavel in one.

"No," again they both echo.

"Very well. Two-hundred fifty dollar fine. Ten days in County," Judge Ellison said with a gavel slap.

Michael looked at Johnathan, who shrugged. The judge seemed in decent spirits. She sentenced the following case just as she had Mr. Jenkins: light but fair. No slap on the wrist or get-out-of-jail-free cards being issued.

The judge rapped her gavel on another case. Sending a forger to her sentence of six months of probation instead of one year in prison, drawing a smile upon Johnathan's face. Johnathan's main point to Michael was that Judge Ellison knew each case. She had either studied them before being seated or was a quick read when she was handed the file. Either way, even the attorneys were surprised at the judge's knowledge of the case files.

"Her knowing the cases could be to our advantage," Johnathan whispered. "With Rachel's clean record, she could be lenient and release her OOR."

"And she could come home?"

"Through the trial, yes."

Their case was slotted next. From forgery to a case of a conversation gone amiss, this would be a walk in the park.

"Next case on the docket. Dr. Marsha Houston versus Rachel Alise Andrews."

"I'm not sure I can do this, Pop."

Michael stood tracing the rim of a cup of tea. It was almost eleven, but he didn't care. He needed something hot, and he didn't drink coffee.

Standing next to him, Frank placed his hand on Michael's shoulder and cleared his throat. Michael understood what that meant. Years of childhood memories and ten years of marriage told him his grandfather-in-law was about to say something, as he would put it, 'worth listn'n to.'

"Michael, we are often put into situations we feel we cannot handle. But it's in those moments we realize we have more strength than we think we have. We just need to find that source of strength. And then move forward in it."

Michael sighed, "I don't know what that is, Frank. I'm at a loss. Between what Dad said and what happened today in court, I'm not sure I have the strength to face this."

"Tell me again what happened," Frank said as he sat at the kitchen table.

"Nothing. That's the problem," Michael said, running his hand through his already tossed hair and leaning against the counter.

"Try. Maybe there are some clues in it that you missed."

Michael took a deep breath and blew it out. He fixated on his cup of tea and let his mind dissolve back to the courtroom.

"The cases for the day started out fine. The judge seemed to be in good spirits. Even Johnathan felt we were in a good position when the bailiff called our case. But for some reason, the air in the courtroom changed."

"Changed?"

"Changed."

"How do you mean?"

"It was like a cold front blew through. You could almost feel it. The chatter behind us quieted, the light-hearted banter between the judge and bailiff stopped, the room seemed to darken… I don't know, Frank. The room just changed."

"Interesting."

"You had to be there."

"I would imagine," Frank said.

"The bailiff called the case, and the side door opened. I almost lost it. Rachel came through, and she looked like she hadn't slept. There were bags under her eyes, and while her hair was brushed, it wasn't like she would normally have it; I mean, not that I expected her to be dressed up."

"Right. She's in prison. It's not like she could shower and get fancied up."

"I understand that, but this was different. It…" Michael huffed. "It was just different, Pop. She wasn't herself. Even for an unslept and unkempt Rachel."

"Okay," Frank nodded, "continue."

"I obviously wanted to say something. It took all I had not to, but I remembered Dad's advice that it could only make things worse for her. So I gave her a half-smile, which I suppose she returned. She sat behind the desk and faced the judge."

"They wouldn't let you talk to her?"

"I will get to that."

"Sorry. Go on," Frank motioned.

"The bailiff reads off the charges, which I was grateful were identical to what was read at the preliminary hearing. Only the

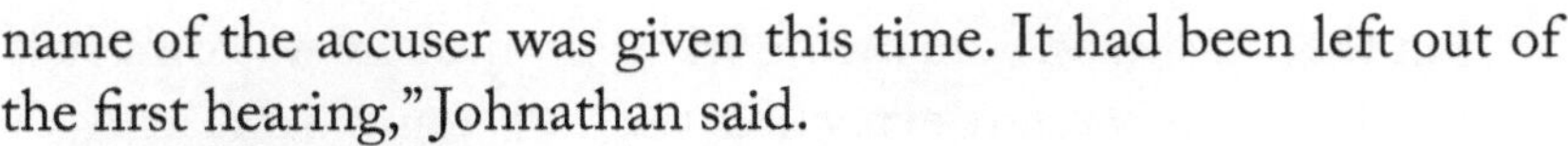

name of the accuser was given this time. It had been left out of the first hearing," Johnathan said.

"Was she there?"

"Finally, yes. Dr. Marsha Houston. I didn't recognize her."

"Houston. Hmm." Frank's brows furrowed. "Doctor, you say? Never heard of her. And I know everybody. I will ask Margaret. If I don't know her, she will. If she doesn't know her, she doesn't exist."

"That's what I figured. And that's what scares me."

"This whole plant idea?" Frank said.

"Yeah. I don't want Dad to be right. But in a way, I do because I don't want the alternative to be true either."

"What? That your old man is losing his marbles?" Frank said.

Michael chuckled. "I know he's not. You guys have been through a lot. And I know he has our best interest at heart. I'm just scared for Rachel."

"So, what happened next?"

"Nothing."

"Nothing?" Frank asked, rubbing his chin.

"The judge didn't even ask for a plea. As soon as the final word of the charges left the bailiff's lips, Dr. Houston's attorney ranted about sufficient evidence to go to immediate trial based on her client's *upstanding reputation* and *role in the community*. She cited two cases where the merit of the offended was sufficient evidence to bypass any evidentiary hearing and go straight to trial.

"Then the judge glanced at Rachel for a couple of seconds, looked back at the doctor, slapped her gavel, and granted her request. She called the lunch recess and disappeared into her chambers."

"She never asked for a plea?" Frank asked.

"Nope."

"Isn't that illegal?"

"I guess not under the updated JSI laws," Michael shrugged, emptying his cup.

"So now what? What did Johnathan say?"

"He was as flabbergasted as I was. Mind you, I had just dumped on him that this was a ruse before we went in, so he was only half prepared. But we weren't expecting not to get any word in at all. We expected them to let us fight, squirm, and force us into a corner, then do something stupid."

"But they didn't?" Frank questioned.

"Not even a jab."

"Interesting."

"All for the best, I suppose," Michael said. "Dad will be pleased. He told me not to do anything that would jeopardize Rachel's safety. Or my own."

"So, what's next?"

"I wish I knew," Michael said, shaking his head. "That's the problem. Rachel's in there, and I have no way of communicating with her. You asked about talking to her? After they dismissed us, I went around and asked if we could get a conference room to talk."

"And they didn't?"

"They couldn't even find her file. And by the time they did, she had already been transported back to the prison."

"And you can't see her at the jail?"

"You know I can't. If she is being held for the reasons we believe, we'd only make things worse for her."

"But you need to see her, Michael. Or she'll begin to think you've given up on her," Frank said. "And I'll be darned if I'll have my granddaughter feeling that way. She's missing her kids enough—don't need her missin' you as well."

Michael knew Frank was right. He had fought to see her at the courthouse. He should fight to see her at the jail. He looked at the clock. There was no way he'd get into the prison this late. Another night of making up excuses for Mommy. He sighed.

Frank must've read his mind; his hand was on his arm. "You need to tell the young'uns."

"I know," Michael said. "I just don't know how to say it."

"Best thing is just to say it. They won't understand it, but you have to tell them. Lyin' every night will just tear your conscience apart and only hurt more should they find out some other way."

Michael nodded. *But how do I tell a five-year-old that Mommy's in jail?* He looked up at the ceiling where the kid's footfalls were making the chandelier vibrate.

"More tea?" Frank offered.

Michael shook it off. "No, it'll keep me up. I should get the kids home. It's almost bedtime. Maybe I can think of something during their bath."

"Stay strong, Michael. Lean on the Lord. He's your strength," Frank said, giving him a couple of firm pats on the shoulder.

Michael wasn't so sure. He and God weren't exactly on speaking terms. He couldn't remember the last time they had a conversation, let alone him opening a Bible or setting his foot in a church.

"I'll try, Pop," Michael finally said. He stood and walked up the stairs to the room where little voices giggled.

"Daddy!" Aiden and Angela said in unison when he opened the door. Maggie sat in a rocker in the corner with her patented smile.

"Heavens, Michael. I still can't get over how much you look like your father," Maggie said. "Spitting image."

Michael smiled. "Not sure if that's a good thing or bad."

Maggie laughed, "Most certainly a good thing, my dear. You are a handsome man. Your wife is a lucky woman."

Maggie put her hand over her mouth, realizing what she had said. She looked over at the kids who were looking for the cat that had hidden under the bed, oblivious to their conversation.

"Don't worry about it. They're fine. She's fine—I guess. I don't know. I didn't get to see her. Long story. Pop will fill you in," Michael said in a near whisper. A bit louder in Aiden and Angela's direction, he said, "I need to get these munchkins home and cleaned up for bed."

"Nooo," again in unison.

"We're having fun, Daddy," Angela said.

"Can we stay the night again?" Aiden asked.

"We have stayed enough nights, buddy. It's time to go home and sleep in our own beds. Now go get your stuff so we can get going."

"All right," Aiden said. "C'mon, sis."

Both children headed out of the room, leaving them alone. "I don't know, Maggie. I'm at a loss. At some point tonight, I need to tell them their mom isn't coming home anytime soon. I just don't know how to word it in a way that a five-year-old would understand it."

"You'll figure it out, sweetie. You should do fine if you have your dad's brains like you have his looks," Maggie said.

Michael grinned. "Thanks. I'm still not sure if that is a good or bad thing."

"He raised you, and you turned out better than average." Maggie elbowed him with a chuckle. "I would say that is a good thing."

Michael hugged her with his goodbyes, loaded the kids into the truck, and headed home. By the time he arrived, both kids were already yawning and dozing in their car seats. Michael had a half notion of tucking them into bed, clothes and all, leaving off the difficult conversation. But the empty driveway drew the questions he hoped to leave until breakfast.

"Where's Mommy's car?" Angela asked through a yawn.

"I'm not sure, sweetie," Michael said, which was the truth. He didn't know what the city did with her vehicle. But not knowing was not going to end the line of questioning.

"Is she still at work?"

Michael didn't answer. He didn't want to lie, and he wasn't ready to have a conversation in the car. "Let's go inside and have our baths and get ready for bed. Then I want to tell you something."

"Is it about Mommy?" Aiden asked.

Smart kid, Michael thought.

He chewed on it for a second before answering, not wanting to scare them. "Yes, but let's get cleaned up and in bed before I tell you the story, okay?"

He hoped the word *story* would snuff the current line of

questioning and get him inside the house. Bedtime was story time, and maybe it would buy him some time.

"There is a story about Mommy?" Angela asked, trying to unbuckle herself.

Michael finished with Aiden, who hopped out of the truck and helped a frustrated Angela. "Yes, sweetie. I will tell you about it after your bath and when you're tucked in. Okay?"

"Okay, Daddy," Angela said, hopping out of the truck like her brother.

"Ha! I jumped farther than you did," Angela said.

"Did not. I landed in the grass," Aiden said.

"So did I," Angela protested, pointing back at where she said she had landed. Michael laughed; it was nowhere near where she did, but he let them have their debate.

"Nuh-uh," Aiden said, "Dad. Who got further?"

Both children looked at him, standing and pointing to the spots they believed they jumped to. "I believe it was a tie. Both of you are amazing jumpers. Much further than I could have jumped. So you both win."

"Yay!" both cheered and ran to the door.

Michael was grateful they were won over that easily and had not given into a debate that one of them had to win. He was reminded of his sister. They bickered quite often, but there was an age difference. Aiden and Angela were identical in age. Could that have been their advantage? It was this evening, and he wasn't complaining.

Michael pulled up a chair two sizes too small and sat looking at his children's clean, smiling faces. It was now or never. Angela was tucked under her paisley-colored bedspread; blue eyes focused on him. Aiden was on the edge of the bed, cross-legged and hands in his lap, holding his stuffed dinosaur, Selly.

"Okay, guys," Michael began. "There's something I need to tell you about Mommy. And I'm not sure how I can tell you in a way you can understand it. I am going to say it as plainly as I can."

"Is Mommy hurt?" Angela asked, gripping her covers.

"No, no. Nothing like that, Angie." Michael patted her leg. "Mommy is in jail. That's as simple as I can put it."

"Jail? Mommy did something bad?" Aiden asked.

Michael wasn't sure how to answer the question. He was working on how to say it in a way a five-year-old would understand. In some sense, it was true that she had broken the law, but on the other hand, she had done the right thing by sharing her faith.

"It's not that Mommy did something bad. It's that as adults, there are some rules you can't break, even if what you are doing is good."

The two crinkled noses showed him that he wasn't getting through. *Maybe this wasn't a good idea.*

"Okay. You know how your mom and I would tell you to be nice to people and say nice things to them."

Both kids nodded.

"And that it's not nice to be mean," Michael continued.

Again, understanding nods met his explanation.

"Well, occasionally, when you are nice to some people, they don't like it."

"Some people don't like you being nice to them?" Aiden asked.

"Unfortunately, not, Aiden," Michael said.

"That's not nice," Aiden said.

Michael half-laughed, "No, that's being mean."

"Was somebody mean to Mommy?" Angela asked.

Michael was glad about the question. It was the main one he was hoping for. "Yes, Angie. Someone was. Very mean."

"And they put her in jail?"

"Yes, Aiden. They did."

"But why?" Angela asked.

Michael wished he could answer the question. Besides being over his kids' heads, he didn't fully grasp what was going on himself. He felt honesty would be his best bet.

"I don't know, sweetie," he said, lifting the curls from her face.

"How long will she be in jail?" Aiden asked. The second question Michael feared.

"That's another one I can't answer. I wish I could. I want Mommy home, too."

Michael was relieved that neither child was crying. But the news was fresh, and the realization had yet to sink in. Once the *missing Mommy* part kicked in, he was sure tears would flow. And he knew some of those would be his.

"Mommy says when we don't know what to do, we should pray. Can we pray for Mommy, Daddy?" Aiden asked.

This was the second time Aiden asked to pray for his mom. Michael felt embarrassed he was again unprepared. He thought back to Aiden's prayer the night before and how impressed he was with its simplicity and how centered it was around God's protection of his mom. His dad once taught him that same assurance. Today, that peace no longer rested with him, but he needed to somehow convey it to his children more than ever.

"I-I'm not sure where to begin. It's been a while, Aiden."

"That's okay, Daddy. I can pray."

Michael was again overwhelmed that his five-year-old could pray with such finesse and boldness. He used words he barely had a handle on, and Michael was ashamed he wasn't the one who had taught them to him. The father was supposed to be the spiritual leader; he learned that from his dad. And he had been lacking in that department.

With Aiden's "Amen," they all shared a group hug.

"I love you guys," Michael said as the embrace broke, and Aiden leaped from the bed.

Michael kissed Angela's forehead, chased Aiden down the hall to his room, and tucked him in. The worry of a mom behind bars was alleviated. He exhaled deeply as he turned out the light and continued down the hall. Calm as he may have shown, his nerves were shot. He opened the door to his and Rachel's room and stared at a cold, empty bed. Not ready to face reality, he shut off the light and headed downstairs to his recliner. At least there he could pretend he fell asleep watching the game and having to answer to an angry wife in the morning.

His recliner was warm and welcoming, as were the sounds of the commentators and squeaking overpriced sneakers on an arena court. He didn't know who was playing or the final score, and he didn't care, just anything to occupy his mind and lull him to sleep. And that it did. Before he knew it, the darkness had been replaced with light, and the morning commentators were discussing how much of a thrashing the home team had taken in the previous night's game. Michael looked around for the time only to remember he had left his watch upstairs, off his wrist because of the bath, and his phone on Angela's nightstand. The ticker on the TV said it was seven-thirty. Time to get up. The kids would be expecting to eat soon.

†††

A loud buzzer and the opening of her cell door woke Rachel from the sleep she had finally fallen into about an hour earlier. While more comfortable than she had expected, her single-bed cell was not a place where she found solace. The room was cold, not only in temperature but in appearance. The monotone grey was off-putting. It wasn't dark, but neither was it lit; it played tricks on the eyes, sucking the life out of you. Even with her eyes closed, she could see it, keeping her from sleeping.

"On your feet. You have a visitor," the shrill voice said as the room illuminated.

Rachel stood as quickly as she could, knowing the penalty for not adhering to an immediate order. However, her sleepiness gave her stance a wobble, and she almost fell back onto her bunk. The corrections officer chuckled as she watched Rachel regain her footing. Rachel wiped the sleep from her eyes and stood upright.

A gentleman in a starch-pressed white uniform stepped in. Rachel didn't recognize him, but being in the enclosed room and not seeing many faces, meeting someone new was not unheard of. He looked her up and down with an eerie knowing glance. Rachel wanted to grab her blanket to cover up; even in her prison coverall, she felt exposed.

His stare continued for a long moment; Rachel wasn't sure if he was ever going to speak. The man finally met her eyes and breathed, "Seems we have an issue here, don't we, Citizen?" He turned to the guard, "We are fine. Thank you, Madame guard, you can leave us. If I need you, I will call."

The guard looked between them, saddened, like she was about to miss out on something. The glance only added to Rachel's nervousness.

After the guard shut them in, the well-dressed man repeated his question. Rachel was not sure how to respond. The court did not allow her to speak to her attorney after the hearing; she wasn't sure what was happening. "I-I'm not quite sure what you mean, sir," Rachel said.

"You're a smart girl. I'm sure you've had time to figure things out by now." The man's lips widened into a sinister grin, and the corners of his eyes forked; he wasn't as young as he appeared to be. "You know why you're in here. They have fully explained the charges against you, correct?"

"Yes, they have. The lady—"

"Doctor," the man corrected.

"Yes, sorry. The doctor I spoke to was not as open to my invitation as I hoped she would be."

Her visitor began to laugh. It was more heinous than his smile. "My dear, you had no *right* to bring up such a subject to anyone. It's not your place. You knew full well it was against her personal rights to hear about *God* or *Jesus* or any of *your...* beliefs, especially in a public forum. It's against the law. If *anyone* should understand these laws, it is you, Citizen."

Rachel's head tilted, "Me? I-I don't follow."

"Don't follow? How could you not? I'm sure you've been told the bedtime stories."

"Sir, I apologize. I have no clue what you are talking about."

"Your family has been making waves in this town for quite some time," the man explained, his face turning a light shade of pink. "One would think the lot of you would have learned your lesson the first time."

"Sir, I apologize. I still have no clue what you are talking about," Rachel said, turning toward the Official but realizing her error and snapping back to attention.

The man went silent as his eyes closed. He took a deep breath and slowly exhaled. "You should ask your father-in-law, Citizen. He will fill you in on all the details. Until then, I hope you enjoy your accommodations," he said with a flourish of his hand. With that, he turned to the door. "Guard!"

"I don't understand, Official," Rachael pleaded.

"You can just sit here and *count* the days until you do," the Official said as he pulled out his pocketknife, releasing its blade; it caused Rachel to yelp. The Official turned to the wall and etched four straight lines, then connected them diagonally. He pocketed his knife and looked back to Rachel. "Does that help you, Citizen? I'm sure your family knows all about it from your father-in-law's bedtime stories."

"What are you talking about? My family? What about my father-in-law?" Rachel asked, relaxing her attention stance again as the buzzer sounded, the door slid open, and the guard returned.

The man remained silent, turning toward the guard.

Rachel grabbed the man's arm. "You need to tell me."

"Unhand me, Citizen, if you know what's good for you," the man said, not flinching or reaching for Rachel's hands.

But the guards did.

"Rachel Andrews, if you do not release the Official, you will be restrained by force," the female guard barked.

Rachael didn't listen. "Please tell me what Jacob Andrews has to do with this, Official."

"Rachael Andrews—" the guard raised her club and knocked Rachel to the ground.

The Official waved her off and knelt in front of Rachel.

"Tell your father-in-law that Official Kendrick Edwards is on this case. He must answer for his crimes against Official *Nathan* Edwards," Kendrick Edwards grinned again, stood, and brushed the imaginary dust from his arms. "There was no need to become unpleasant, Mrs. Andrews. We can do this as civil as we can."

"How civil is using me as the pawn in this game you're playing when I don't even know the rules?"

Edwards laughed again. "Fair enough. I was being facetious anyhow. You could tell your attorney, not that it would matter."

"How's that?"

"From this moment forward, this trial will be held within a closed courtroom. Completely private. No public for any of you to poison with your God-talk. Judge Ellison has placed a gag order on everyone. All I've just said to you is confidential. You can tell your attorney that Kendrick Edwards has a watchful eye over you and your family, but he can't tell them. He would be breaking a court order and end up here with you, and what good would that do you?"

"Where is the fairness in that?"

"Fairness?" the Official's laugh echoed in the small cell. "Who said anything about *fairness*? But I assure you, this is all perfectly *legal*. Well, skating on the edges, maybe, but I'm well within the parameters of the law. But my dear, this has nothing to do with being fair. Jacob Andrews took family from me. Now it's my turn to take family from him. Only I have a heart. He will get to see you from behind bars and not visit a grave marker as I have had to these past quarter century."

Kendrick Edwards turned and walked out of the cell, the guard at his tail. She locked up behind them and dimmed the lights back to their twilight ambiance. Rachel sat on the edge of the slab she called a bed and tried to remember the stories Jacob had told her while she and Michael were dating. She hadn't really heard much from her grandfather about the old days; Frank Dunham wasn't a very talkative man about such things. She knew he was part of a group of men who started the church Michael's dad pastored. She remembered vaguely that Jacob had taken over the pastorate when the original pastor died. *How did he die? And what was all that about Nathan Edwards?* She couldn't remember—or didn't want to remember. But now it seemed as if it was the most important thing in the world.

"Closed door?" Michael said, reading what was handed to him. "What does that mean?"

"It means, Mr. Andrews, that moving forward, your wife's proceedings will be held behind closed doors," the man with too firm of a pressed shirt and blue tie explained.

"But I'm her husband. I should be allowed in the courtroom."

"You'll have to take it up with the judge on Monday morning. All I am is a service clerk."

Michael read the document again as the man turned and walked back to his vehicle, on his way to ruin someone else's day.

"What is it, Mikey," Lindsay asked, coming to the door behind him. Lindsay was Michael's kid sister. Kid meaning four years younger. She peered over his shoulder. "Uh oh. Court order?"

"Yeah. You can say that," Michael said, then looked up at the car driving away. He nodded to it, and Lindsay's head followed his gesture. "Rachel's hearing is going to be closed door. I can't go anywhere near it."

"Can they do that?"

"Apparently," he said, holding up the paperwork.

"But you're her husband."

"That's what I said."

"Or yelled," Lindsay said. "That's what brought me down here. I thought you were gonna take the man's head off."

Michael chuckled. "No, I'm fine. Well, I'm not *fine,* but I wasn't going to hurt him."

"He sure scampered away."

"Didn't notice," Michael read the notice a third time. "Why would they keep me out of the courtroom?" As he asked, his pocket buzzed causing him to jump, and Lindsay echoed his yelp. He looked at caller ID and started to step away.

"Sorry. It's Johnathan Clarke, Rachel's attorney. He must've been served, too. Perhaps he has more answers."

Michael answered the call as Lindsay excused herself, waving toward the kids in the house. He nodded with a thumbs up. "Hey, Johnathan. What's going on here? I was just served."

"Yeah, same here. We need to meet. I'm near your house now. Can I stop by?"

Michael looked down at his plaid PJ pants and bear slippers. With a half-hearted smile, he answered, "Sure. Come on by. How far are you?"

Right on cue, Michael looked up to see a silver sedan pull up in his driveway, "How about ten seconds?"

Michael chuckled. "Do you like toaster waffles?" he asked.

"I already ate. But thank you." Johnathan laughed, parked and met Michael on the stoop, and the two shook hands.

"You didn't have to dress up on my account?" Johnathan said, taking in Michael's appearance.

"Only the best for the one who's going to get my wife out of this jam. Or I guess it is molasses by now?" Michael said, holding up the paperwork. "What the heck is going on, Johnathan?"

"Let's go inside," Johnathan motioned toward Michael's feet, then the house. "Before you attract hunters."

✝✝✝

Lindsay was cleaning up in the kitchen, and laughter from full tummies could be heard from upstairs. Michael led Johnathan to a freshly cleaned kitchen table.

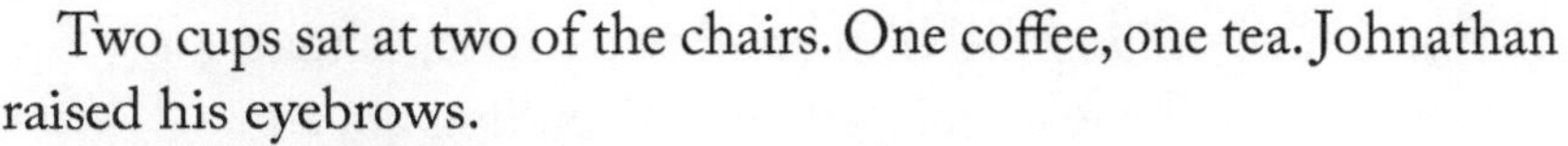

Two cups sat at two of the chairs. One coffee, one tea. Johnathan raised his eyebrows.

"Johnathan, this is my sister, Lindsay."

"We've met," Johnathan said, shaking her hand. "How are you, Lindsay?"

"Fine," Lindsay said flatly, exiting the room.

Michael looked over his shoulder and then at Johnathan. "Dare I ask?"

"Best you not," he said.

Michael raised his hands. "Fine by me. Your business."

"Let's just say attorney/client privilege. Anyhow, we need to focus on Rachael and this court business."

"Right," Michael said, shaking his head. "So, what in the hell is going on here, Johnathan?"

"I was served this morning just as I arrived at my office. So I jumped in my car and headed here. I was hoping to head off the server. Guess they had a separate one for you."

"What does this mean? Closed door? Can they do that?"

"It appears so," Johnathan said, pulling the copy of his order out of his briefcase.

"Is there anything we can do? Can we fight it?"

"I plan to. That's why I came here. We need to talk about how to go about this, what exactly we want, and how hard we really want to push. If this is like your dad says and there is more going on here than meets the eye, pushing back will only make things worse."

Michael rubbed his face with his hands into his hair. "I don't know. I just don't know. I don't want to make things worse for Rachel. But where's that line? How far is too far?"

"At this point, raising our hands could be too far," Johnathan admitted, "if these people are as bad as I've heard."

"But that was decades ago. You'd think they would've matured by now?"

"I think they would've wised up enough to make it look like she initiated the incident."

"You're really filling me with confidence here, Johnathan."

"Just trying to be real," Johnathan said, pulling out a pen. "What do you want me to do?"

"Do what you need to do. You're the expert. I just want to help Rachel without getting her in deeper or hurting the kids in the process."

Johnathan began to scribble on a notepad. "Would it be okay to talk more with your grandparents?"

"Frank?"

"Yes. He may have better insight about what we may be dealing with."

"Sure." Michael saw Johnathan's hands pause after he had written the names and numbers, he had given to him. He knew what was next. "You want my dad's info, too, don't you?"

"He has more details than any of us. Especially if this is about the past."

Michael knew he was right, and if he saw vehicles and people in the shadows, they needed to get ahead of whatever was happening.

"You have his information. Go ahead and give him a call or stop by the gym or church, whatever he chooses to call it now," Michael said.

Johnathan nodded, pulled out his phone, and noted the information it contained for Jacob Andrews. He closed his phone, sat back in his chair reading over all he had written and nodded.

"Does Margaret still work at the diner?"

"Maggie is partial owner now. She works a shift now and then, but not really as a job. More as something to do to get her out of the house. She does well enough as Frank's wife."

"Mmmhmm," Johnathan said, adding to his notes.

"What about other acquaintances who may have known your father and Frank Dunham."

Michael walked to the fridge and pulled a business card from beneath a magnet. He handed it to Johnathan. "Roger Mills and his wife, Jessica."

"Mills Motors?"

"Yeah, that's them. They have a shop in the middle of of town. They've owned it for years. Since before I was born. Heh. Like everything and everyone else in this town, people don't go very far."

"You know them well?" Johnathan asked.

"Yes. I work in the hardware store across the highway. I've been a manager for nearly eight years now. My dad used to work there. He was a parts runner. It's how I got the job. I started in the same position and just worked my way up. After the owner passed away, Roger took over, and he kept me on. He asked me to take over managing the place, I accepted. We have an office manager who does all the billing and paperwork, but I take care of the place."

"Hmm. Interesting. Small towns."

Michael laughed. "Yeah. Hey, New Braunfels isn't so big."

"We are nearly a hundred thousand, not ten thousand. That's quite a difference."

"I suppose. Well, other than the Mills and Dunham's, that's about the extent of the circle who were around back then."

Johnathan clicked his pen closed and set his pad on the table, "It's a start."

"You don't think this will dredge up old memories? Stuff that should remain in the past?"

"Do you think I should leave it alone if it means leaving Rachel in prison?" Johnathan said.

Michael ran his fingers through his hair again. He knew the answer. He didn't want to hurt his family or friends, dredging up old memories, but this was his wife. He had to take the chance that their Christian attitude would be willing to help him despite what it may rehash.

Michael nodded. "It is something we need to do."

"I agree," Johnathan said. He stood, placing his notepad in his briefcase. "Is there anything you need?"

"Do you write doctor's notes for work?"

Johnathan laughed, "You're on your own there. You'll get through this, Michael. Maybe going to work will help. I know you want to be in that courtroom. But if they want to play this out in a negative fashion, your best bet is to stay as far away as you can. It is my job to get Rachel out. I promise I will do my best to do so and keep my cool doing it.

"Just remember that I will most likely be placed under a gag order. Please don't ask me any questions. If you do and I answer them, we can both get into trouble. I could be removed from her case, even from answering one question. We will know more after the hearing on Monday. I will share with you as much as possible, but stop probing when I stop talking. Got it?"

"I understand," Michael said.

"I mean it," Johnathan stood, picking up his briefcase. "Not even a second try. I know how…" he paused, looking for the right word, but Michael understood.

"Johnathan, I got it. We don't take *no* for an answer. I promise. I won't press."

"Alright. As long as we are on the same page. I only want to keep both of us from harming the case and your wife."

Michael saw Johnathan to the door, and they agreed to meet later that evening while Johnathan prepared a new approach that would exclude Michael.

Not having the official word from the judge, they took the risk of having another meeting before their court date to discuss what would happen going forward. Each scenario made Michael even more nervous. The cases Johnathan presented to him were dark, and he seemed embarrassed by how the legal system treated the accused. Nonetheless, Michael was grateful for his candor and the preparation for what they might be heading into.

Two case files were sitting off to the side. It was apparent Johnathan was saving them for last. Curiosity got the best of Michael when the stack of files hit its low point; he nodded to the two folders.

"So, what's the story on those two?" Michael asked.

Johnathan glanced from the folders and Michael, reluctance on his face. Michael saw through him as if he were a Wi-Fi relay station; the files were of his parents, or at least his father—he was the one with a criminal record.

"Let's see them," Michael said, waving his hand.

Johnathan reached for the folders and placed them on top of the stack they had made between them.

"My mom has one too?"

"That isn't your mom," Johnathan explained. "She was never arrested or detained. One is your father. The other is a copy of the employee file on one Official Nathan Edwards."

Michael's eyebrows raised, "Isn't he the—"

"—the Official that was tied to *the incident*," Johnathan completed his sentence. "He *died in the line of duty*. Or that was the authorized story tied to the incident. Of course, your father was cleared of any wrongdoing. It was blamed on his deputy, Jesse Durrant. CCTV shows the struggle they had before the device went off. Even though your father fled, he was not being detained at the time, and he did phone authorities about the fire at the Department, so no charges were filed."

"I knew he was involved, but I didn't know he was actually there," Michael said.

"Your dad never told you any of this?"

"No. And I've never asked."

"Well, maybe it's time."

"Thank you, everyone, for attending this morning," Jacob said, closing his sermon. Michael glanced around the room. It was more filled than he anticipated. He had trouble finding a chair when he arrived. One of the women recognized him and quickly led him to the front row, where she found him a seat. He didn't want the spotlight, but it had been placed on him with a fatherly smile the entire service. His dad continued, "May God be with you. If any of you need anything, I am always here, and you have my contact information. Let's pray."

Everyone stood, and another gentleman he only knew by face said a prayer. Frank played a closing hymn, something Michael knew only the tune. There were no lyrics to be seen. Everyone else seemed to know the words by heart. He felt out of place and a bit ashamed—the preacher's kid not singing along. After a few glances around, he closed his eyes and feigned prayer until the music stopped.

When the final chord played, Frank said, "Thank you, friends. See you next week."

The crowd started to exit the building. Some remained behind, chatting as they returning the room to the gym-like atmosphere it had before the service. Michael stepped back, waiting for the room to clear and for his father to break away from those around him. The scene took him back to when he was little. He remembered how the crowd would gather around his dad. Someone always wanted to talk to him or shake his hand. To a kid who was either hungry or just wanted to get home and play, it seemed like it took forever. Today, with all the questions he had about the past, that childhood anxiety returned; it seemed to be taking an eternity.

Jacob glanced his way and must've noticed his impatience because he ended his conversation and made his way to him.

"It's good to see you here, son," Jacob said—a smile as big as Texas on his face.

"It's not what you think, Dad," Michael said. He knew his dad wanted him to return to the church and God. But religion was the last thing on his mind right now. Getting his wife out of prison was the priority. And if the secret of his past held the key, this was where he needed to be. "I need to talk to you about what happened with Jesse Durrant." No need to dance around the issue.

The smile on his dad's face disappeared, and he looked at the men stacking chairs. They hadn't looked their way. "Let's go into the office."

Jacob directed the chair stackers on what to do with the room as they left through the facility to the office they had been in a couple of days prior. It was much cleaner than it had been, more organized, and smelled of cleanser.

"Please sit," his dad said, pointing to the same chair.

Michael sat.

Jacob sighed. "Okay, why do you want to talk about Jesse Durrant? Rather, who mentioned him to you that you want to know about him?"

"I'm not sure what's happening, Dad. First, from what you and Frank have said, we have been watching our backs. But I received a court order barring me from the courtroom during the hearing. This was after Johnathan did a little research in preparation for tomorrow's hearing. He came across older cases and found that you were there when Official Nathan Edwards died. That it was blamed on his deputy, Jesse Durrant. The reports showed that you were there moments before that event happened."

"I didn't—"

"I'm not saying you did," Michael said, cutting off his father. "I'm just trying to piece together everything that happened back then. All I know is the pieces of a three-year-old mind and the case files Johnathan and I have gone over. I want to be prepared for what may come next."

Jacob sighed but didn't answer.

"Dad. I'm in the dark here. We don't know why Rachel is being kept from us. Something is going on beyond our control. There seems to be more than meets the eye with this hearing."

"I don't know what to tell you, Michael, other than what I've already told you."

"Tell me about what happened when I was two years old," Michael said.

"What do you want to know?"

"Everything," Michael said, sitting back and folding his arms. "I want to know who Official Edwards is."

Jacob matched his son and sat back in his chair, stroking his chin.

"C'mon, Dad."

"Hold on, son," Jacob said with an extended hand. "I'm just trying to figure out where to begin. It's been over twenty years. I've pushed that man out of my mind," Jacob paused. "But there isn't a week that goes by that his face doesn't sweep across my mind. I'm just grateful you were young enough that you don't have to go through such memories."

"Let's begin with the jail. What law did you break that put you in prison with him?"

Jacob chuckled.

"This is funny?" Michael said.

"No, Son, it's not. Sorry. But, when I look back at how I was, I can only laugh because God saw me through it. I was young and stupid. I was a hothead and thought I could get away with anything. It wasn't too long after the laws became enforceable here. Edwards was the Official appointed to our area. To make a long story short, your mom and I were separated at the time. I went to the house and made a scene. She called the police, but Edwards showed up. He and I had an altercation, and he took me into custody."

"How long were you in jail?"

"Three months."

"So, what happened after that?"

"It is not so much what happened after that but inside that prison cell."

"Is that where you met Eric Lassiter?"

"Yes. Yes, he was in another cell in the jail with me. He is the man who led me to Christ. If it weren't for him, I wouldn't be where I am today."

"Hmm," Michael responded.

"We talked through a vent at the top of our adjoining cells. Eric helped me see that I was full of hate and needed to change, or I would die trying to live the life I wanted to."

"Was he right?"

Jacob sat lost in thought, looking into the distance, then back to his son. "Yes. I was determined to see you and make things right on my terms. I didn't want to fail, and I was trying so hard to do it my way that I was pushing your mother away. And getting in the face of that Official that day—" Jacob shook his head. "And now, knowing what he was capable of. Yeah, my life was in danger."

"But Jesse was the one who ended up dying," Michael said, not sure how his dad would react to the comment. It wasn't well.

Jacob's eyes began to tear up. "Yes. He sacrificed his life so I could get away. Edwards wanted to pin Eric's death on me, then murder me and say it was an escape attempt."

"But how did the authorities know it wasn't you?"

"CCTV. That and before Jesse came into the room, he videotaped a confession about his involvement and Edwards cruelty and what he had done to Eric. It was enough to exonerate me."

"Where was Mom?"

"Home," Jacob said, wiping tears. "She had no idea what was

going on through most of this. We had gotten back together, and you two had stayed with me in my apartment until…"Jacob paused.

"What?"

"…until your mom was ready for me to move back into the house. We had things to straighten out."

Michael knew his dad was leaving something out. But he could tell it was a sensitive matter, so he left it alone.

"So, what happened after Edwards was gone and things returned to normal?"

"That took about a year," Jacob said. "By then, local police were back in charge of the area, and we haven't seen an Official since. That office was torn down. It's a car wash now. I won't go near it. Neither will your mother."

"The Spik and Span?"

"Yeah, that's it,"

"Dad, I go there twice a week to wash my car. Sometimes, I have the kids with me." Michael suddenly felt sick. Not that the man meant anything to him, but shining up his rims over a double homicide didn't sit well with him.

"It was a long time ago, Son. I figured it didn't matter. It's in the past," Jacob sighed and walked to the window. "In the past, where it should stay."

"When did you first notice the SUVs again?"

Jacob's head turned to the side. "Why does this matter all of a sudden?"

"If you and Frank are seeing SUVs, something is about to happen. It may already be happening. Rachel's arrest may not be an isolated incident."

"You think it's connected?"

"I don't know," Michael said. "But when you consider all the subtle hints we have been receiving, from the comments Xavier has been making to Johnathan, you, and Pops sightings, and now with Rachel's closed-door hearing? You must admit the coincidences are piling up fast."

"What do you want from me?"

"I need to know what to expect next."

"I don't know, Son. The laws have changed. All I knew was what Edwards could and would do. I have no clue what's going on now. Edwards is gone, so he poses no threat to us or Rachel."

"What about those SUVs?"

"What about them?"

"When was the last time you saw one?"

Jacob looked out the window again and didn't speak. Michael knew what that meant; his father was hiding something.

"Dad?"

"This morning."

"Today?"

"I think," Jacob said. "I don't know. It all happened so fast."

"Tell me about it."

"I was outside helping a couple out of their car when I saw the reflection of Denalis in the window. By the time I spun around, they had disappeared into the traffic."

"Could've been your imagination."

"Two of them? Back-to-back? Same color?"

"Could be."

Jacob shook his head and sulked back to his chair. "I don't know, Michael. I felt uneasy, but not to the point of canceling services."

"Johnathan mentioned something Xavier said as well. Something about *plants?*"

"Hmmph," Jacob said with a smirk. "Not likely. We had no visitors this morning, and everyone here I know personally."

"So, the plants back then were visitors?"

"For the most part. You can sense when one is around. They just seem out of place. The good ones can blend in well. But I think I could sniff them out now. They go too far. They are overly enthusiastic and get close to what is happening too quickly. If they are smart, they will find a balance before going too far, or they will be accused of breaking the very laws they were sent to expose."

"Which are?"

"Even that has changed. Back then, things were simple. Voice your opinion publicly against someone in authority, and you could be arrested. But Official Edwards took it too far and made himself judge and jury. He had the right to arrest me. He just went about it the wrong way."

"Is that why we don't have Officials down here now?"

"Part of it, yes. The Nathan Edwards name became synonymous with brutality. It gave Officials a bad name. They still operate and function as their own entity alongside law enforcement. That much hasn't changed. Only the laws have."

"So, these law changes are why Rachel was arrested?"

"Michael, you have to understand, if she was just talking to someone and mentioned God, Jesus, or even faith, and they were offended, then they had every right to have her arrested. It's the law now. I'm not saying it's right or that I agree with it, it is just how it works now."

"So, she's in real trouble then?"

"Yes, she is. I'm not going to lie to you. Things can get worse if this has anything to do with religious plants. You need to pray for an understanding and lenient judge who will see past the game and maybe even a judge who is saved themselves."

"What happened with your judge?"

"Heh. That is where you're lucky. I never saw a judge. I was arrested and immediately taken to jail. Where Rachel is now is part of the Nathan Edwards improvement plan on the Federal Speech Act. His actions caused its rewriting, or rather amendments to it. But with the additions, the rules also became stricter. The lines clarified what can and cannot be said and done."

"So, Rachel seeing a judge protects her?"

"If she sees the *right* judge."

"Guess we will have to pray about that." Michael swallowed hard as he spoke. It had been a while since he had said those words. It was one thing to pray with his children—another to talk to God himself. He was reminded of his son and how he prayed. His guilt returned, and looking back at his father, he realized that he hadn't lived up to the example that had been set for him. He had been shunning it for so long. It was about time to embrace his past. He needed it, his kids needed it, and now his wife needed it more than ever.

The kids were still asleep when Michael woke up. He was already on his second cup of tea when Lindsay entered the kitchen. Lindsay had slept on the sofa and was just getting out of the shower. She was also an early riser, one of the few qualities they shared. Other than that, they were night and day. She was like Rachel, but different. Rachel had grown to love their differences. To Lindsay, his idiosyncrasies were a childhood annoyance that brought back memories of a bully who'd pull her ponytail and blame it on the dog.

Lindsay saw the kettle on the stove and the crumpled tea bag. She let out a soft grunt, remembering her brother's tea preference. "So, no coffee then?"

"There is freeze-dried in the cupboard." Michael chuckled.

Lindsay grunted again.

Michael knew his sister hated freeze-dried coffee even more than tea. He pointed to the corner of the counter. "Coffee is made, Sis. Rachel drinks it. And I know you can't function without it."

Lindsay gave him a cold glance. Michael knew better than to toy with a coffee drinker before their fill of caffeine, but messing with his kid sister was just too much fun.

"Creamer and milk are in the fridge. Sugar and Splenda are in the cupboard above the coffee maker."

No thank yous were uttered. She shuffled to the maker and

found the cup that was waiting. After a few sips, she shuffled and sat at the table next to him.

"Good morning," he said.

"Good morning," she echoed.

After she drank a few more swallows, Lindsay spoke again. "So, what are you doing since you aren't allowed inside the courtroom? Are you still going to the courthouse?"

"That's my plan," Michael said with a sigh.

"Are you going to behave yourself?"

Michael's brows furrowed. "What is that supposed to mean?"

"I know you, brother. You can get a little heated when things don't go your way. I just don't want you to overreact when this goes down."

"I'll be fine," he said, taking a sip of his tea.

"As long as you're sure. Your attorney is good, but there is only so much he can handle."

"Sis, I'll be fine.

"Gotcha."

Michael understood what Lindsay meant. He was even questioning himself. Not being able to talk to Rachel was wearing him down. All he wanted was to see her and make sure she was okay. Even five minutes with her would do.

"What time is the hearing?"

"The courthouse opens at nine. I can be in the lobby, but that's as far as I can go. Johnathan says we will see the docket, but they don't post any times. It just depends on where your name is on the list, I suppose. I will call you. Thanks again for staying with the kids."

"No problem. It's not like I have a life I need to live."

"Lind!"

Lindsay laughed, almost spilling what was left of her coffee. "I'm just teasing, big bro. You know I'd sell everything to help you. You're family. I love you."

Michael smiled. "Sell everything? Yeah. Your cat and that boring column that no one reads."

"Hey! That column goes to 500K of San Antonio. And can I help it if my cat doesn't like you? Maybe if you'd visit more, he'd recognize you."

After a good laugh, the room quieted. The coffee pot beeped, telling them the warmer was shutting off. Michael excused himself and headed upstairs to get dressed. He was grateful for his sister. He was reminded of how protective they were of each other. They both knew how eccentric their dad was. Lindsay wasn't even born when their parents struggled. His memories exist only in spurts. And concerning the spiritual, his dad was protective of everything that dealt with God.

Michael was sure to check each room before he left the house. Both Aiden and Angela were asleep, lost in dreams of a better time and place. Maybe even dreaming of Mom. He thought of waking them to hug and kiss them goodbye, but that could raise questions he was not prepared to answer. Let them sleep. He, in a way, felt guilty because those questions would be passed on to Lindsay. But she was the writer. Maybe her story would be more convincing than his.

✝✝✝

"Call Johnathan," Michael told his Bluetooth, which obeyed his command. The ringing buzzed through the car speakers.

"Good morning, Michael. On your way to the courthouse?"

"Yeah, just left the house."

"Take your time. Rachel is the final case on the docket. They just posted it. Meet me in the lobby. There is a bagel shop around the corner I want to try. Park in the garage of the Justice Building. It was practically empty when I pulled in. That and we need all the mojo we could get."

Michael chuckled, "I think you and my father would have a difference of opinion."

"Yeah, well, I'm praying, too, if that means anything."

"I'll be there in ten minutes."

Michael disconnected and made a left onto the street that led to the highway. He noticed the vehicle behind him did the same. It pulled up closer to his bumper than he cared for. Its squared headlights lit up, causing Michael to squint. *What is this guy doing?*

High beams flashed again and passed on his driver's side—it was a GMC Denali. Michael went numb as he watched it pass; its windows were tinted. Then, he was immediately blinded by a second pair of high beams through his rear-view mirror, closing in. Returning his attention to the road, he had to slam on his brakes. The first Denali was now in front of him and at a near stop. The second truck on his tail resembled the first. The three of them were driving in tandem down the highway, less than a vehicle's length apart. Michael was trapped.

"Call Johnathan," Michael hollered to the Bluetooth.

"I do not understand the command," the vehicle responded. "Do you wish to make a call?"

Michael took a breath and enunciated his request, and the call went through. "That was fast. Are you here—"

"Johnathan. I'm being chased by the Denalis. Those trucks my dad and Frank described. They are real. They exist. I don't know what to do."

"Call the police," Johnathan said.

"What if they *are* the police? We don't know who we can trust."

"What do you want me to do then?"

"I don't know. You're the attorney. If anything, you are a witness if anything happens to me," Michael said as they drove through a red light. "Johnathan, these guys are getting dangerous. We just blew through a light. Luckily, there was no traffic."

"Just stop. Pull over or something."

"And then what?"

From the silence, Michael knew Johnathan didn't have an answer. "I don't know how these guys are getting away with this. Traffic is picking up."

At those words, the second Denali behind him pulled onto a side street, allowing Michael to slow down, then the second switched lanes, made a U-turn, and headed in the opposite direction.

"Johnathan. They are gone. I guess the traffic spooked them, or they feel they made their point."

"You okay?"

"No," Michael said, hands sweating, his nails digging into the wheel. "But yeah, I'll be there in a few minutes." Michael disconnected the line and realized he was trembling. He wanted to pull over to recenter himself but didn't want to give his visitors the opportunity to return. Completing his trip and getting to the courthouse would be his best bet, where Johnathan, and better yet, unbiased witnesses would be.

After he pulled into the garage across from the courthouse and rounded the second turn, he found Johnathan waiting. As he had stated, it was fairly empty. He held out the number four and pointed ahead. He found Johnathan's car and a spot not too far from that fourth slot. Michael was still shaking when he turned off his engine. He sat with his eyes closed and took several breaths. A knock at the window startled him. Michael rolled down the window.

"Now, why in the world would you do that to me?" Michael half snapped.

Johnathan surrender-posed. "Sorry. Just making sure you're okay. Guess not. Want me to leave you alone?"

"So they can come back? No way. I need to be with people. Let's go inside," Michael said, unbuckling.

"What happened?"

"Not now. Let's get inside, where it's safe. I don't want to be caught out here if they followed me."

Johnathan didn't argue but followed Michael into the office building and down an elevator. Once in the lobby, Michael scanned the room, making sure no one was paying extra attention to them. But it was just a typical Monday morning of busy executives and tired clerks rushing to their jobs on the floors above. Traffic rushed by the windows, but none were black or SUVs.

The two men reached the front doors, pausing to scan what they could of the street, glad to see no parked vehicles. Luckily, a crosswalk in front of the building led to the courthouse. A group of suit-clad men stood around the light pole as the light above them turned yellow, then red. The crowd entered the intersection.

"Let's go," Michael said, taking control of their movement.

Johnathan followed close behind, nearly holding hands. "Michael. Calm down. We're fine. Those vehicles are gone now. If they are secretly following you, why would they show themselves in public?"

"I don't want to take any chances. Who knows what their intentions are? If they were bold enough to corner me on the open highway…" Michael bumped into a briefcase-holding female in front of him, entering the building.

"Hey," she hollered.

"Oh. Sorry, ma'am." Michael stopped where he was, stepped aside from the path, and took a breath.

"You okay?" Johnathan said, placing his hand on Michael's shoulder.

"Yeah. No. I don't know."

"You're shaking," Johnathan said.

"You would be too if you were nearly run down."

"Yeah, I suppose you're right. Let's get inside and sit down."

Michael and Johnathan found a coffee shop on the first floor and ordered. They sat as far away from the window as possible but with a view of it at Michael's insistence.

"So, what happened exactly?" Johnathan finally asked after receiving their drinks, and Michael had a few sips.

"They appeared out of nowhere," Michael began, then took a long sip. "I'm not sure. The next thing I knew, I was boxed in, and they wouldn't let me speed up or slow down. We ran two lights. The one in front of the mill and the one just outside of town. Then they took the turnoff, and I lost sight of them. I thought they would appear again at the light, but I guess they didn't take that right. That's when I hightailed it here. I didn't see them again."

"Well, now we know one thing," Johnathan said.

"What's that?"

"Like you said, the SUVs exist," Johnathan shrugged.

"A helluva way to find out." Michael chuckled, glad for a bit of levity.

"Now we have a problem, though. We know that there could be more to this than a simple arrest. Or Rachel's arrest triggered something bigger."

"You said her case was later on the docket?"

"Yeah, the last one for the day. There are three ahead of her. Two are jury trials, so who knows how long things could take. We may not even be seen today. It's wait and see."

"And hope the lenient judge we witnessed the other day makes a return. She sure pulled a one-eighty when she saw Rachel's case file, though. And she was speaking, like in code. I don't know. Maybe I'm just paranoid."

"No. You're not. There was something odd about that hearing. I'm not looking forward to going back in there. I don't know what to expect. And after what you just went through, I'm not sure I want to go in there."

"But you/I have to," they said in unison.

"Yeah," Johnathan said.

Michael suddenly realized he was drinking coffee. He never drank coffee. It was always tea for him. He felt invigorated and took a breath, "Okay. It's time to get back up there and see where we stand. We need to get you prepared. They most likely did this to shake us up. Let's let them know they failed. We need to be strong for Rachel. She needs us; she needs you. *I* can't be in there, but you can. So, let's forget this morning happened and move on to what you are going to do when you step into that courtroom to outwit your opposition and bring Rachel home."

With their case being the final on the docket, the halls were nearly empty; no one else had reason to be there. The case that had exited the courtroom was in the far corner, speaking in a hushed whisper. One of them was in tears. *That couldn't be good.* Michael's stomach was regretting his coffee and danish. He looked up at the sign for the restrooms and considered a visit, but was worried that if he left, Johnathan would come out with word about Rachel. So he sat and waited in an uncomfortable knot, trying to catch a comment or two about what happened to the lady in tears.

The day had gone by slower than anticipated. He and Johnathan were ready to pack up for the day when the bailiff requested that Johnathan enter the courtroom. Johnathan looked at his watch and shrugged; it was ten minutes until the end of the day.

Johnathan pouted to Michael, "Guess we see what happens. Maybe this will be quicker than we think," he said and followed the bailiff into the courtroom.

That was an hour ago. Michael began to pace; the crying family had left, the mystery of their burden unrevealed.

The courtroom doors rattled, and Michael's head spun around; *just a clerk.* Her heels clicked on the tile as she walked around the corner, fading into the distance, leaving him within the humming of the AC.

What could be taking so long? Michael was hoping they wouldn't turn the lights off on him. He walked toward the doors, hoping to get a peek inside. As he reached for the handle, the door swung open, almost smacking him in the face.

"Michael," Johnathan called out. "You okay?"

"Yeah, I'm fine." Michael rubbed his face from the injury that almost was. He blinked a few times and turned to Johnathan, who was getting out of the way of the others exiting the courtroom. "What happened? What took so long?"

Johnathan looked and pointed toward where they had been sitting, "Let's sit down."

Michael followed his lead.

"At least this time, I was able to get a response on the record. At first, it felt like I was going to get a quick, *This is how it's gonna be, and you're going to like it*, but I went in there having decided that I was going to say something whether they liked it or not."

Michael could feel Johnathan looking at him for a reaction. He nodded.

"Yeah, sorry. I know we didn't discuss that. I know we chose not to rock the boat out of fear of what it could mean for Rachel. But I figured we needed to fight because if we don't give a solid defense, we have nothing to appeal. If she is being railroaded, perhaps a higher court could see through what is decided here. And speaking up gets it on record."

Michael nodded. Johnathan was right. Standing aside and letting them steamroll them was a bad idea. They needed to push back in some way. Rachel may not know what's happening, and seeing her husband and attorney do nothing in her defense would be confusing and disheartening.

"What did they say?"

"Same thing as before, only more in legal terms. They are trying to make this completely about JSI2399. Mainly over the amendments added concerning secondary offenses. Which ones makes little difference. Just know they are basing all of this on laws that are on the books, which, unfortunately, Rachel *did* break. She mentioned God to a person who was not willing to receive it. That is illegal, technically."

Michael shook his head. Part of him kept wondering why his wife could be so careless, especially about God. She knew the laws. But he also didn't share her enthusiasm for faith. He realized that through his experience with the kids. They had that spark. A zeal that made him jealous. Could that spark have caused someone to throw caution to the wind and talk to someone despite the dangers that exist? Would his wife take that risk?

Johnathan continued, "They laid out their case against her, even letting Dr. Houston speak. But this is not like any case I've ever tried. It doesn't seem like it will be *a witness takes the stand, and the lawyers examines and cross examines* type of case. At least, that isn't what it was like today. I've never seen an accuser give an opening statement. I don't know if it was legal or if it has precedent. But she spoke with legal terms, eloquently, and held the jury's attention."

"That can't be good," Michael said. From the look on his attorney's face, he agreed.

"By the time she was done, even I was convinced of her guilt," Johnathan shrugged. "Sorry. I know that's not what you want to hear, but hearing it from the victim's mouth has that much more power. They instructed her well, Michael. I don't know how else to put it."

"And you? How did you counteract her sinking our ship?"

Johnathan sighed. He pulled out a manilla legal pad and read it over. "First, to set your mind at ease, I didn't lose control, nor did I mention anything about what we think we know. I did, however, question the method of the proceedings. I wanted an explanation as to why you were excluded from the list of allowed parties in the courtroom. I asked why on two occasions, imperative documents were missing from what the court had and what I had received. I informed them that this left me unprepared and caused me to lose credibility before the jury."

"That is toeing the line, questioning the court's integrity," Michael said.

"I know, but I'm only stating this to get it on the record. It's walking a fine line, but it needs to be documented that I'm not receiving all the paperwork I'm entitled to, and I am not able to provide Rachel with the best defense due to it."

Michael nodded. "How did they respond?"

"Appropriately. They objected."

"I thought you couldn't object to an opening statement."

"You can't. But they did."

"Did the judge allow it?"

"She looked to the prosecution's bench and lifted her hands. They matched her pose. I thanked her and continued. She did inform me that I was close to being in contempt for questioning the court's integrity, which appeased Mr. Ford. I asked again for an explanation. She blamed it on a court clerk or my ineptitude again."

"So it didn't work."

"I wouldn't say that. From my side glances, I think it struck a chord with the jury that it happened on more than one occasion."

"You mean you hope," Michael said.

"Don't be so negative. We need to take each moment as it comes. Judge Ellison knows someone messed up, and the only way she can cover up that someone screwed up is to shovel the blame back onto us. We can hope that some of the jury will see through the crap. If they do, we are good."

"And if—"

"Michael!"

"Right, negativity. Sorry. Anything else?"

"I asked about ORO. As expected, they are not going for that. They fear she will flee the country. Understandable, but I felt I needed to ask. For the kid's sake."

"Thank you," Michael said. "Opening statements were all that happened then?"

"Basically. A few housekeeping comments from me since we

were not allowed to speak at our previous hearing. I asked about visitations and the possibility of amending the current order of keeping you out of the hearing."

"And?"

"No-go on allowing you in the courtroom. As for seeing her, they feel it would compromise the case and confuse her. What that means, they would not elaborate. I asked, but they just stated it was a matter of privacy. I plan to look into it further and see if I can find laws or precedents that would overrule their judgments to get you in there."

"Don't rock too hard. You can't get thrown off this case. They may not allow anyone else as good as you or could appoint some staff flunky just to appease the paperwork and send Rachel away for the full term, or worse."

"Trust me. I know what I'm doing. I think I've found the line and am playing their game well enough not to cross any lines. Rachel is in good hands."

"Were you able to talk to her?"

"Just the customary hello and legalese questioning. I haven't determined who is listening. We sat about five feet apart. A liaison sat at the end of the table; I was not a hundred percent sure what that was about, but I figured it was from the prison to ensure she behaved. They did allow her to sit uncuffed, but she was still in her prison uniform, which was off-putting. That communicates guilt to the jury."

"How did she look?"

Johnathan was quiet. Michael remembered the last time he saw his wife. The look on her face was gut-wrenching. The empty eyes and disheveled appearance made him want to cry. He wanted to see her today in hopes of seeing Rachel in better spirits to wash that memory out of his mind. Even if she were still saddened and confused, at least it would be a better picture of what his memory held of her.

"She looked good," he finally said through a forced grin.

Michael saw through the exaggeration. He knew it was for his benefit, and he appreciated it. "Thank you," he said.

Johnathan nodded. "Anyhow, after a little back and forth about procedure, our opening statements are complete. Now, that's all I'm at liberty to say. I was permitted to share that much with you. From here on out, I've been expressly warned that I'm forbidden to share any case information unless the judge herself grants me the authority, and that's highly unlikely. But I believe we're doing fine so far."

Michael nodded. His life and wife were now in the hands of his attorney, and whatever game was being played out behind the doors in front of him was beyond his control. He tried to believe things were going to work out, but his confidence in others was shaky at best. He liked being in control, and having someone else behind the wheel of his life didn't sit well with him. Just the thought of one of those forces not having his best interests at heart only made things worse.

$$\text{\LARGE ||||\ ||||\ |||}$$

Jacob was wiping down workout equipment. The dust layer on some unused pieces was not doing well for the front of an active gym. He needed to encourage more church goers to visit during the week. *Feed the spirit, feed the body.* Jacob chuckled. *Sermon topic, perhaps.* He provided each member with lifetime gym memberships, but few took advantage of them. The church was, after all, well-funded, to the point where the gym was self-sustaining. The parishioners knew the importance of keeping the church alive and safe. Jacob was grateful for that.

He was in the middle of spraying down an elliptical when a knock came at the front door—rather a clink—the sound of metal on glass. Jacob looked up at the clock. It was still an hour from opening, and he wasn't expecting Michael and the kids for another two hours. He gave the equipment room a quick glance and headed to the door.

Passing his office, he caught a glimpse out of the window and saw a sight he would rather not have seen. He froze in disbelief. It was a black SUV.

Tink. Tink. Tink.

The frosted glass revealed the shadow of a tall figure holding what appeared to be a nightstick. A cowboy hat completed the ominous tower.

"Open the door, Citizen," the man called out. "I know you're in there. I saw you through the office window, and I can see your piece of crap pick up in the parking lot."

Citizen?

Jacob stood, not sure what opening the door would bring. He wanted to call someone, but his cell was in the office. What if someone was watching the office through the window? He couldn't chance it. Now, he wished he had listened to Renae and put that second line in the storage room. But it was too late for regrets.

Tink. Tink. Tink.

"I can think of three reasons to break this door down, Citizen."

Jacob could think of a few more than that. He had no choice. He approached the door and unlocked it.

The patented white uniform of an Official stood before him. The grin behind the reflective lenses seemed all too familiar.

"Now, was that so hard, Mr. Andrews?"

What can I do for you, Official?"

"I was just in the neighborhood and saw the car parked in the lot. It was early, and I wanted to ensure you were not in distress. We've had reports of unauthorized activity in the area, and I wanted to confirm your safety." The Official's eyebrows raised as he nodded back at Jacob's truck. "Sorry about the comment about your vehicle. I just needed you to open the door."

"I'm sure you meant no harm," Jacob replied in a monotone cadence.

"Of course not," he shrugged. "I'm here to serve and protect. After all, when law enforcement isn't available, I'm your only hope. But I'm sure you understand the responsibilities of an Official, don't you, Mr. Andrews?

"All too well, Official—? I don't believe I caught your name."

"I don't believe I gave it."

"Mmhmm."

"It's quite all right. You will understand who I am soon enough, Citizen. I'm just around to ensure our neighborhood remains secure. You want that, right? You wouldn't want any *illegal* activity to occur around your place of business, would you, Mr. Andrews?"

"No, I wouldn't. And you are here to ensure that doesn't occur."

"Now you are catching on," the Official said, patting Jacob on the shoulder. "As long as we have an understanding, you and I should be good friends."

"I have enough friends," Jacob said.

"Now see, why would you say that? I'm trying to be friendly, and you're being difficult."

"I'm just trying to find your angle."

"Why would I have one?"

"We haven't seen an Official around these parts for fifteen years. Why now?"

"For that very reason, Citizen. Your area doesn't have an Official to monitor activity. We can't have folks creating havoc and disobeying local, or worse, *federal* laws, now, could we?"

Jacob hated the way the Official glared at him behind his lenses. He hated the way his expressions would reflect and reveal his own contempt. That was not who he was, but this branch of law just brought it out of him. This Official saw what it was doing to him, and he was milking it.

"Official, you have nothing to worry about here," Jacob stretched the truth as far as he could. "We are a fitness center, and the days you are insinuating are behind us."

"Insinuating? I have no clue what you are referring to. I am simply here to check on your well-being. I saw your car in the lot and thought you could be in distress. Nothing more." He smiled again, tipping his hat. "Seeing that you are well, I will bid you a good day."

"Thank you for your concern, Mr. Official. I appreciate your concern. I *am* well. May I get back to opening my gym?"

"Of course. Have a blessed day, Pastor," the Official said.

"Thank you. You as well," Jacob said and closed the door.

Jacob took a few steps into the gym and froze, nearly passing out. He realized what he had just done. He turned back toward the door—he could hear laughing, an all too familiar voice walking away from the door. He shook in fear. *How in the world could it be?* He saw that man die. He ran to the window, but all he could see was an SUV driving away.

†††

"What are you talking about, Jacob?" Renae asked. "Slow down. You're not making sense."

"I told you. He's back."

"Who's back?"

"Edwards."

"Jacob, Edwards is dead," Renae said with a sigh. He knew that sigh. She had given it to him before. It was the one she gave him after his bad dreams to reassure him that the boogie man was gone.

"Renae, this was not a dream. There was an Official here. He said that he was going to keep an eye on us. When he left, and I shut the door, I distinctly heard Edwards laughing."

"Jacob, maybe the Official was laughing, and he *sounded* like Edwards."

Jacob sat in silence. The thought never occurred to him. The sound grabbed him so quickly any other option fled his mind.

"It was so close, Renae. I was convinced it was him."

"Maybe he was doing an impression to scare you?"

"Pretty dang good one. He had me going," Jacob said, peeking out the window again.

"Honey, it's fine. You're fine. We're fine," Renae said. "It was inevitable that Officials would make their return to Carrolton. Just be glad they're out of hiding now, and we can stop wondering."

Jacob took a deep breath. As always, his wife was right. He had been looking around corners and watching his back far too long. For them to finally make their presence known would be a relief. He could recall when Edwards would have his two cronies sit in the school parking lot just watching them, he wouldn't feel fear. He knew where they were. Now, he could have that same relief. It was the one thing this unknown badge didn't realize. He thought the pressure would cause apprehension. It would be quite the opposite. Their visual presence was a relief.

"You're right, babe. Thanks." He smiled and walked away from the window back toward the gym. "Will you be by for a workout after work today?"

"Yes, that's the plan. I'm getting in the car now. See you later, love."

He blew kisses into the phone and ended their call.

Jacob walked through the gym, ensured it was as clean as needed, and unlocked the front door. He had two regulars waiting.

"Good morning, Laura. Hello, Timothy. How are y'all this morning?"

He was welcomed with excited stories of being ready to begin their day and the goals they were aiming for. He smiled with words of encouragement and waved them in. Jacob walked the sidewalk outside the parking lot, looking for signs of his visitor. When he was sure that he was free of the eye on him, he paced back toward the building. When he stepped up on the sidewalk, Michael pulled into the lot. Once parked, one bouncing redheaded girl and a brown-haired boy ran his way, hollering his name. It only added to the comfort he needed. He wished the straight-mouthed man walking behind them would add to the comfort they gave, but he would need some work. Yet, the look in *his* eyes had changed; it held fear. Something had happened. He wondered if he had a similar story to what he had just experienced.

"Good morning, Michael." Jacob did not want to assume. His son had a way of hiding his emotions or reflecting them poorly. Better to let Michael approach him with news, good or bad.

"Dad, we need to talk. Do you have a moment before you begin your day? It will only take a minute," Michael said, looking around.

Jacob knew then he was looking for the same thing. "We better go inside. If your story is anything like mine, indoors is better than standing outside in the open."

Michael's eyes widened. Jacob just nodded, giving his son a knowing glance toward the building. He turned toward the door, half-listening to the kids trying to explain about Mommy being in jail, but God was with her, and she was going to be okay. Jacob looked back at Michael; he could only shrug his shoulders. But Jacob understood. What else could his son do? Sleepovers and being sick can only take you so far. If the truth was bound to come out, even to a four-year-old, better come from a parent than a stranger.

Once inside, Jacob directed them to the play area. The room was sometimes used for aerobics and other group exercise activities, but not on Tuesdays. Today, it would be used for daycare. Parents came and went through the day as they worked out around busy schedules. They also came and went as they visited him as their Pastor. The church still ran secretly while the gym did its business. Jacob still felt the sting of the sin of law-breaking, but desperate times called for drastic measures. He was taken back to the secret church meetings in the school's basement. This was no different. Only the laws were different, stricter. He knew how bad the situation was and how much trouble he could get into, something Michael constantly reminded him of. But the good he was doing, he felt, outweighed it all. So he remained in the shadows until this morning. Now, all he was doing was in danger of being exposed. And the little ones he was bringing into this place—what would it mean for them? It was probably what his son wanted to address this morning.

Emily took the kids, and Jacob led Michael into the office and closed the door.

"I'll show you my hand if you show me yours," Jacob said, sitting in his office chair and directing Michael to do the same.

Michael sat and took a breath. Jacob could tell Michael's story could be more harrowing than his. "You okay, Son? Do you need anything? Water?"

"No," Michael extended his hand, "I'm fine. I just have a story you won't believe." Michael paused and shook his head. Jacob understood his faux pas. "Sorry. You will most certainly believe what I'm about to tell you. And I'm only sorry I didn't believe you sooner. From your expression when I walked up, I can see you have a story yourself, Dad. Let me tell you what I've been through the past twelve hours, and we can compare notes."

$$\text{卌 卌 IIII}$$

By the time Michael and his father had exchanged stories, he felt guilty for ever doubting him. He relived every moment that he had let his facial expression get the best of him and saw the hurt on his dad's face. He wished for those moments back. He would've done a better job of listening and at least trying to believe. Michael now understood his fear, not knowing what would be waiting for him when he pulled out of the parking lot. He felt it was a miracle he made it to the gym that morning. Would they attempt anything with the kids around? Were they that bold? Were they when he was little?

"You don't have to apologize, Michael," Jacob said. "I will admit. I was paranoid for many years. I put you, your sister, and your mom through way too much. It's a miracle she hasn't left me. I don't blame you for our estrangement. That's on me. I think it's even driven your sister to do some of the stuff she's done," Jacob added.

Michael started to ask but thought the better of it. He didn't need to know. If it was bad enough to need an attorney, it was something no one was proud of. If he didn't know about it, that's the way people wanted it. Best to leave it alone. If they wanted him to know, they would tell him.

"Regardless, Dad. I put you in an awkward position. You needed me to believe in you. And I failed you. I'm sorry."

His Dad smiled. He hadn't done that too much lately, at least one that seemed genuine. He looked back at the door and then up to the clock. Two hours had passed; his brows furrowed.

"Yikes. I need to get out there," Jacob said. "I'm surprised they haven't checked on us."

"I'm sure they figured it must be important with you closing the door."

"True. But I have a lot to get done out there. I have to meet… *training sessions*," his father corrected.

"Ah, I see." Michael chuckled. "And I need to get to the courthouse. I didn't tell Johnathan I was stopping by. He may be concerned if I'm late with all that's going on. With your story, we may need to change our approach."

"What about Rachel?"

"I will talk to him. Right now, our best bet is to keep a low profile," Michael said, a bit slower so his dad could catch his hint.

He must have because Jacob let out an exasperated sigh. "Michael, you know I can only do what God leads me to do. I can't hold back because a little bit of danger arises. And I think Rachel would agree. If she didn't, she would not have spoken to the lady in the supermarket."

Michael knew his father had him there. Although he still didn't fully understand it, God had His way of working. Keeping a low profile was not always on His agenda. If the stories about his dad and his group were true, a time came when they stepped out of the shadows and took their stand. Would this be true of him as well? He knew his dad was firmly planted. He was even convinced his kids had a stronger rooted faith than he did. He looked out the window and wondered what would happen if an SUV pulled up and tried to challenge him. What would his stand be?

"You are both stronger than I am," Michael said. "I don't think I could ever be as tough as you two are."

"Faith takes time, son," Jacob said. "It isn't something you can turn on overnight. It takes testing. One can say they have it, but unless it's been proven, you're just going through the motions. But don't worry. You're being tested right now. Your faith will strengthen through this trial if you allow it. Stay strong, Michael; trust in God."

Michael never considered what he was going through as something that would draw him closer to God. If anything, he thought adversity usually drives people further away from God. But if there was one thing he knew about his dad, it was that he never blamed God for the bad things in his life. He always taught that pointing fingers and screaming at the sky did nothing to solve the problem. He needed to take something from that.

Michael sighed, "I should let you get back to work. I need to get to the courthouse. Johnathan is waiting, and I still need to drop off the kids with Frank."

The men stood. Michael extended his hand, and Jacob pulled him in for a hug.

"I will be praying for you and Rachel. You *will* get through this. Your mom and I are here for you. You know that, right?"

Michel nodded.

"I know you've kept your distance from us, but there is no reason to anymore. We're in this together. You, me, and Frank should meet soon. We need to talk about what we can do now that these Officials have made things public."

"And to see if they have made things *official* with him."

"I should give him a call," Jacob said, picking up the phone.

Michael headed for the door. "I'll call you later with an update."

As soon as Michael stepped outside, his phone buzzed with a couple of notifications. One voicemail, another text. Both were from Johnathan, wondering where he was. He returned his call and let him know he was on his way. There were no signs of anyone following him, but that did nothing to comfort him. According to his dad, they could hide in the shadows, and one would be oblivious to their presence. He had no choice but to go about his business as usual. He said a quick prayer as he turned toward the courthouse.

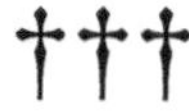

"Fourth is better than last," Johnathan reassured him as they sat on the same chairs they had sat the day before.

"It still means the rest of the day sitting here guessing," Michael sighed.

Michael shared his father's experience with his attorney. Johnathan could only shake his head. Other than the document service, it appeared they were leaving him alone. It made little sense to Michael; why not scare the attorney away? It would be his first move; scaring Johnathan enough to drop the case or run away. Maybe they had other plans. His Dad said they were smarter than that. Even though a reaction may get the case stalled, it wouldn't get it thrown out; it would only cause a delay. They wanted the case to proceed. A conviction is what they wanted, and since they held all the cards, why would they need to frighten the attorney? Leaving him alone was a threat enough.

"Who do you think this Official is?" Michael said. "We haven't had any of them around Carrollton in over a decade. Interesting with Rachel's arrest, he suddenly appears."

"You said our mystery guest stated they are reentering the area after being away for so long," Johnathan said. "We need to find the trigger. It can't be a coincidence Dr. Houston was in that market at the same time Rachel was."

"Rachel told us the same thing," Michael said. "Remember, she said she felt it wasn't a coincidence they kept passing in the aisles. She said it felt like God was speaking to her. But what if Dr, Houston instigated the interaction and Rachel misinterpreted that as God's hand?"

"It's possible," Johnathan admitted. "But there is no way to ask her about that right now. I can't get ten feet near her without some sort of liaison. So, all we have are assumptions."

"At this point, does it matter when you talk or what she says when you do?"

"According to the legal system, yes. The world changes the moment I walk through those doors. You think it's bad out here? It increases tenfold when I walk in there."

Michael stood and paced. "I want to be in there. I need to be in there," he said with growing frustration.

"The tension in your voice is why you shouldn't," Johnathan said. "Especially after your ordeal. You'd most likely lose it in there. Let me handle it. *I* am your voice, so let me do my job. You can trust me, Michael. Just be patient."

The doors swung open, and the second case walked out, frustration on the faces of the men exiting. "Can you believe that judge; the audacity," said one to the other.

Johnathan shrugged. Michael paced to the end of the row of chairs and sat, turning away from the doors, burying his face in his hands.

As Johnathan watched Michael wallow, the doors to the courtroom opened again, and the bailiff nodded to him. "Attorney for Andrews?"

"Yes, sir."

"Judge Ellison is continuing the case before yours. She is ready for you. Is your client here, Counselor?"

Johnathan looked at Michael, "Hey, Michael. I'm up."

Michael looked up, confused.

"They continued the case before ours." Johnathan met him halfway. "The judge is ready to call us. I'm heading in before she gets even more upset."

"She's upset?"

"She is if those attorneys were any indication. I don't know what to expect, but better to expect the worst and hope for the best. I'll talk to you later," Johnathan said, then entered the courtroom.

The doors swooshed behind him, and he followed the bailiff down the aisle. The judge was wrapping up the case being continued. She seemed agitated that the prosecution did not have their star witness in the courtroom. From what little he heard, there had been an incident at the jail, and the witness was unable to appear.

Johnathan sat in the second row while they set a date for the next hearing, which would take place upon his release from the infirmary and return to the jail.

Johnathan cringed at the mention of infirmary and the thought of Rachel in the same predicament. How would he explain something like that to Michael? How serious were these people? If they were willing to nearly drive Michael off the road and threaten an eighty-year-old man, how far would they go within the prison where the blame could be easily passed off? He feared Rachel's appearance, rather feared more the lack of it with the story behind the case of the gavel slap that just occurred.

The attorneys left the courtroom, the offended attorney at a slower pace, his head shaking toward Johnathan. Johnathan shrugged with a grimace.

"Is there a problem, counselors?" a voice called to them.

Johnathan looked up. The judge was standing at the bench, looking in their direction.

Wide-eyed, the caught-in-the-act attorney turned around, "Nothing at all, Your Honor."

"Not at all, ma'am," Johnathan echoed.

"I would expect not, gentlemen. Please clear the courtroom if you do not have business here."

"I am Johnathan Clarke, Your Honor, attorney for Rachel Andrews," Johnathan said, as apologetic as he could manage.

Judge Charlene Ellison picked up the case file on her bench, lowered her glasses, and read it over. "I am aware of who you are, Mr. Clarke. Please step forward. The *accused* will be in shortly."

Johnathan was tempted to shake his head again at the judge's sneered address, but he was able to catch himself. He looked to the prosecution side; there was no sign of Dr. Houston. He wondered how much leeway Judge Ellison would give her this afternoon. He opened his case file and studied it for the umpteenth time, hoping to gain fresh revelation. Hoping there were no added addendums that were conveniently left off. He was getting tired of surprises.

The side door opened, and Dr. Houston entered with her attorney, both in freshly pressed suits. *Probably Dior or another high-priced designer. I wonder what she worn that day in the grocery store to mislead Rachel.* They sat, and Xavier opened his briefcase, placing his files on the desk. Johnathan looked over to him with a nod. Xavier returned the half-hearted gesture. He turned to the judge, who was conversing with the bench bailiff. She was looking through the case file, then lowered her glasses.

"Are we ready to proceed, gentlemen?"

"Yes, Your Honor," Johnathan and Xavier said in unison.

"Mr. Ford. We heard from you and your witness yesterday. Do you have anything further before we proceed?"

"No, Your Honor, but I would like to refrain from resting to have the option for rebuttal."

"Granted, Counselor," the judge said. She turned to Johnathan. "Are you ready to present your case, Mr. Clarke?"

"Yes, your honor."

"If we are ready to proceed, you can bring in the accused and jury, bailiff."

On cue, the side door opened, and the jury entered and took their seats. The courts had done a decent job mixing juries, at least at face value: both men and women, a decent mixture of color. Johnathan felt encouraged by the faces he saw. However, if a doctor could be bought, so could a juror and for a lower price. He prayed that they would be able to see through the game being played.

Once the jury was seated, another bailiff entered, escorting Rachel by the arm. Her wrists were cuffed in front of her, as were her ankles. The shuffling of chains echoed through the room. Johnathan fought off another reaction, but when he saw the fresh bruise across Rachel's cheek, he could no longer keep silent.

"Your Honor, what's happened to my client?" Johnathan stood and said a bit too loudly.

"I'm not your client's keeper, Councelor."

The bailiff spoke up, "Be wary of your tone when addressing the judge. You can and will be held in contempt."

"I mean no disrespect. However, I would like answers regarding my client's condition."

"Perhaps your client is an instigator just as she has been accused of here, Mr. Clarke? Do we need to take this into consideration?" the judge inquired.

Johnathan stood in silence. The judge did have him there and in front of the jury. *Any appearance of evil.* He looked to the judge, to the prosecution, to the jury, their faces contorted with confusion; then to Rachel, hers with fear. His mind went back to his discussion with Michael. *Don't rock the boat.* And that is precisely what he was doing. How he was acting out here meant reaction for Rachel back there. He turned back to the judge.

"Forgive me, Your Honor," Johnathan said. "We can proceed."

Johnathan sat as Rachel was uncuffed and led to her assigned position on the other end of the table, court liaison next to her.

"Very well. Now, if you are ready, you may present your case."

"Thank you, Your Honor."

†††

Michael sat in the hallway as the mumbles from the court invaded the silence. He wondered how long he would have to wait this time. It was only one-thirty—plenty of time for the case to go long; plenty of time for the prosecution to condemn his wife for something that shouldn't even be a law in the first place.

The thought of his wife being behind bars for twenty years had yet to register with him. But now that he had the time to sit here alone, outside where those questions were being deliberated, it was the only thought on his mind. He would be forty-seven. The kids would be... Michael had to hold back tears at the thought. They would through college and possibly married, maybe even with their own kids.

No. He shook the thoughts from his head. *This has to end here,*

99

he told himself. *There was no way Rachel can be found guilty.* The kids needed her; he needed her.

Michael stood again and walked the length of the hall. He looked down the corridor toward the elevators. He could see the wind blowing the trees through the window on the other end of the hall. Daylight was dimming; a storm was blowing in. He thought about the kids. Aiden was afraid of thunderstorms. Angela, not so much. He considered giving them a call but didn't want to have to answer questions about Mommy. *How selfish is that?* He heard a rumble of thunder and pulled out his phone.

"Hey, Pop. How's Aiden?" Michael asked, skipping the pleasantries.

Pop laughed. "Nothing out this way. Sky is dark, and the wind is blowin', but the heavens haven't opened up. Yet. Kids don't even know about the weather."

"Good," Michael said. "Sometimes, if you turn up the TV, Aiden won't even know what's going on."

"Yeah. I have a baseball game on. When they are in here, it should drown out anything God dishes out."

Michael snickered. "Who's winning?"

Pop sighed. "Them."

"Sorry."

"It's okay. They end up winning. Come back in the ninth. It's a replay of Sunday's game."

Michael laughed.

"How's it goin' over there?" Frank asked.

"Johnathan's in the courtroom now. I was walking around to keep my mind occupied when I noticed the weather."

"Aiden's doin' all right. Angela too. Peanut butter and jelly for lunch and *VeggieTales* on the TV in the den. Maggs makes a mean sandwich. So blessed to have her."

Michael could hear a rumble of thunder and a child holler through the line.

"Well, that is my cue. Maggie stepped out to the store for some ice cream. I'm on duty," Frank said and called to Angela.

"Alright, Pop. I'll talk with you later. Give them my love." Michael ended the call.

The sky outside the window lightened up, and the winds died down. A beam of sunlight glared off the floor causing Michael's eyes to squint. He could feel its comforting warmth hugging him with hope. He knew his children were safe with Frank. That thought made him smile as he walked back around the corner toward the courtroom.

†††

Johnathan stood. "Defense calls Rachel Andrews to the stand."

Rachel stood and slowly walked to the podium and sat. The bailiff asked Rachel to raise her hand.

"Do you swear the testimony you are about to give is accurate and without fallacy?"

Rachel rubbed her wrist as she raised it, "I swear."

The bailiff sat, and Johnathan approached the witness stand. "How are you this morning, Mrs. Andrews?"

Rachel's eyes narrowed, "I'm okay, I suppose."

"I see you have bruising across—"

"Objection," Xavier interrupted.

"Sustained," the judge agreed. "Mr. Clarke. Stick to the case."

"Yes, Your Honor," Johnathan said.

He looked to the jury to take in their reaction. It was a sea of varied expressions. Some watched him. Some examined Rachel's injuries, others were indifferent. It was those indifferent ones he would need to win over. He paced from the witness box back to his desk and picked up the file. He played like he was reading it while flipping over its pages.

"Mrs. Andrews. I'm looking over your arrest report. I do not see any mention of injuries to your person. Can you—"

"Objection. Your Honor."

"Sustained," the judge said, her voice gaining an edge, "Once more, you will be held in contempt, Mr. Clarke. Either ask a question

101

that pertains to the facts of this case or close your case. Anything else and I will close it for you."

"Understood. Thank you, Your Honor."

This time, he had all eyes on him. Mission accomplished. His heart was racing, bringing him to the envelope's edge. Now, it was time to present his case. *Let's hope it was worth it,* he thought.

"Mrs. Andrews. Can you explain in your own words what happened in the Shop and Save market on the date in question? First, take us through your day. How did it begin?"

"I dropped my kids off with my grandparents. I planned to take them with me that morning, but I just wanted to get in and out of the store. And Pop…"

"Who?" Johnathan asked.

"I'm sorry. My grandparents, Frank and Margaret Dunham, wanted to spend the day with the kids. It wasn't long, so I dropped them off and headed to the market."

"Once you arrived at the Shop and Save, what happened?"

Rachel looked at Johnathan, then to Xavier and Dr. Houston, then up to the judge. Johnathan picked up on Rachel's apprehension.

"Your Honor, may my client speak freely without fearing consequences? I believe she fears that her testimony may cause further repercussions."

"Counselor?" the judge looked to Xavier.

Xavier turned to his client, who shrugged. Xavier said, "We will allow the accused to testify freely without further implication."

"Go ahead, Mr. Clarke."

"Thank you, Your Honor," Johnathan said. Then to Rachel. "What happened while you were shopping at the market, Rachel?"

"While walking through the market, I kept passing Dr. Houston. While I didn't know who she was at the time, I did feel the urge to speak to her the more times I passed her."

"Did you speak to her at any time before your contact in the produce section?"

"No."

"Any eye contact that would give you the inclination that approaching her would be welcomed?"

Rachel looked up at him with a questioning scowl. He knew what it meant, not a question a defense attorney would ask, but he knew where he was going with it.

"No. We made eye contact but didn't say anything to each other. We didn't say anything until we spoke in the produce department."

"And how did that exchange take place?"

"I asked her about a type of onion."

"An onion?"

"Yes. I asked her about the difference between a sweet and a white onion."

"And she was able to help you?"

"Yes. She gave even gave me a great recipe for fajitas."

"And what happened next?"

"She mentioned she was new in town."

"Objection," Xavier stood and stated. "My client has testified and is above reproach that living conditions were never mentioned."

"Overruled," the judge stated. "But noted. Let the accused give her testimony, Counselor. You can dispute it through cross-examination. You may continue, Mr. Clarke."

"Thank you, Your Honor. Okay, Rachel. Dr. Houston. Did she mention she was from out of town?

"Yes. She stated that she had recently moved from Atlanta and was just getting to know the area."

"And then what happened?"

"I asked her if she had found a church to go to. She said no. I then extended an offer to visit the church I attend."

"And you are aware that by talking to people about God to someone who is not receptive is illegal?"

"Yes, I am aware."

"So why would you take that chance?"

"I felt that Dr. Houston would be receptive. We were having a friendly conversation, and I just felt God leading me to speak to her."

"Objection," Xavier said. "We can only give so much latitude, Your Honor. I ask you to draw the line here. A god speaking to someone is going too far; please put an end to this."

The judge looked to Dr. Houston, then to Rachel. "Sustained. Your client's latitude is paper-thin, Counselor. Tread lightly."

"Understood, Your Honor."

Johnathan paused for a moment, then eyed Rachel, raising his eyebrows. "When you felt this...*urge*...to speak to the plaintiff, and you crossed that line, were you aware of the danger you put yourself in?"

Rachel swallowed and closed her eyes, "Now that I've had the time to think about it, I don't think I was really considering the consequences of my actions at the time. I was just being obedient to what I felt I should do at that moment."

"Can you explain that?"

"No. Not without upsetting the court."

Johnathan felt a pull that more needed to be said. He backed up and turned to the jury; they had his full attention, as did the judge and both attorneys. A burning inside overwhelmed him, and the compulsion to speak took over.

"Mrs. Andrews, would it be fair to say you felt it was God leading you to speak to Dr. Houston, and that is why you chose to speak to her despite the existing laws? And this is why you are on trial instead of an issue of a simple offense? In addition, could it be that Dr. Houston is known as a plant and is being used by a hidden party to use you as a pawn to harm your husband and father-in-law?"

"Objection, Your Honor," Xavier said. "Pure speculation!"

"How dare you accuse me of such atrocities," Dr. Houston pushed back her chair and shoved her attorney. Xavier took hold of her arm and pulled her back. Pointing her finger at Johnathan, she continued, "I will have you up before the ethics board and have your license, you insolent fool!"

The judge slapped her gavel, "That will be enough, Dr. Houston—my chambers now Counselors, both of you. Bailiffs, escort the accused to holding and take Dr. Houston back to the waiting area."

$$\text{\Large ||||\ \ ||||\ \ ||||}$$

With a loud slam, the courtroom doors flung open, and Johnathan darted out. His eyes were bloodshot and darting back and forth. He paid no attention to Michael, who had been near the exit; he jogged past him toward the restroom.

"You okay, Johnathan?" Michael asked, following close behind.

Johnathan didn't reply. He swung open the door to the first stall and kneeled into it.

Michael stood back, giving him space. His mind returned to the earlier attorneys exiting the courtroom. Their case must've not gone as planned. He let Johnathan finish business and regain his composure before asking any case-related questions and, more pressing, how Rachel was.

Johnathan flushed the commode and cleared his throat. He walked to the sink and wet his face, dabbed it with paper towels, and turned to him. He began to speak and stopped himself.

Michael remembered. Johnathan was under a gag order not to speak about the case outside the courtroom. Johnathan turned and looked toward the stalls and peeked under each of them. When he was sure that no feet were present, he whispered, "I am not permitted to tell you what happened in that courtroom, Michael. Not only through the paperwork we've been issued but with what just occurred inside the courtroom just now, including the judge's chambers." Johnathan sighed roughly. "I've already said too much.

I need to get out of here. Too many eyes and ears." Johnathan brushed him aside and headed out the door, not waiting for a response.

"Wait," Michael called. "What about Rachel?"

Johnathan stopped at the door. He slowly turned around, "Rachel is fine. I'll meet you later this evening. I need to get a couple of things together for the case. It's four o'clock now. Let's meet at your grandfather's at six." He turned around and exited the restroom.

Michael's mind was swimming with questions. But if he was going to learn anything, he knew the courthouse was not the place. With Johnathan in his current condition, he knew now wasn't the right time. Besides, it was time for him to check on the kids.

†††

"Did he give you any inclination of what happened?" Frank asked.

"Nothing, Pop," Michael said, sipping a cup of coffee.

Frank's eyes narrowed at Michael's beverage choice. "Since when did you start drinkin' coffee, Son?"

"Don't remember. It grows on you, though," Michael said, taking another drag of his mug.

"What time will Johnathan be here?"

"Any time now," Michael said, looking at the clock. It was half an hour past the time Johnathan said he'd be there. He had already texted him twice with no reply.

"I hope he didn't run into any trouble?" Frank said, raising his bushy, ashen brows.

"They haven't done anything to suggest they would threaten him. So far, they've only made moves on us three."

"That you know of."

"You think Johnathan is holding out on me?"

"If I were trying to comfort my client, I would hold back the fact I was receivin' threats, is all I'm sayin'."

"With all that's happened, I think he would be open and honest. He knows the danger and understands the risks."

Their conversation was interrupted by a knock on the door. Maggie answered it and led their visitor into the kitchen.

"Sorry I'm late, gentlemen," Johnathan said. "I got drowned in paperwork. I wanted to make sure I had everything under control before I headed over. And that I wasn't tailed."

"Did you see anything?" Frank asked.

"Nothing that I noticed. I circled the highway twice and then took a back road. No one followed or seemed interested in where I was headed."

Frank nodded. He had been there. He scratched his head and pouted. "Glad you made it okay, John. Take a seat. You want anything?"

"Water would be nice. I need to catch my breath before we begin. I have a lot to cover." John opened his briefcase and took out several folders. Some Michael knew as the case files; others were new, all color-coded.

After drinking a couple of glasses of water and a few pleasantries about the weather and the restaurant, Johnathan suggested they get down to business.

"Everything I am about to tell you could get me disbarred. Even saying I have knowledge of this information is dangerous. But I'm telling you because I believe what is going on is borderline illegal, which is saying a lot considering how strict the laws are."

Johnathan pulled out a file and opened it.

Michael knew Johnathan had a process, but he needed answers. "Why did you get sick this afternoon? What happened in that courtroom?"

"Michael, I know you're concerned for Rachel, but please be patient. I'll get there. I've been preparing for this all evening. I have everything organized so you will understand the conclusion I've come to. And better yet, what I plan to do to get Rachel out of this situation, so please, bear with me."

Michael nodded. The confidence in Johnathan's eyes encouraged him. The nervousness he had regarding his tardiness was now alleviated. He was ready to hear the battle plan to fight for his wife's freedom.

Johnathan finished his glass and took a breath. "Okay. Let's get to it. First, the hearing began poorly. I think it started the moment I stepped into that courtroom. Judge Ellison is hard to read. One minute, she was all over me; the next, she was giving me a favorable ruling. But impartiality can be faked to lessen the chance of being accused of favoritism. Either way, if accused, she would be labeled as fair and impartial.

"We have to remember, Michael, Rachel broke the law. So what we need to prove is she was coerced. That is much harder to do because individuals have a choice."

Johnathan reached over the table and grabbed a folder with a blue tab. "I have color-coded each of these. Blues are the ones that are safe to share with you. Yellow are the iffies, and red are the ones I've been forbidden to share."

Johnathan sipped at his water again. "Don't worry. By the end of the evening, you will know everything I know. I'm tired of all this secrecy. It's wrong, and I now understand that it's not the legal system behind it but the ones trying to keep Rachel behind bars."

"Who is doing this?" Frank asked.

"I wish I could tell you. But right now it all appears to be legal and tied up in a bow." Johnathan exhaled. "I will be honest. If I can't do my job and perform a miracle, Rachel will go away for a long time. But I don't intend for that to happen. I will do my best to find out who is behind this and find a way out of it. We can only pray that the judge is not in on it. If she is, we've already lost."

"Okay, John. Quit dancing around it, and let's get to it," Frank said with a playful slap to the table. "What do you know?"

"I'm getting to it. I have to explain all of this because I need you to understand what we are up against."

"I *know* what we are up against," Frank said as he stood. "I've been here before. I will help as much as I can. *Heh.* I may be older, but I can still fight with the best of 'em."

"Okay. Let's move along," Johnathan said.

"What happened in that courtroom, Johnathan?" Michael asked.

Johnathan paused and fixed Michael with a stare. "Don't get excited, Michael. But something happened to Rachel. She came into court with a bruise across her cheek."

Michael swallowed, doing his best to keep his composure. "Did she say what happened?"

"No. Nor was I able to ask her."

"Right. The liaison you mentioned."

"Exactly. But I needed to get it on the record that Rachel came into court wounded, so I asked her on the stand why she had the bruises."

"Can you do that?" Michael asked.

"No, but I did."

"And how did everyone react?"

"Just as you would expect. The prosecution objected. The judge upheld it. I pressed the issue, and after the second objection, I was threatened with having the case thrown out. So I stepped back."

"I seem to remember you giving me warnings *not* to rock the boat. That sure sounds like boat rocking to me," Michael said, leaning back in his chair.

"It was. But I needed to get Rachel's condition on the record should we get a hung jury and need a reason for appeal. Her getting roughed up in prison is a good start. I'm sorry that it happened, but it is a reason to put doubt in a jury."

"And Rachel? How is she?"

"Bruising across her cheek. She seemed a bit shaken up. I won't lie to you; the place is wearing her down, but there is still strength in her. She is a fighter. I think me standing up for her gave her a bit more stamina."

"Standing up for her?"

"I'm getting to that."

"Why do I get the feeling I'm not going to like this," Michael said as he stood and started to pace.

"Relax. In a way, it's a good thing."

"If it's what sent you storming out of the courtroom and into a commode to lose your lunch, I'm not so sure."

"I will give you that. But it wasn't what happened in the courtroom that hit me like that; it's what happened after. But I will get to that."

"Go on." Michel nodded.

"After the judge threatened me, I paced the front of the bench, and something hit me. A sudden warmth inside. I can't explain it any better than that. It was like I was outside myself but in full control of my mind. I *knew* what I had to do. I walked to the bench and began asking Rachel a series of questions involving her belief that Dr. Houston is a plant."

Both Michael and Frank sat slack-jawed. "You can't be serious," Michael spoke.

"I almost wish I were kidding," Johnathan said, both arms raised.

"How did Rachel respond?"

"She never had the opportunity. Her attorney objected, and the judge sustained even before she had the opportunity."

"But Rachel has no idea what is going on with our plant theory, does she?"

"I haven't had the opportunity to discuss it with her. It was Mr. Ford who mentioned the subject to me, and you and I discussed it, but Rachel and I have barely spoken since our meeting. They won't let me speak to her without the liaison."

"So, was this another one of your *let's get this on the record* stunts?"

"No. Not at all. It just came out. I began to speak, and the words flowed. It was after the gavel slap that I realized what I had said. That and Rachel's wide eyes."

"That's when they took you back to the judge's chambers?" Michael said.

"Yes. They escorted Rachel back to the holding area, and the doctor went—I honestly don't know where the doctor went."

"So?" Frank asked.

"The bailiff escorted me back to the judge's chambers. I could hear the raised voices even before the door was opened. The judge told Xavier to wait until I was present to make any ex parte arguments because anything they would say would be inadmissible without me being present."

"That's good, right? Shows she can be impartial," Frank said.

"Yes. So far, so good," Johnathan admitted.

"The bailiff knocked on the door and opened it before getting an answer. She announced me, and the judge pointed to a chair opposite Mr. Ford. Now, I have known Xavier for the better part of a decade. I had never seen him so upset. His face was beet red, which is difficult for a Black man. Seriously, he was livid.

"I sat, and even though you could tell he wanted to explode, he allowed the judge to take the wheel. She asked why I had done what I did. By then, the adrenaline had worn off, and I didn't have an answer for her. But honestly, I don't think she was looking for an answer. Her question was more rhetorical. She didn't even pause for an answer."

"What did she tell you?" Michael asked. "Did she say anything about Rachel?"

"No. Nothing. It was quite the opposite. It was a warning about accusing the court of impropriety. It was one thing to accuse the jail and the guards of mistreatment, but to accuse her or her courtroom of any type of wrongdoing was grounds for my imprisonment without proper evidence.

"Even Xavier was taken back by the judge's candidness. His red had faded to pink. The judge finished by asking me if I wanted my cell next to Rachel's or if I wanted to be in another block. There wasn't a smile on her face, nor was there a hint of sarcasm."

"How did you handle that?" Frank asked.

"Without the boldness I felt in the courtroom, I did the only thing I felt I could do. I asked for forgiveness. I didn't even try to explain my position because anything I said would offend her and make things worse."

"Did she give you an opportunity to speak?"

"Not a chance, other than to apologize. Once I did that, she wouldn't let me get a word in edgewise."

"And Mr. Ford?" Frank asked.

"I think he had his say before I arrived. She heard enough and was done with the issue. I was glad that I avoided a few nights in a cell. Or worse."

"So that's why you got ill?" Michael asked.

"Wouldn't you? To get that close to going to prison and avoid it by the skin of your teeth?"

Michael shook his head. He looked back at the table. So far, Johnathan had shown them the green and yellow files. "So, what's in the red file?"

Johnathan grabbed it with a sly grin. "This, gentlemen, is my plan to get Rachel out of jail. It won't be easy, and we will have to go out on a limb to get there, but if all goes well, we won't be the ones on defense. Doctor Houston made one error in that courtroom. She tipped her hand in that she could be set off. Right now, I'm confident she is being counseled that she can no longer lose control of her temper in the courtroom. We just need to find those hot buttons.

"Come tomorrow, when the case resumes, we focus on Dr. Houston and what gets under her skin. When we discover that, we find out how to get her to admit she was coaxed into cornering your wife, and if we are lucky, maybe we can even get her to admit she is a plant."

$$\text{卌 卌 卌 |}$$

"We're not scheduled until third. Better than yesterday, but still a wait," Johnathan said through the phone. "Take your time and watch your back. I'm not sure if my behavior yesterday will have triggered anything. It was the one thing I failed to think about. I'm sorry."

"Don't blame yourself," Michael encouraged his attorney. "You said you felt led to do what you did. If you're anything like Rachel, you would probably say it was God leading you, and you wouldn't do anything differently, so don't apologize. I now know they're out there. I didn't yesterday. They no longer have the element of surprise. We're good."

"Okay. But don't get comfortable. We don't know what these guys are after. If they were willing to nearly drive you off the road, we can't let our guards down."

"I understand. I have no intention of letting them get the best of me again."

"Just get to the courthouse and don't make any unnecessary stops. You're fueled up, right?"

"Yeah. Half a tank."

"Good. I'll see you when you get here."

Michael ended the call and finished getting ready. The kids stayed with his parents, so he didn't have to worry about them. He called and spoke to Angie and Aiden, reassuring them their mom would be okay. After a quick check in the mirror, he was out the door.

He checked the street for parked cars or anyone standing where they shouldn't be. When satisfied, he got into his truck and headed for the courthouse. He was careful driving past the location where he had noticed the tail the last time and again around where he had lost it. Taking in his surroundings, he saw nothing at all. Still, he didn't feel at ease until he parked in the garage at the courthouse.

Johnathan was in the same parking spot he had been in before. He held up three fingers. Michael parked accordingly and met him at the elevator. "You okay?"

"Yeah. I wasn't followed, if that is what you mean. I think they've made their point," Michael said.

"I didn't see anything on the street. Either they're that good, or they aren't there," Johnathan said.

"I will rest on the side of not there. Let's get to the courthouse. We can stop at the coffee shop and rest up for the hearing," Michael said, nodding to the elevator.

Johnathan laughed. "Coffee is growing on you, methinks."

"I think it is the only thing keeping me going right now. I can't sleep. All I can think about is, if Rachel can't sleep comfortably, what business do I have to?"

The two men entered the coffee shop, placed their orders, and stepped aside.

"So, are you in the bed?" Johnathan asked.

Michael shook his head. "No. Downstairs recliner. It's comfortable enough. I've fallen asleep in it enough during a ballgame. But now, I can barely catch a wink. The bedroom I can't bear to enter. If I didn't have to go in there to shower and change, I probably wouldn't go in there at all."

"My dad was like that after my mom passed. It took him a month before he could sleep in the bed again. But then—" Johnathan paused mid-sentence, realizing what he was doing. "Damn, I'm sorry, Michael. I didn't mean anything by that. Please, forgive me."

"Please," Michael said. "Nothing to forgive. I didn't think you were insinuating anything. I know you meant well. And I appreciate it."

"We're going to get through this."

"I know. And you're the one who will fight to get us there. I fully believe that," Michael said, hoping more to convince himself.

The street sounds through the window and other patron's conversations filled the silence.

Michael finally spoke. "So, what brilliant strategy have you concocted for today? Make fun of the judge's hair bun? Call her mom a name or two?"

"No, but I do have a list if she gets feisty."

Michael laughed, glad for the levity. He needed it. His mind was swimming with fear of what could be happening to Rachel; even just a brief respite from that was relaxing.

"Thanks, Johnathan. I needed that."

"Don't worry about Rachel. She is strong. She'll get through this. If she can manage birthing twins, an unruly cellmate won't be an issue. Just think of what the other person looks like, *eh*?"

Again, Michael released a belly laugh. Johnathan was right. Rachel could sure handle her own. He wasn't a small man, and there were times when he wanted to cry mercy when she handled him. He exhaled and sat back. "So, what did your dad do to get back into his bed?"

"You don't have to do this," Johnathan said.

"No, I want to know."

"He washed the sheets and sprayed his cologne on the bed. It wasn't that he wanted to forget her, but he needed to break free from the constant reminder.

"Now, I'm not saying you should do that. His wife wasn't coming back. For you, it should be the opposite. You need the comfort of her being there. So, I don't know—spray hers? It could help you feel that she is there. Maybe enough for you to get some sleep anyhow. Yeah, you may wake to the realization she's not there, but it will be easier each time you do. Just a thought."

Michael nodded. He admitted to himself that the idea could work. At this point, he was willing to try anything to get a good night's sleep. Staring at infomercials and replays of his team's repeated losses was wearing thin.

Their order was called, and they discussed the consequences of Johnathan's outburst on their way up the elevator. Johnathan explained that they would pick up from where they left off; Rachel would be back on the stand with the stern warning that any further questions about her condition or any attempt to smear the defendant without evidence would lead to an immediate mistrial and his removal from her case.

A familiar face greeted them when they arrived. "Mornin' gentlemen," Frank Dunham said, hat in hand.

"Pop, what are you doing here?"

"Figured you could use the support."

Michael smiled. He was grateful for his in-law's appearance. He could use someone to talk to while Johnathan was in the courtroom. It would help keep his mind occupied.

"Yes, Pop. It is indeed welcome. Thank you."

The men exchanged pleasantries and sat.

Michael sipped on his coffee, feeling the dark concoction replenish his tiredness. He was saddened by the time missed that his wife had consistently urged him to share with her. It was a silly thing, something like a beverage that you would regret the most.

"We need some privacy," Johnathan said, tapping on the red folder he held.

"Men's room?" Michael joked. "We can't be sure anywhere else would be monitored."

Johnathan nodded, stood, and walked in that direction.

"I was joking," Michael said, but before Johnathan could respond, he was off in the direction of the facility where he had released his tensions the day before.

Michael stood and nodded for Frank to follow them.

Johnathan was either a master sleuth or employed one. He

knew where Dr. Houston was born, where her parents were born, what schools she went to, her class rank, and that she had a puppy named Sparks. He found that she lived in four locations after graduation, three after acquiring her doctorate, and that the home she currently lived in was not owned but subleased, and within the last month.

"That is odd for a doctor," Frank said in a hushed voice. "You would think someone with a doctorate and a practice would want to set down roots and have enough money to buy something."

"Odd indeed," Johnathan pointed out. "She has had three residences in the past three years—one here, one in El Paso, and one, ironically, in Houston. None owned. All rented or, like this one, subleased."

"Have you looked into those cities?" Michael asked and paused as two men entered the restroom. The newcomers exchanged looks with the three men, used the facilities and left.

"Looked how?" Johnathan asked.

"Has she attempted to do anything like this before? You know, cause accidents only to collect the insurance money. Maybe this is something like that. Remember—plant."

"Would make sense," Frank said. "No home. She smashes and grabs."

Johnathan scratched his head. "Why didn't I see that? I was too busy chasing her family and residential history that I didn't see the obvious right in front of me."

"Well, we know it's a possibility now. Have your crack staff look into it," Michael said.

Johnathan pulled out his phone, "Let me text my clerk, Meredith. Get her started on tracing her history in those cities. I always figured it to be job-related. There was usually a title change associated with the relocation. Some sort of accolade that came with it."

"Yeah, a payoff," Frank said.

"Let's not get ahead of ourselves," Johnathan whispered. "We don't want to get it in our heads that someone did something wrong without proof. We wouldn't want that for Rachel. We shouldn't do that for Dr. Houston."

"Just sayin', where there is smoke, there's usually fire," Frank said.

"I can understand that, and I agree, but let's play it safe until we know something solid. Then, we can make our move. Remember, this is family we're talking about."

"You're right. You're right," Frank said. "We can't go jumpin' the gun. No matter how much we don't like 'em. Their guilt or innocence is just as at stake as ours is."

"Exactly. So, we approach this from a legal standpoint and wait until all the evidence is in. Then we make our move."

Johnathan thumbed through his red tabbed file again. He examined the dates to see if he had missed anything. He looked at the door and then handed a few packets to Frank and Michael. "Look at each of these. Look for anything out of the ordinary."

"What are we looking for?"

"You might know it if you find it. Just mention anything that looks out of the ordinary," Johnathan said as he started to read through his stapled packet.

The sound of pages turning and concern filled the room, but there were no epiphanies.

"If I knew what I was looking for, then maybe I could find it," Michael said. "I'm not an investigator. She rented a house, paid her bills, worked for a firm, had a side job for a public relations firm, did some charity work for disabled childr—"

"Wait," Johnathan said. "Go back."

"To what?"

"The side job?"

"It says a public relations firm?"

"Does it give a name?"

"Not that I see on the ledger," Michael said.

Johnathan riffled through the file. He didn't have the details there. They were in the larger file back at his office. All he had was the summary with him. "I need to get back to my office."

"Do you have the time?" Michael asked.

"I don't have a choice," Johnathan said.

"Can't you just call Meredith?"

"She is busy looking for the other information. Plus, I know exactly what I am looking for. It would be quicker."

"If you think it's best," Michael said.

"No time to argue," Johnathan said. He felt for his keys in his pocket and headed for the elevator. "I'll be back."

"How long should you be?

"If there is no traffic? An hour at most." Johnathan said, collecting his files.

"Just remember, I'm not allowed in there, so I can't stall for you."

"I know. Just stall the clerk if they should call the case."

"What should I say?" Michael said.

"You'll think of something. Be creative. You're a dad. Improvise."

Michael looked at the open door and then back at Frank. He had a smirk on his face. He patted him on the shoulder and nodded toward the courtroom.

"Let's grab a cup of coffee, Son. Looks like you could use it."

$$\text{卌 卌 卌 ||}$$

Johnathan tossed his keys onto Meredith's desk. It made a *clank* that echoed through the empty office. He cringed, remembering how tidy she kept her desk, and anything nudged out of place would be recognized the next time she came in. He grabbed them, moved the paperclip holder back to where he assumed it had been, and placed his keys in his pocket. His desk was the exact opposite of the decorum of Ms. Street's: unkempt and overfilled. But to his credit, he knew exactly where everything was. His *disorganized, organized mess*, so he called it.

Luckily, Mrs. Andrews file was not within the Mt. Everest of his desk but on the nightstand under the lamp where he studied current case files. Here was his Milani chair that hugged him every time he sat in it. He wished he had a couple of hours to review his file again, to get a dose of inspiration from the chair's comfort. But he didn't have that luxury. He picked up the file, found his notes, and read over them.

"Myles, Lynn, and Taylor. Well, I'll be da—"Johnathan was cut off by the office door creaking open. "Oh, good. Meredith, you're back. I need you to look into something. I need to get back to the courthouse. I—"Johnathan turned around, but it wasn't Meredith.

A tall, thin man in a white uniform, sunglasses, and a brimmed hat stood with a steely grin. There was a silver badge on his upper left shoulder.

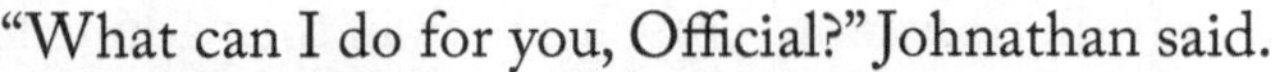

"What can I do for you, Official?" Johnathan said.

"Edwards. You can call me Official Edwards," he said, removing his glasses.

"Official Edwards, sir, what can I do for you?"

"Aren't you supposed to be at the courthouse?"

Johnathan's eyes squinted, but he went along with the line of questioning, "Yes, sir. I left a file here that I needed. I have to defend my client to the best of my ability."

"Right. Right." Edwards nodded. "You plan on showing that file to Mr. Andrews as well?"

"I'm sorry? I don't follow?"

"The file you are holding. You are bound by a court order not to show anyone any pertinent court documents. Are you not?" Edwards nodded to what Johnathan held in his hand. "You have sworn an oath to keep every piece of evidence within the confines of the county court walls. Now, Counselor, you would not have willingly violated Judge Ellison's direct order, would you?"

"Of course not. But that does not bind me from taking files out of the courtroom. I am just not allowed to share them with my client."

"Ahh, that's right," Edwards nodded. "Just that we are clear on the matter of a gag order."

"We are clear. Now, if we are done here, I need to get back to the court. I am not sure how long I have before our case is called, and I need to be ready for my client."

"Just wanted to let you know we will be wat—"

Johnathan cut him off, "And I will have *you* know, Official Edwards, that if you keep coming near my clients, I will have you brought up on charges. I know the law, and what you are doing is borderline harassment and unappreciated."

"As you say, Counselor, it is *borderline*," Edwards said. He replaced his sunglasses and peered at him, his sinister grin returning. "Have a good day, sir. You be safe out there."

Official Edwards turned and exited the office with a growling laugh, shutting the door behind him. Johnathan stood and waited a long moment. He didn't want to cross his path in the parking lot. He turned his back to the door and started to read over the file again.

The door opened and creaked again.

"What is it this ti—" Johnathan snapped as he turned to a startled Meredith. "Oh, I'm sorry, dear. I thought you were someone else."

"I should hope so. Greetings like that would soon see me turning this piece of tail out your door for good, Counselor."

"An Official was just here. Did you see him?"

"Must've just missed the pleasure," Meredith grinned through her green eyes. Meredith had been with Johnathan's office for over fifteen years. She was to him what Della was to Perry Mason. Her spunkiness was one of the reasons he hired her and why he kept her around. "Now tell me why you are snappin' at me."

"I've already apologized for that. But I'm sorry, and I will get into that later. I don't mean to seem rude, but I need you on something, stat. I have something for you to dig into. Do you remember the name Myles, Lynn, and Taylor?"

"Aww, yeah. That crooked firm up in Seattle. They were known for taking bribes to get clients with a rather clean reputation harsher sentences through questionable testimony. But nothing could be proved. Still can't from what I know."

"Still can't," Johnathan confirmed. "They don't practice anymore. They got too close to the fire, and I think whoever was financing them, shut them up or relocated them. You no longer hear about the firm trying cases."

"And what do they have to do with our case?"

"The prosecution's star witness was a witness in one of those cases," Johnathan said.

"Well, not to rain on your parade, but that doesn't prove anything. MLT was never convicted of anything."

"I realize that. That is where you come in. If the good doctor has sat on the witness stand of one bogus case, she has sat on more. I need you to find them." Johnathan handed her the file in his hand. "Go fishing, Miss Street."

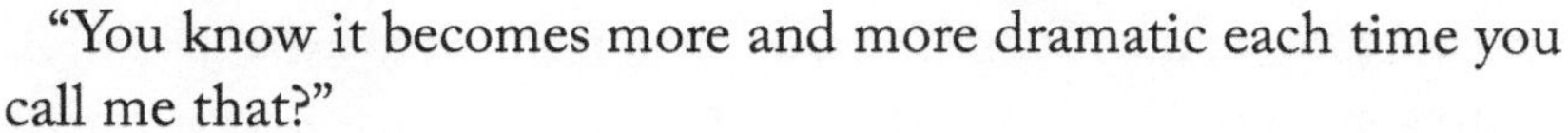

"You know it becomes more and more dramatic each time you call me that?"

"It is your name," Johnathan said, emphasizing the file in his hand.

Meredith rolled her eyes and snatched the file. "I guess it could be worse. I could be named Moneypenny."

"That's my girl," Johnathan patted her on the shoulder. "I need to head back to the courthouse. I really need something before I enter the courtroom. Wave your wand and pull something out of that hat of yours like you always do. Send me anything as soon as you find it. Encode everything FMYO."

"*Hmmph,*" she said, flipping on her computer screen. "And don't think I didn't notice you moved my paperclip holder, mister," she called after him. He gritted his teeth as he closed the door behind him.

By the time he hit the parking lot, there was no sign of any GMC Denali trucks that everyone had seen. Either Edwards was gone or hidden somewhere. In any case, he had no time to worry about a stalker; he needed to get back to the courthouse. He slipped into his vehicle and spoke to his navigation system.

"Call Michael Andrews."

The system responded.

"Hey, Michael. I am on my way. How are we looking?"

"We are next up. No telling how long the case in there will take. It has only been about ten minutes, though." Michael said. Johnathan could hear the tension in his voice. "Just get over here. This is making me nervous."

Johnathan could hear Frank in the background but couldn't make out what he said. Probably some reassuring words to his grandson-in-law because Michael sighed and replied in kind to him.

"I will let you drive. Be safe. Just get here."

"I'm on my way. Be there in fifteen," Johnathan said and disconnected—no need to bring up his law enforcement encounter—no reason to get him riled up. Let them get through today; he could mention it after today's hearing. He still needed to figure out what he was going to do. *Edwards knows things, and now we're in danger of being exposed.*

Johnathan looked in his rearview mirror and saw a silver SUV a few car lengths back. *Guess I'm on their list now, too.* His status of untouchable had worn out. He just hoped he wouldn't face the encounter Michael did. With all the traffic, he doubted they would go that far. And with his Edwards experience, Johnathan figured he wanted to be seen. Officials knew how to remain hidden. This was a mind game to let him know they were watching, just as he had said in his office.

Perhaps their confidential restroom visit wasn't so confidential. He wondered if someone was spying from the lobby or if the room itself was bugged. If there were listening devices, he was done for. If the judge got wind of that, he would definitely get thrown off the case and most likely disbarred. He suddenly felt ill. *I should've known better.* He broke his own rule of no discussion of the case at the courthouse. Now, it could cost him his license *and* the case.

He made the final right onto the street with the parking garage. The Denali followed and pulled up closer. Even the front window seemed tinted, but Johnathan couldn't see inside well enough to make out the driver. He could see the hands on the wheel enough to tell that it was male. There didn't appear to be a passenger. Which meant either Edwards was driving or he was in the rear as a passenger.

Johnathan turned into the parking garage, and the SUV drove on, not slowing down. Johnathan exhaled in relief. Then he remembered that they drove in pairs. He wondered where Edwards' pair was. With caution, he drove up to the second level where he was accustomed to parking. Four slots in, as usual, and no signs of a second Denali, but that didn't mean one wasn't near, and he wasn't going to wait around to find out. He parked, set his alarm, and headed to the elevator as fast as his feet would take him.

Without looking to see who was watching, he pressed the button for the elevator. "C'mon, c'mon," he willed. When it refused to open, he jogged to the stairwell and headed down the single flight to the lower floor, skipping steps as he went. As he reached the door to the lobby, he stopped to catch his breath. Johnathan opened the door and peered through it, not quite sure what he was looking for; guys in sunglasses with a finger to an earpiece, perhaps searching the lobby for the man they had lost sight of. He looked back and forth, suddenly realizing how ridiculous he looked. "What in the world am I doing?" Johnathan exhaled; it echoed in the stairwell. He released a small laugh, entered the lobby, and walked across the street to the courthouse, not even giving a second thought to the SUV that had followed him.

"What happened to you?" Frank asked as he saw Johnathan come out of the elevator. He had been pacing the hall. "You look like you've been through hell, Son."

Johnathan ran his hands through his mussed hair, not realizing how disheveled his appearance was. "I'm fine. Took the stairs in the garage, got a bit winded, I suppose."

Frank squinted, reading him like the morning newspaper. He hated that feeling.

"Where's Michael?" Johnathan asked to change the subject.

"In front of the courtroom entrance. Pretty anxious if you ask me. Seein' you should bring some relief." Frank's eyes returned to normal. "I'm goin' down for coffee. You need anything?"

"No. I'm alright."

"You sure?" Frank pressed.

"Yeah," Johnathan sighed, then looked toward the corner of the hall. "I ran into an Official at my office."

"*Ahh*. I see now," Frank said.

"Don't say anything to Michael. We don't need him anymore on edge than he already is. Please."

"Secret is safe with me. I get ya."

"I will tell him and explain what happened after the hearing. I promise. Let's just get through this."

"You don't need to explain to me. I've been with the boy while you were gone. You are right. Don't need to add coal to the fire."

"Thank you."

"Sure, you won't take anything?"

"Bottled water would be nice," Johnathan admitted.

"Will bring it up." Frank tipped the hat in his hands.

"Thanks again," Johnathan said and headed toward the courtroom.

Johnathan could see Michael sitting in front of the doors, his knee bouncing—a nervous tick he had seen from countless clients. Michael stood and headed his way when he saw him.

"It's about time," Michael said. "I was beginning to think you weren't coming."

"I told you it would be a quick run. Just needed this file so I'd have information for the judge." Johnathan held up the file he retrieved.

"So that will get Rachel off?"

"I didn't say that. It will point us in the right direction of proving that Dr. Houston has a history of being a star witness in similar cases. It could cast doubt on her testimony, but it will be up to the jury to decide whether they find her credible."

"And then Rachel can come home?"

"That is all I can say, Michael. I have already said too much. Please don't ask me any more questions. It's for Rachel's sake and your own. If I give you too much information, it could cost me my place on this case. I am already in hot water as it is."

"What does that mean?"

"I can't tell you. Please, that is all I can say. Don't press."

"What do you mean?" Michael asked.

"Michael, *don't press.* It is for both of our sakes."

Johnathan could see that Michael was processing his words, but wanted to say more. To his credit, he left things as they were. The two men sat in silence for a long while.

Frank eventually returned with the water. He picked up on the tension of the moment and refrained from speaking.

Johnathan hoped he hadn't cost them Rachel's chances of freedom with his choices. He trusted that what he found would change the course of the case. He hoped the threats from Edwards were idle, and he was only pressing to see if he would break under pressure. Maybe he didn't know anything. Perhaps that restroom wasn't bugged after all, and Edwards knew nothing. He knew now that he needed to talk to Jacob. Only he knew how far the Edwards family would go to get what they wanted.

Johnathan looked up as the courtroom doors swung open, and the bailiff peeked his head out. "People vs. Andrews. Judge Ellison is ready to continue your case. Attorney for the accused, please enter the courtroom."

⫿⫿⫿⫿ ⫿⫿⫿⫿ ⫿⫿⫿⫿ ⫿⫿⫿

Johnathan sat still and as quiet as he could. The opposing counsel and jury were not present, and the bench was empty. He could hear voices approaching and the shuffling of chains; Rachel was on her way. How an innocent was treated until proven guilty for such a minor crime made him cringe. It was an embarrassment to the system. At least today, the jury would not see it.

The door opened, and the bailiff followed by Rachel and her liaison entered the courtroom. Rachel looked better than she did the previous day. She looked as if she had bathed and was given the opportunity to at least brush her hair. It was up in a ponytail. He was grateful because it made her look younger and, to be honest, more innocent. Her bruising was more apparent, however. If the jury bought into her being the instigator, that could hurt, but if the innocence of her appearance helped, she looked like the victim even more.

Rachel's shackles were removed, and she sat at the end of the table with her appointed liaison. Johnathan turned and leaned over toward her.

"How are you today, Rachel?" he asked, just above a whisper.

"I'm okay," she said in kind, her eyes meeting his, probably for the first time. "I'm still a bit confused about yesterday. I know you have a plan. I just wish I were in on it."

Johnathan looked to the liaison, who paid no attention to their conversation—or seemed not to. "Part of a bigger plan. I had a

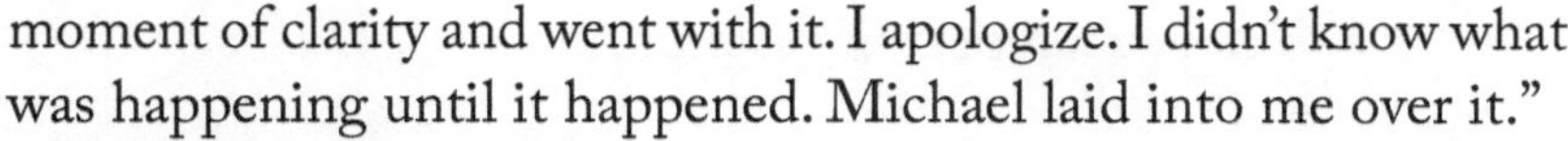

moment of clarity and went with it. I apologize. I didn't know what was happening until it happened. Michael laid into me over it."

"Michael. How is he?"

"Missing you."

Rachel smiled for the first time. It made him smile. They gained the attention of the liaison for the first time. She cleared her throat.

"We… I mean, I am doing the best I can to get things straightened out. Please be patient and go with the flow. I know you have a lot to deal with back there," he said, nodding at her bruises. He lowered his voice to a near whisper, "But keep praying, and God will see you through this."

Her liaison still must've heard because it elicited another clearing of the throat. But it was soon drowned out by the door opening and the jury entering the courtroom.

"Stay strong, and don't react to anything." Johnathan leaned closer again and said, "It's the one thing they will notice. I will do the best I can, Rachel. Just believe in me."

"I will," Rachel answered and sat back in her chair.

The side door opened, and again, in formal wear, Dr. Houston and her attorney entered the room. It was like they intentionally waited for the jury to be seated to make a grand entrance. He wondered how she could appear so well dressed and gain the pity of the jury while her client was essentially in rags and looked down upon. The impressed look on the jury's faces said it all. There was no such thing as the little man, in the right or not. Dr. Houston looked impressive and reeked of authority. Who would accept the story of a woman in rags over hers? They were doomed.

"All rise. The Honorable Charlene Ellison presiding."

As soon as the judge entered, she was handed the case file. She lowered her glasses and read over it, then nodded.

"Please stand, Mr. Clarke," Judge Ellison said, still looking through the case file.

Johnathan stood, straightened his tie, and flattened the panels of his suit jacket. "Yes, Your Honor."

"Are we to expect a repeat of yesterday?"

"No, Your Honor."

"And I was clear about my expectations through our conversation in chambers?"

"Yes, Your Honor."

"And we can proceed without further outbursts?"

"Yes, Judge Ellison."

"Excellent," she said. "One final warning. There will be no additional warnings. One slip up, and if I slap my gavel at you, it means you are removed from the case, and your client will need to find a new attorney. Am I clear, Mr. Clarke?"

"Perfectly, Your Honor," Johnathan said. Nervous as he was to agree, he had no other option.

"Very well, we can proceed. You may recall the accused to the stand."

Johnathan motioned to Rachel, and she stood. The bailiff escorted her to the stand, and she sat. He mouthed, *It's okay,* to her. She nodded.

Johnathan paced the front of the bench to the jury box, made eye contact with each juror, and stopped in front of their box. "During our last meeting—"

"Objection, Your Honor." Xavier stood.

"I haven't even—" Johnathan began.

"Might I warn opposing counsel that what happened during our last meeting has been stricken from the record and is inadmissible?"

Johnathan grinned. "So noted, Mr. Ford." He had wanted to remind the jurors of what had happened during yesterday's session. Even if it was inadmissible, he wanted it fresh in their minds. Xavier had played into his hand. "Women and men of the jury. I want to talk to you today about my client and her mindset during her encounter with the plaintiff. I want to ask you a question—a question I want you to consider without prejudice.

"I know many of you may already have an opinion of Rachel Andrews. You look at her and see a woman in a prison jumpsuit, battered and bruised. I don't care about your opinion about how you feel she received those scars. What I do care about is what you do with that information. Are you the type of person who can look beyond the outer and see the inner, or do you make a judgment call based on what others tell you what you should think?

"Rachel Andrews is on trial today for what happened in that grocery store. Not for the condition you see before you. So, get that out of your head right now. Look at me. If you look at her, be willing to see the truth."

"Are we going to get a question anytime soon, Your Honor?" Xavier said.

"He's right, Mr. Clarke. Opening remarks are made. Ask your first question, or do you intend to go straight to your summation?" Judge Ellison said.

"Sorry," he turned to Rachel. "Rachel, let's pick up where we left off. You had walked through the store and passed Dr. Houston several times, then felt the urge to speak to her. You talked with her about being new in town and onions. Then what happened?"

"We were having such a friendly conversation, and she was new in town. I asked her if she had found a church," Rachel said, looking to the floor.

"A church? You realize that is borderline violating the Federal HSA Act?"

"Yes. I'm aware."

"But you continued to talk to her."

"Yeah. I just felt comfortable with her," Rachel said, finally meeting Johnathan's eyes.

"You felt safe talking to Dr. Houston," Johnathan said, pointing toward Xavier and the doctor.

Rachel sniffed and nodded.

"Please, we need an audible answer," the judge stated.

Rachel looked toward the plaintiff's bench. She had tears in her eyes. "Yes. She seemed friendly, and I felt we were hitting it off. I trusted her."

"And you took it a step further?"

Rachel nodded again.

"Rachel," Johnathan reminded.

"Sorry," Rachel wiped a tear away. "Yes, I did. I think I may have mentioned God to her."

"Think?"

"Yes. The more I replay it, the more it changes. I know I invited her to church, but I'm not sure beyond that. I think I said God bless you when we parted."

"That is against the law. You are aware?"

"I am aware," Rachel said.

Xavier stood. "Your Honor. What more do we need? The accused admits on the stand that she broke the law. I make a motion we immediately move to sentencing and administer the full weight of twenty years that my client is requesting."

"I am not through with my examination, Your Honor. If it pleases the court, I believe my client is entitled to a full defense. I think the court would not want any reason for appeal."

"Motion denied, Mr. Ford," the judge announced. "You may continue, Mr. Clarke.

"Thank you, Your Honor," Johnathan said.

"I'm sorry for the interruption, Rachel," Johnathan said, placing his hand on her arm. "I just have a couple more questions.

"I am okay, Mr. Clarke. Go ahead."

"First. At any point did the plaintiff tell you she was offended by you asking her about church—"

"Objection," Xavier said. "My client doesn't need to protest at the time of proposition."

"Oh, but doesn't she? If she is claiming how much damage my client has inflicted upon her and claiming she had to be hospitalized, filing a two million dollar claim, and trying to imprison my client for twenty years, wouldn't there be some forceful evidence?"

"Overruled," the judge said.

"Thank you, Your Honor. Rachel, did Dr. Houston at any point say or do anything to let you know that she was opposed to you mentioning your church during your conversation?"

Rachel's brows furrowed, and her eyes darted. "No. Not at any time. In fact, she was smiling. She was, like me, enjoying our conversation. We exchanged recipes. It was one of the reasons I felt comfortable talking to her about God. She was receptive to it. In fact, I remember now. She placed her hand on my arm and patted it like an aunt or grandmother would. She said, "Thank you, dearie." Then we parted ways.

"Second question." Johnathan took a breath. He knew he had to get this one off fast and that Rachel would have to pick up on it quickly to get it on the record, at least for the jury to hear. He placed his hands on the witness stand and looked into Rachel's eyes, "Rachel. Have you at any point been threatened to give testimony that would favor the plaintiff's case, or if not, harm would come to you or your family?"

Everyone in the courtroom froze for an instant. Both Xavier and Dr. Houston's jaws dropped, and the judge nearly dropped her gavel. Rachel was shocked, but Johnathan's focus remained on her for the entire speech as she took in every word, knowing exactly what to do.

"Yes," Rachel said. "I was threatened by Official Kendrick Edwards."

In the ensuing cacophony, the judge slapped her gavel repeatedly, Xavier shouted, "Objection!" and Dr. Houston yelled in exasperation.

"Mr. Clarke?!" the judge snapped.

"Your chambers," Johnathan said. "I know."

"I will have an engraved seat waiting for you, Counselor."

$$\text{卌 卌 卌 IIII}$$

"Give me one good reason I shouldn't send you packing right now, Mr. Clarke? Because I must live up to my word. Unless you can convince me in two sentences why I would be wrong for doing so, you are hereby relieved of your duties as counsel for the defendant," Judge Ellison said raising her gavel over the block on her desk.

Xavier stepped in before Johnathan could even speak, "Your Honor. You cannot begin to consider giving him *another* chance after that display? After that mockery? His client flat out admitted she was guilty. Then she went on to accuse an officer of the law of willful and blatant strong-arming, trying to convince the jury that an Official inflicted her wounds."

"Counsel, he did nothing of the sort," Judge Ellison snapped. "Now, will you sit down? This is *my* chamber, and *I* will ask the questions and get to the bottom of this. If I require your assistance," she turned to Dr. Houston, who had opened her mouth as if she were about to speak, "or yours, Dr. Houston, I will ask for it. Are we clear?"

"Yes, Your Honor," Xavier said.

"Dr. Houston?"

"Yes, Your Honor."

"Thank you. Now, if there are any further outbursts out of any of you three without me asking a question first, I will dismiss this case *with* prejudice, and there won't be a case, Mr. Ford. And your client, Mr. Clarke, will be lucky to be released by Christmas, waiting for the paperwork to clear. So let me do my job and get to the bottom of what's going on.

"Now, Mr. Clarke, what just happened in my courtroom?"

Johnathan was unsure if the two-sentence rule still applied, so he weighed his words carefully. He wanted to make his point, and he wanted to make it in a way where he would be able to remain Rachel's attorney. He held up one finger to signal he was in thought. In reality, all he needed to do was deliver two sentences that would warrant follow-up questions.

"We haven't all day. Make it quick, Mr. Clarke."

"The past two weeks since my client has been arrested have been interesting for my client, myself, and others involved with the case."

"That's one. So far, I'm not impressed. Every client faces challenges while incarcerated, and their families have to deal with the ramifications of their family member's decisions that got them there. Why should your client be any different? Your second sentence."

The judge's expression did not waver. This one had to be good.

"That is true, Your Honor, but other clients do not have their family members threatened or run off the road by members of an organization not to be named and have their attorneys verbally threatened to leave a case alone or suffer the consequences."

The judge nodded, her eyes never leaving his. She was weighing the truthfulness of his statement or if it was just smoke-blowing to help his client. From what he could tell, she believed him. Her lips pursed, and she leaned forward in her chair, "I think that was more than one sentence, Counselor."

"It was full of commas, your honor, but I assure you, it was one statement," Johnathan half grinned.

Judge Ellison returned the gesture. Xavier didn't say a word. Nor did Dr. Houston. They both knew the consequences. The judge looked at everyone's faces. Then stood. "I find sufficient reason to allow Mr. Clarke to remain counsel for Mrs. Andrews."

Xavier raised his hand, "Your—"

"Remember my warning, Counselor," the judge said, raising her gavel. "This piece of wood still works in here. Ask Mr. Clarke."

"Yes, Your Honor," Xavier nestled back in his seat.

"Mr. Clarke," the judge paced around her desk and stopped next to him. "You may remain in your position, and you may continue your line of questioning. But I warn you, if you continue, you go down a dangerous path. Accusing an Official of any kind of wrongdoing is grounds for imprisonment. It's even dangerous to do it here with me. And you just took the gloves off in open court. You're lucky we're in closed-door proceedings, or the whole world would know it by now. Are you sure you want to follow this path?"

"I have to, Your Honor," Johnathan said. Then he turned toward Xavier and Dr. Houston. "My client may be guilty of breaking laws, but she was coerced into doing so. And that is what I aim to prove. And now we are all being threatened because we are trying to defend her. And that isn't right."

"Now, I must caution you. You are close to smearing the reputation of an upstanding member of society," the judge said. "You may be able to say that here in my chambers, but try that out there without sufficient proof, and I will let Mr. Ford nail you to the cross you are trying to bear."

Xavier chuckled, "Thank you, Your Honor."

"Don't get too cocky, Counselor. I'm just doing my job. I must remain fair and impartial," the judge said as she walked back around her desk to where Dr Houston sat. She looked between the two of them. "I can't stand those who take advantage of the system to gain a buck, Dr. Houston, nor do I like suits who choose to use my courtroom to grandstand to make a point, Mr. Clarke. So, both of you will settle the hell down and try this case, or I will dismiss the jury and decide this case for you. And so far, neither of you are impressing me enough to give you a decision.

"Now, let's shake hands, get back into that courtroom, and act like reasonable human beings. No more surprises. No more shock moments. No more grandstanding. Are we clear, everyone?"

"Yes, Your Honor," both men agreed, then shook hands with plastic grins.

"Now I want the both of you to go in there and act like we had a pleasant conversation and continue where we left off.

"Don't forget, Mr. Clarke. You opened this can of worms, but Mr. Ford still gets his cross-examination. You are dismissed, gentlemen." The judge circled back to her desk then looked up at the clock. "As a matter of fact, it's already late, and I'm famished. We're dismissed for the day." The judge slapped her gavel and removed her robe, placing it neatly over the chair behind her.

"Good day, gentlemen. The bailiff will see you out," the judge said, then disappeared through a side door.

Both men exchanged glances. Xavier shrugged and motioned to Dr. Houston, and they left the judge's chambers. Johnathan followed the bailiff to the courtroom, which was empty except for the briefcase he had left behind. He packed up the folder and notepad and stared down the aisle—a voice called to him.

"What did we do to get into this mess, John?"

Johnathan turned. It was Xavier.

"Just lucky, I suppose."

"Never thought it would get this complicated that day we initially met. I figured your client would try and plea. Why fight this so hard?"

"She did nothing wrong, Xavier. I've told you that from day one."

"I know that now."

"So, you believe her?"

"I can neither confirm nor deny that statement."

"So why did you take this case?"

"A two-million-dollar case, which was supposed to be open and shut. I didn't know the details. I saw the numbers and the payout. I couldn't say no."

"But you regret your decision?"

"I can neither confirm—"

"Nor deny the statement. Right. But we are not in a place where we should be talking about this. The walls have ears."

"So, I've been told."

"So, I know. Experience," Johnathan said, rotating his head.

Xavier only nodded. "Same ole place?"

"Same ole time."

Xavier nodded. He turned and exited the way he came.

Johnathan turned and exited the courtroom. He found Frank and Michael where he had left them in the lobby unaware of what had transpired in the courtroom. He had another story to tell and just over an hour to do so. Then he had an appointment at an old Irish pub in downtown San Antonio to get to.

†††

For once, Johnathan had the advantage of not having to lay out every detail to a client. With the gag order in place, he just nodded to Michael and Frank when he left the courtroom, and they understood. He finished their brief meeting with an *everything is going to be okay* and left it at that. He explained that they were done for the day and the judge would reconvene at 9 AM. She would likely see that they would be first or second on the docket. He suggested they all go home, get a good night's sleep, and meet early. He assured them all was well and left it at that with an eye raise that assured them that more info would come when privacy was available.

†††

It being the middle of the week and still early, the crowd at Tilly's Tavern was light. He recognized a few law clerks from the county office gathered at the bar. He nod-waived at them. They returned the gesture and went back to their drinks and appetizers. The games on the TVs behind bar were in in full swing or pregame interviews for West Coast games. A waitress came up to him smiling. "Pretty empty still. Sit wherever you'd like, sweetie. I'll be right back."

138

"Thanks, Jasmine," he said. Not seeing Xavier yet, Johnathan found a tall-stooled table near the front window. He picked up a menu and looked it over already knowing what he would get, but it was there, so he perused. Although it had been a while since he and Xavier had eaten together, they were creatures of habit.

A couple of minutes later, Jasmine returned with a pad. "Alone tonight, Johnny boy?"

Johnathan laughed. "No. Xavier will be along soon. Guess I'm still faster than he is."

"Slow down, sweetie. It's still early," Jasmine said.

"Oh, brother," Johnathan said. "Driver. You know what I meant."

"Sure, that's what you meant," she said with a wink. "What can I start you off with? Appetizer? Or are you going to wait for the Xman?"

"No. I'll go ahead and order so it's here when he arrives—the usual. Two talls, dressed, and the bucket of wings. Spicy."

Jasmine scribbled on her pad, and with another wink added, "Gotcha. Any chips or pretzels while you wait?"

"Pretzels sound good."

"Comin' right up."

Teams were stretching for the seventh inning on some screens and warm-up pitches for West Coast games on others.

"Football season is comin'," a man turned to him from the bar. "Then these silly boys throwing rubber waving at it with sticks will be gone, and we will see real sports of pigskin and gridiron."

Johnathan laughed. "Can't wait. Go, Cowboys!"

"Darn right!!" the man said, pointing to the lone stars on his chest and hat.

"Mingling with the locals, I see?" Xavier said as he sat, taking a sip of the beer that had been placed at his seat. He let out a relieved exhale as he set down the glass. "How long has it been since we've done this?"

"Too long, *Xman*," Johnathan laughed.

"Oh hell," Xavier waved his hand in the air. "Don't start up that crap." He laughed, taking a pretzel.

"Don't blame me. It was Jasmine who brought it up."

Jasmine arrived at the table with their wings and placed them in the middle of the table. "Are you two talking about me? It better be good."

"Just reminding Xman here of his moniker and the old days."

"Well, if he didn't like it, he shouldn't have shared it with me. Now he's branded. C'mon, boys. Never share details with your waitress. Especially if you're a frequent flyer."

"Our mistake," Xavier said.

Jasmine laughed. "Enjoy your meal, boys," she said, placing extra napkins on the table.

Xavier looked around, then back to Johnathan. "I hope these aren't as hot as this case we have before us."

"Yeah. No kidding. I need oven mitts every time I enter the courtroom. Let's eat a moment before we dive into the deep end, though."

Xavier agreed. Both men ate for a few minutes and talked about anything but courthouses, laws, or abrasive clients. They were reminded of times like this, just not on opposite sides of the courtroom. While it was not their first time opposing each other, it was the first time it seemed to carry this much weight. They talked about Xavier's growing family. His wife was expecting again. This would be number three for them. Xavier was wondering how no woman had lassoed Johnathan yet. Johnathan admitted he just hadn't found love yet.

"Time is ticking away, my friend. We're not as young as we were when we started this journey. What about that frisky secretary in your office?"

"Who, Meredith?"

"Yes, Meredith! Who else has been by your side the last decade?"

"No one, but don't let her hear you call her a secretary. I don't need to be defending another client."

Xavier raised his grease-covered hands in surrender. "My bad. What would you have me call her?"

Johnathan thought about it for a moment, "I don't know. She's Meredith."

Xavier laughed, nodding. "I gotcha. Sounds like you are already married."

Johnathan smirked and took a swig of his beer.

Xavier wiped his hands on a napkin, took another swallow of his drink, and surveyed the room again, which was now much fuller. "Okay. We need to get down to business. I need to talk about this, or I am going to explode. This gag order and this client are making me want to—" Xavier held his hands in front of him choking the air; he gritted his teeth. "You know?"

Johnathan laughed. He nodded. "It has been frustrating. Imagine what I am going through. All you have to do is speak the words. You have the law on your side. I have to defend my client."

"Well, in all honesty, Johnathan. She did do what she is being accused of."

"True. But I wouldn't call her guilty. There's a difference here."

Xavier downed the last of his beer and set it down just in time for Jasmine to set down its replacement.

"Damn. I love this place. You are on top of it, Jasmine."

"Got to keep my Xmen pleased."

"*Pssssh.*" Xavier waived her off and took a sip from his fresh glass. He looked into the distance, then stared through the TV screens. The West Coast games were in the third inning. He looked down at the empty plate of wings and then rotated his beer glass.

"Of course, there is a difference. But I can't admit that in the courtroom. Even right here is a gamble. It would be unfair to my client to talk trash behind her back."

"But isn't that what we are doing?"

"Indirectly, but I won't do it directly. You know how it is. If any word gets back to her that I've said even half the things I've already said, my license is gone. She has that much power."

"So why defend her?" Johnathan said.

"As I've said, I have no choice now. If I stop, I get disbarred or worse. Besides, guilty or innocent, clients get the best defense, or in my case, prosecution, that an attorney can give. Like it or not, I am getting paid to send your client to jail. And that is what I aim to do. So you better pray for a miracle to get her off, or it's lights out. And from the ace you pulled out of your sleeve today, you are halfway there.

"For the first time, I saw fear in Dr. Houston. The pride that was there before, was shaken. So whatever shaking you are doing, keep doing it, Counselor. That is all I can say about that." Xavier sat back and took a long swig of his beer.

Johnathan leaned in his chair, taking in his friend's advice. Was it really working? Was his gut paying off? It had given Rachel the confidence to stand up for herself. That had paid off with the judge. It had affected Dr. Houston. Now it was impacting Xavier. The tide seemed to be shifting in this case and moving in their favor. He just needed to keep the momentum moving forward and keep himself from getting thrown off the case for crossing any other fine lines the law had in store for him and Rachel.

||||| ||||| ||||| |||||

After arranging to meet Johnathan at the downstairs coffee shop downstairs, Michael turned toward Frank who shrugged and asked, "You hungry? Maggie's got some lamb chops at the house. Said she saved us a plate."

"I would, but I really need to get to the kids. I haven't spent any solid time with them since this whole thing began. With the bomb I just dropped on them, I think I need to be around them as much as I can. I can just make a sandwich at home. Who knows, maybe Mom has made me something. I do appreciate it, though."

"You don't know what you're missin'," Frank said as they walked toward the elevator.

"Oh, believe me, I do. I've had Maggie's lamb chops. But my little lamb chops must come first. I just wish I had something to tell them. I hate having to explain every night that Mommy's not coming home again. I mean, neither one has shed tears yet, but it's only a matter of time. It's been almost a week now." The bell sounded, the doors opened, a couple exited the elevator, and they stepped inside.

"They are just questions. True, they miss her, but once they get their minds focused on something else, Mom drifts into the distance. It's not that they forget about her; they just become kids again. Which is fine. But still, be ready for it to hit them and then your shoulder when the tears do come."

"I know. And I will," Michael wondered what his dad might be telling them. He had always been blunt and honest. He shivered at the thought of him telling the kids about their mom's prison stay. But he also knew his father would take into consideration their age. He tried to remember how he was with him when he was their age. The laws didn't swing until he was eight, he remembered. That was when religion took a big hit, speeches and sermons began to be monitored. He recalled his dad mumbling to his mom that he would not comply. He wasn't sure if anything was ever said to him directly, but he did remember that nothing was ever hidden from him.

"I just want all of this to end. I don't understand why laws are so against people talking about God or talking to others about Him."

"*Hmmph*," Frank said. "It's been like that for decades, unfortunately. It was behind the scenes at first, with more and more people taking a stand against Christianity. At the same time, fewer spoke up to defend their right to talk about God and defend the faith. The louder voices are won out. Now, the anti-discrimination movement has become so strong that faith has no place anywhere, I'm afraid. We have become the minority."

The bell sounded, and the doors opened. Frank and Michael exited the elevator and walked to their vehicles. They shook hands, and Frank headed to his home, Michael to his waiting kids. The trip was incident-free. No SUVs that he could see. Frank did not call him, so he was hopeful that his drive was also Official-free. The house was lit up with a welcoming glow of home. He had to smile as he thought of his redhead and a crooked smiled boy.

Michael knocked on the door, and Renae answered. "Hey sweetie, long time no see." She pulled him in for a hug. Michael was still always healed through his mom's hugs. There was just something about them that no matter how down he was, a healing balm ran over him and warmed him up each time she held him.

"Hey, Mom. How are you?" Michael laughed as he heard his kids yelling his name from upstairs.

"Exhausted. I can't believe the empty-headedness of the managers at some of these branches. You train them to do a job, and it's like the moment you leave, they do their own thing. I cannot," Renae said, waving her hand in the air.

Michael again laughed at his mom's candor. "Well, that is what they pay you the big bucks for."

"*Hmmph.* I don't know sometimes, dear—enough about me. How are you?" she said, placing her hand on his arm.

"I'm doing okay. Johnathan seems to think we are heading in the right direction. But I don't know. Yesterday seemed like a bad day. He got sick over what happened in court."

Renae gasped. "Oh my. What happened?"

"He toed the line with the judge. Remember, they've made our case closed door. But Johnathan does share some of what happens. In fact, he shared some interesting details about our case just recently. He is fed up with how the laws are keeping this doctor safe while Rachel is in prison for doing nothing wrong. But I guess the judge was offended by the way he did it. She almost threw him off the case."

"Well, yeah. That would do it. We know about *offending* people," Renae rolled her eyes.

"Did you guys go to court?"

"Never had the opportunity. Edwards held your dad here. From what it seems, he never reported anything to the higher authorities. He took the matter into his own hands. He played judge and jury. I think a vague stipulation in the law allowed him to do that. He just stretched his authority. But laws have been amended to prevent that now. *Heh,* I think it's even called the Edwards Amendment."

"Seriously?"

"That's what I hear," Renae said. "But your father would know more about it than I would. I'm just glad that part of our life is in the past."

"Or is it?"

"How do you mean?"

"He hasn't told you?"

Renae raised her eyebrow and pursed her lips.

Michael wasn't sure what he should do. His mom didn't know what was going on. Why Jacob had chosen to leave her in the dark was beyond him.

"The SUVs"

"I know he has said he thinks he has seen an SUV or two," Renae's voice strengthened.

"Mom, relax. I'm sure there is a reason he hasn't said more. Maybe he didn't want you to worry."

"Jacob!" Ranae called to the other room.

"Mom. Don't get mad. Please. This is a tense situation. We need to remain calm."

"Yeah. What's up, babe?" Jacob said, entering the room.

"Don't babe me. What's going on?"

Jacob exchanged glances with Michael and Renae. He saw Michael's deer-in-the-headlights look and Renae's, you have some splain'-to-do look. He knew what was going on.

"Look, I was going to tell you, but I wasn't sure what was going on myself."

"So, what is going on exactly?"

"You already know I was visited by an Official yesterday," Jacob said. "And that I was terrified because he sounded exactly like Edwards."

"Yes, and I told you there is nothing to worry about, so what's the problem?"

"There is something to worry about," Michael said.

Renae's head snapped to Michael, and her eyes narrowed, "Go on."

"I don't know if it is the same Official, but I had two Official vehicles, GMC Denalis, nearly run me off the road the other night."

"It probably wasn't, because the one that visited me drove a grey Denali. The two that around Michael were black."

"I'm sorry, Dad," Michael said. "I thought you had told her."

"It's okay. I should have."

"Yes, you should have. I am a grown woman; we have been through this crap before. You, above everyone, should know I can handle these laws and whatever they choose to throw at us. So, who are *they*?"

"We don't know. Some new Officials assigned to the area," Jacob said.

"You *did* say that he sounded like Edwards," Renae said.

"Yes, but that doesn't mean anything. Like you said, the voice sounded like him. But Edwards is dead. I was there and saw him die. I was just spooked by seeing an Official, that was all."

"Does Johnathan know about this?"

"Yes. He knows everything."

"Have they tried anything with him?"

"Not that I am aware of. From what I know, they are keeping their distance. But today, he did seem a bit distant. I don't know," Michael said, shaking his head.

"You need to talk to the judge," Renae suggested.

"And say what?" Jacob said. "That Officials are attacking us? Yeah, that will go over well."

Renae bit the corner of her lip. "Yeah, I suppose you're right." She elbowed Jacob. "Still, you two should have let me in on what was going on. What if something had happened and you had disappeared again?"

Jacob lowered his head and nodded, "You're right. I'm sorry. We should've told you. We just didn't want you to worry."

"Well, hell yeah, I'm worried. It's my job to worry. I'm a mom. When did this happen?"

"The other morning. I was headed for the courthouse. They cornered me, and I don't think they were trying to run me off the road. Just trying to scare me. The moment we got into town, they vanished."

"And you, my love? You have any other encounters you are hiding?"

Jacob shook his head. "No, just the one that you know of."

Renae looked at his Jacob just like Rachel looked at him when she wanted the truth and was going to press it out whether he liked it or not. His dad's face showed he was telling the truth.

His mom nodded. "Okay. If either of you has any more encounters. I want to be the first to know. I care about both of you and don't want anything to happen to either of you—especially you, Michael. You have your two angels to take care of right now. Rachel needs you with them more than ever. Don't make any mistakes with anyone out here."

"Yes, Mom," Michael said.

"And I need you to come home to me, mister," Renae said to her husband. "Your church needs you, too. Think about them. Be careful out there."

"Yes, dear," Jacob said.

"Okay. Now that we have that settled, how are we going to handle this situation?"

"There is not much we can do but keep to ourselves and try not to upset anyone," Jacob said. "Our Official stated he wanted to ensure that our neighborhood was to remain safe."

"Whatever that's supposed to mean," Michael said.

"It means that he is watching us. He knows we are using the gym for church activities," Jacob said.

"But that doesn't explain why he was chasing me," Michael said.

"Unfortunately, it does," Jacob said. "He is using you to get to me. And Rachel's arrest is the same thing. To get to our family."

"But why?"

"Because they are Officials, and that is their job. Since the laws have gotten stricter, they have looked for ways to shut down churches. Especially ones that don't adhere to Federal laws."

"Does this have anything to do with you and your sermons?" Michael asked.

"It might," Jacob said, sitting on the stairs.

"Dad. How difficult would it be to submit your sermons?"

"If I hand those over, they could dictate what I preach. They could tell me what I say from the pulpit. And that is not right. I am called to preach the gospel. And for me to be unable to do that is against who I am and against a higher law."

"How would they know if you would preach something different than what you handed them?"

"That would be lying. And that would be against who I am. God would not want me to do that either. Hiding is not the right thing to do, Michael."

"But that is what you have been doing. Hiding behind the façade of the gym."

"That's different. It is not handing in a sworn document with deliberate intent. The gym is a legitimate business. Plus, the words on the door and building have a dual meaning. And on Sunday, it's not like we are hiding. We hold our services in the open. We just have never been questioned."

"Yet," Michael said.

"Yet," Jacob echoed.

"What's that?" Renae said, looking behind the men to the front door.

Both men turned, and red and blue flashes lit the foyer through the frosted glass. All three adults' eyes met and froze in realization.

"What do you think he wants?" Jacob said.

"I don't know," Renae said. "I'll check on the kids. You two find out."

"Yeah, thanks," Jacob said as Renae headed up the stairs.

The *tink tink tink* of a baton rang against the glass of the door.

"Don't they ever use their hands?" Jacob asked.

"First time dealing with one at the door," Michael said. "Well, first time dealing with one face to face. Last time, one tried to run me off the road."

"Well, here's your chance, son," Jacob nodded toward the door.

Tink tink tink. "Are we going to go through this again, Citizen? I know you're in there," the voice called.

"That's the same Official that was at the gym," Jacob said.

"The one you told Mom sounded like your dead Official?"

"Shut up," Jacob said, stepping toward the door and unlocking it.

The flashing lights lit up Jacob's face, briefly blinding him. The Official grinned.

"Well, that was easy enough. Sorry for the lights. We had a report of a disturbance in the area. Just wanted to ensure you and your family were okay. Can't be too careful."

"No, you can't. Thank you, Official. I still don't have your name."

"No, you don't," the Official said. All in due time," the Official said.

"So, it's just you and your wife here?"

Jacob stepped back, opening the door wider as Michael stepped behind his father.

"No, sir. I am here. I'm Michael Andrews, his son."

"Mr. Andrews. Yes. I have heard of you. It's a pleasure to finally meet you," the Official extended his hand. Michael reluctantly accepted it.

"So that would mean your children are here as well?"

"Maybe they are, maybe they aren't. I have other family as well. I don't know you well enough to share that type of information, if you don't mind."

The Official laughed. "Is that right? Understandable. You should be careful with whom you trust. You never know who would betray that trust and create complications for you, Mr. Andrews. Ask your father. He knows about trust's complexity. Don't you, Mr. Andrews?"

Jacob's eyes narrowed. He looked into the now familiar face of his visitor.

The Official extended his hand to Jacob.

"Let me officially introduce myself, Mr. Andrews. My name is Kendrick Edwards. You may have known my uncle, Official Nathan Edwards."

"It's not like you didn't know it was me, Citizen," Kendrick Edwards said.

Jacob looked him over. The grin was there, but the stature was not. Kendrick was a hundred pounds lighter than his predecessor. But Jacob had to admit, his demeanor was nearly identical. "I guess so, Official Edwards," Jacob cringed, saying the name.

"There is a penalty for your crimes. I'm here to ensure you pay for them," Kendrick said as he removed his glasses. It didn't help his appearance. The icy stare from his sunken eyes only enhanced his devilish appearance. "Your petulance must be paid in full. I'm here to collect, Citizen."

"I don't understand?"

"You know very well what I am referring to, Mr. Andrews," Kendrick said, looking back and forth between father and son.

Michael and Jacob exchange glances.

"Who are you talking to?" Michael asked.

"That depends on who is willing to talk to me first."

"Official Edwards, we have no clue what you are talking about," Jacob answered. "All I know is that you have been sniffing around my gym, and your officers nearly ran my son off the road the other day."

Kendrick grinned, "I have no knowledge of your son's incident. And I was merely protecting your investment, Mr. Andrews. Doing my duty as an officer of Carrelton. Your gym has a high membership rate, Mr. Andrews. To what can we attribute this? And don't tell me you provide a service to the body *and* the soul. I don't need to be misled. I'm smarter than you take me for."

Jacob nodded. He looked at Michael and shrugged. "What do you want to know, Official?"

"You are secretly holding services there. Aren't you?"

"I wouldn't go as far as saying they are secret. I never attempt to hide what we do. We accept anyone who wants to visit. I apologize, Kendrick. Would you care to attend one of our services?"

"Don't patronize me, Mr. Andrews. Do you realize I could arrest you right now for such a suggestion?" the Official sneered.

Jacob stepped back, realizing his error. He knew the rules had changed. Laws had become stricter than when he had insulted the first Edwards. The first time he chose to mouth off drew three months of confinement. But since the Edwards fiasco, both sides of the law were now under the microscope. He didn't want to enter that arena again. He looked to the ground, then back up to the Official.

"I thought you might have a change of heart," Edwards said, then continued, "Now, might I remind you I know about your extracurricular activities. But being the kind-hearted gentleman I am, I will give you one final service to tell your loyal followers you will be shutting down operations and no longer conducting your illegal activities. Your get-together will run fifteen minutes, from the time you say, 'Good morning' until the time you say, 'Thank you for coming,' that is all, Citizen."

Jacob nodded.

"Is this understood?"

Jacob again nodded.

Kendrick nodded with a grin, returned his glasses to his face, and headed toward the door. He stopped short and turned around.

"And don't even think of trying to plan another place to meet. You never know who will be listening," Kendrick tapped his ear and completed his exit, shutting the door behind him.

Michael finally exhaled; he didn't realize he had been holding his breath. His palms were clammy, and he could feel the back of his button-up shirt sticking to his back.

Jacob walked to the door as the brightness of flashing lights and the growl of a Hemi faded into the distance. He opened the door slowly and then shut it.

"Now what?" Michael asked.

Jacob shrugged. His ashen face looked up; Michael followed his gaze, and his two little ones held onto his mom's side.

"We can't go through this again, Jake," Renae said. "Be careful what you say, alright?"

Jacob hadn't realized Renae had been listening to their exchange. So had the kids. Renae looked down at them; their arms were clinging to her side.

"I'm sorry, Michael," she said, her hands going to their sides, then rustling their hair. "I could hear everything. I couldn't help but come out. They just followed."

"It's okay, Mom. Don't worry about it. They will be fine. I'll be up in a second."

Renae disappeared into the room. The swoop and sweep of cartoons could be heard, then the shutting of a door.

Michael repeated his question. Jacob motioned to the kitchen area. He poured a glass of tea for himself; Michael found the pot of coffee was still warm. He chuckled. "We just go on, Michael. We live day to day and don't let what he does get to us. That's what we do."

"But—"

"But what?" his father said. "We go to a higher agency?" Jacob shook his head. "There isn't one. Not when it comes to an Official. Trust me, Michael, I know. I'm just relieved we know who we are dealing with now."

"He doesn't scare you?"

Jacob grunted. "When I first made the connection, I had a brief frightening thought. But then I remembered that God gives us our strength. I remembered I got through the situation with his uncle, and if God led me through that situation; He will lead me through this one as well."

"But I thought Edwards gave you nightmares," Michael said, then sat back, wondering if he should have mentioned it. It was something his mom had told him in confidence.

"True. But it wasn't anything I couldn't handle. My final moments with Nathan Edwards were not fearful ones. I stood up to him. If anything, he feared me *because* I stood up to him. He didn't like me because he couldn't get me to bow to his overbearing and abusive authority.

"You may not know this because I've only told your mom, but he threatened to kill me that day. But God stepped in through a friend. Now he's gone, and I sit here alive. Maybe it was because of you. I don't know."

"I didn't know that," Michael said.

"How could you," Jacob said. "But don't go fearing Kendrick Edwards. He's no stronger than the strength you give him."

"But Rachel—"

Jacob sighed. "Yeah, there is that."

"What do you plan to do?"

Jacob looked down at his glass. "For Rachel's sake, I will comply. It will only be temporary. Our church family will understand. I'm sure they will find a way to meet. I will talk with Roger and Jessica Mills. Maybe they can help find a way to meet. They have a couple of shops now. Josh has the one up North some can meet in." Jacob chuckled, taking a sip of his tea. "It will be cramped, but it will feel like the old days."

"Y'all really met in an auto shop?"

"Yep. There were five or six of us back then. Ask Frank about it. He can tell you the stories."

"I will have to do that," Michael said, vaguely remembering Frank telling him a story or two. He may not have been listening too well, drowning out the past because anything having to do with his dad's history at the time irritated him. Now, it was all that seemed to matter.

Michael stood and downed the rest of his mug, causing his dad to laugh. "What?"

"Never thought you'd be a coffee drinker, Son. In all my years, you'd always been a teetotaler."

Michael chuckled. "Yeah, it took my wife going to prison and a crazed officer looming over me to drive me to drink the stuff."

"Could be worse, Son," Jacob said.

Michael agreed. He was grateful he had never given over to alcohol. The flavor of it had never appealed to him. After turning of age, he had a couple of buddies try to get him to go out with them. He agreed and hung out a few times. But he never found that life attractive. The more they were drawn to it, the less they hung out. Then the kids were born, and they stopped hanging out altogether. Family became everything. The strongest thing that he drank now was two tea bags of Earl Grey.

Michael called up the stairs to the kids, who gave him their disapproval of his summons. Renae laughed and appeared a moment later with two children in tow with *but Dad* looks on their faces.

"C'mon, you two. It's time to go home and let Grams and Gramps get some rest. You two need your baths, too."

"Aww," they both sang.

"You can come back later."

"Tomorrow?" Aiden asked.

"I'm not sure. You might go to Pop's house tomorrow. We'll see."

"Yay!" Angela said. She liked going to Grandpa Frank and Grandma Maggie's. They had animals they could help care for.

Michael was grateful they had a supportive family they could balance between. He had been so clouded, and the family love was helping.

Jacob walked Michael to his vehicle and buckled Aiden into his seat. He hugged his grandpa tight, giving him a raspberry on his stubbled cheek, then giggled, making Angela laugh.

"Hey now," Jacob said with a bellowed laugh.

"Thanks, Dad," Michael said. "We'll see you later."

After tucking in the children with little fuss about where Mom was, Michael opened the door to his and Rachel's room. It had a faint, stale air to it. The perfume that had once floated in the room had faded. While he had been in it to change his clothes, he hadn't used the restroom. He was using the downstairs guest bathroom for showering and getting ready.

He recalled the voices of the wise men who had spoken into his life. *What better time than now,* he told himself as he pushed the door open. Michael had grown tired of his once comfortable place of solitude. He could remember the nights when he would sit in that chair watching a game or the tail end of a movie Rachel couldn't finish and fall asleep. He wished he could take back those moments, go to bed with her, and lay by her side. He wanted her by his side now. Who knew when the next time he would be with her? Twenty years? They would be near fifty, then.

Michael released a *now's-the-time* breath and entered the room.

Michael turned on the light in the bathroom, which was still reasonably clean. It was the one room in the house that always stayed clean. Rachel saw to it. She was a germaphobe who had seen too many videos and read too many articles on the dangers that lie in the recesses of your bathroom. The end result was that he didn't have to worry about a dirty sink, shower, or commode. The thought hit him that this could end up being his job. He turned around, shut off the light, and plopped belly first onto the mattress.

"What am I going to do?" Michael said into the pillows to no one.

"You can tell me a story," a tiny voice answered his rhetorical question.

Michael shot up, looking to the door at a curly-haired girl.

"What's wrong, Angela?" Michael asked, not sure he heard her question.

"I can't sleep. Will you tell me a story like Mommy?"

Michael wasn't sure what stories his wife told their children. Did she make them up? Did she have books memorized? He found another reason to be amazed at how connected Rachel was to their children—and saddened by how disconnected he had become from them.

Michael took a deep breath and picked himself up onto the bed, laying his back against the headboard. "Come up here, sweetie," he said, patting the bed.

Angela hopped onto the bed and curled into Michael's side.

"No one can tell a story as good as your mom. And I don't dare to try. But you are her big girl. And since you are a big girl, she is teaching you to be a mommy. Some day, you will be telling stories to your little girls. So, why don't you tell me a story? I would love to hear one."

"Really? You think I'm big enough to tell a story?"

"Of course, you are, Pumpkin," Michael said.

"What should it be about?"

"Anything you want it to be about. It's your story," Michael said. "Tell it like you think Mommy would tell it. But make it your own."

Angela sat up and put her hand on her chin. She looked up with her tongue sticking out of the corner of her mouth, deep in thought. "Okay, I'm ready," she said, laying back in Michael's arm.

She began with a pretty princess, as most little girls would, and told a very well-thought-out story of a magical kingdom being attacked by a mean dragon named Aiden-Saurus. But the handsome prince Joey, who turned out to be a boy in daycare, came to rescue her from the evil jail the princess was being held in. Joey came along, but instead of attacking the Aiden-Saurus, he distracted him with a giant bowl of ice cream, Aiden's favorite flavor, and rescued the princess, Angela, without anyone getting slain.

When Angela finished her story, she laughed so hard that Michael was afraid she would be wide awake and unable to get back to sleep. He kissed her forehead and walked her to her room. After tucking her in, he turned around at the door to say good night. Before turning out the light, to his surprise, Angela was already sound asleep.

Just like her mom…

He shut the door and walked back to his room, hoping to have the same luck. He looked at the bed; he saw Rachel lying there in his mind's eye. He laid next to her and whispered how much he missed her. And like his daughter, before he knew it, he was lost to sleep and whatever dreams awaited him.

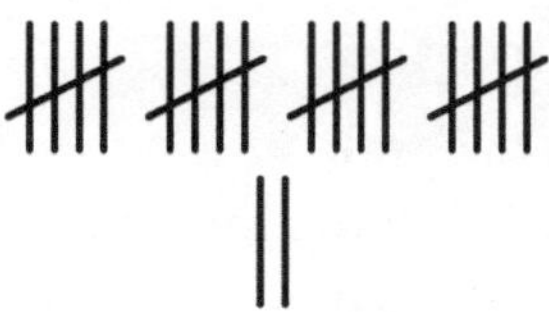

"Why would the judge continue the case?" Michael asked, pacing the small office.

"She didn't say," Johnathan said, following him behind his back, "and would you quit your pacing? You know I can't focus when you do that. You're going to make me sick."

Michael stopped and froze in place, not sure what to do next. "Oh, sorry. I'm just—"

"We both are," Johnathan pointed to a seat across his desk. "Just sit down. We'll figure this out together."

"Are you sure we should be talking about this?"

Johnathan nodded. "Being an attorney in today's day and age, I routinely sweep for listening devices. And after recent events, I swept this room twice before you arrived. We're clear to speak freely."

Michael sat in a chair across from Johnathan and sighed. "Do you think Judge Ellison is on to you talking to me about the case?"

"I don't believe so, but anything is possible."

"So, this delay could be about Edwards' visit then."

"Possibly."

Michael leaned forward. "Do you think she sent him?"

"I don't believe so. I think Judge Ellison is clean."

"How can you be so sure?"

"Just a gut feeling. She seems genuinely neutral. She was just as in the prosecution's face as she was mine. And Dr. Houston's reaction? She was afraid of her. If the judge were on their side, Dr. Houston would have known how she would react and respond accordingly." Johnathan shook his head and leaned back in his chair. "No, Judge Ellison is impartial. I'll stake my reputation on it."

Johnathan's ease relaxed Michael. He sat back in his chair and exhaled. "What about Rachel?"

"As before, Michael. We wait and see. As long as she is in there, she should be fine. This is nothing like what your father went through. It's not a pit with chains, beatings, and gruel to eat. Most of what your father went through was unsanctioned. Half of the laws on the books today were written because of Nathan Edwards' actions. Honestly, I feel Rachel is safe."

Michael nodded. "So, we have to wait until Monday, then?"

"That's what the bailiff said. All cases for Judge Ellison have been continued until Monday. Let's use this downtime wisely. My advice to you is to go see Rachel. Don't talk about the case, about getting out, or her defense—talk about you, the kids, anything but what's going on. It's not the best setting, but she needs her mind away from where she is.

"If she's half the mother you say she is, her thoughts are on her kids. Hearing about them may give her mind the rest it needs. God knows she won't get much when this train starts rolling again. And if this is Edwards-related, any possible access to Rachel will be shut off. Now may be the only time you get to see her. Go do it now."

"Should I just go to the jail?"

"Couldn't hurt." Johnathan shrugged. "Worst case, they tell you that you need to schedule an appointment. The best, they make you sit for an hour while they bring her up. I say go for it."

Michael stood and shook Johnathan's hand. "I think I'll do that. I'll let you know how it goes."

Michael exchanged pleasantries with Meredith as he left the office, then drove across town to the prison where Rachel was being held.

†††

The county jail holding facility wasn't far from the courthouse. The building was plain, yet he assumed it was under full surveillance. No external guard was posted, but that didn't mean one wouldn't appear should something out of the norm occur. Michael had heard stories of those ignorant to security measures on the outside and inside. They both paid dearly. He made sure to proceed with caution before finding his parking space.

He held his driver's license as he approached the reception desk. He had his passport in his back pocket just in case they asked for a second form of identification or tried to be difficult. Michael entered the first door, and there were two guards behind a pane of shielded glass. One looked up from her screen, the other continued with whatever he had been doing. The first pressed a button. "Name and purpose of your visit," she said, in perfect officer monotone.

"I wanted to see about visiting my wife. She is being held here." Michael said. He couldn't lower himself to label Rachel as a prisoner.

"Name and offense?"

"Rachel Andrews," Michael said. "Why does the offense matter?"

The guard rolled her eyes in a huff, "It would matter where she is held, sir. Different offenses are kept in different parts of the prison. Petty offenders are in the East Wing. Criminal offenders, the west wing, and so on. What is Ms. Andrews' offense."

"She is being held on Free Speech Act offenses, not sure what that would fall under," Michael said.

"Oh," the officer stated. "Those are federal crimes."

"I don't know. I suppose so," Michael said, not sure if the guards' reply was a bad sign.

The guard released her button so Michael couldn't hear her conversation with the other guard. She pointed to her screen, then the other guard came to her and typed on her keyboard and shook his head. The female guard pressed the talk button. "Can you spell the name for me?"

Micheal spelled it for her.

"Date of birth?"

"March fifth, Nineteen ninety-seven."

"Thank you. One moment."

More typing. More shaking of heads.

"Are you sure you have the right prison, sir?

"Quite certain. Unless there's another prison in Carrelton."

"No, there isn't. We're the county seat. All prisoners are brought here, so no, she wouldn't be transported anywhere else unless she were a violent criminal."

"No, Rachel isn't violent."

"Then she would be here. But we have no record of a Rachel Andrews being incarcerated here or ever was held here."

"I don't understand. We've been in court all week?"

"Mr. Andrews, I don't know what to tell you. Your wife is not here. Talk to your attorney. Maybe he knows where your wife is because, I am truly sorry, she is not here."

Michael was lost in the moment. The guard's eyes showed no sign of deception. They revealed she was concerned about his confusion. Her partner had his hand at his belt. He was ready for Micheal's reaction. He knew he needed to let it go and leave.

"I'm sorry. You're right. I will speak with my attorney and find out what's going on. I apologize for bothering you. Have a good day, miss." Michael slightly bowed his head, turned around, and walked back to his car. By the time he arrived, he already had his phone in his hand. He dialed Johnathan's number. It rang three times and went to voice mail.

"Perfect," Michael muttered, pulling out of the parking lot.

Once back onto the highway, Michael saw two SUVs parked at a fuel station. As soon as he passed, their headlights illuminated; he hit the gas. Thinking about where he was, he had a couple of possibilities. One was just pulling into any of the local businesses about a mile up the road, but being chased by an Official was not a good scenario to be in. His other option was a couple more miles up the road, into the heart of Carrelton. Michael nodded, figuring it was the better option; it was family.

Michael sped up and made it through the two lights, both were green allowing him passage. When Michael hit the right turn, he could see both of his followers closing in. Heading into the bend, he sped up, well above the speed limit, hoping not to attract a local authority's attention, which would be the last thing he needed, but with his stop being less than a mile up the road, he took the chance. He knew with the curve in the road, he'd be hidden, and the pursuing SUVs would not see him pull into his destination.

Michael watched his rearview mirror as he made the curve. He saw the two SUVs make the turn just as he disappeared around the bend in the road. He accelerated again, holding his breath. He saw the sign for Mills Motors on his left and entered the turn lane. Two of the three bays were open. He hoped there was space in the back for him to park, maybe even in the closed bay. He remembered his dad spoke of the unwritten code of Mills Motors when a church member was in need; he just prayed it still worked..

Michael pulled into the lot and behind the shop. The final bay was indeed empty, and the rear door was open. A worker who Michael hoped was Josh was sweeping the bay out. Michael lowered his window and yelled out, "Code Black, Code Black." The teen leaped into action, repeated the code into the office, and waved him into the bay. He ran into an adjoining room and pulled out what looked like a tarp.

"Drive onto the rack and get out. Quick!" the grease-covered worker said.

Michael hoped he could do what he was asked to. Driving that straight made him nervous, but he complied.

The teen covered the car with a cover and raised the vehicle as high as it would go and went underneath it. His shirt had his name on it; he was indeed Josh, "What are you doing? Go inside," he said, pointing to a door.

Michael didn't argue but followed where Josh had pointed.

"Michael! How are you?" Jessica Mills said, pulling him in for a hug. "Well, I guess not good if you are calling a Code Black. Don't worry. We got this. Follow Janice, and we will get y'all when this is over. Now go."

Janice, who was about Josh's age, probably his girlfriend or wife, took his arm and led him into the office and through a waist-high door into a smaller room. She closed the sliding door behind them and turned out the light. Michael could hear something being moved in front of the door—they were in a safe room.

"Hey, Michael," Janice whispered. "I'm Josh's wife, Janice."

"Nice to meet you," Michael said, finding her hand and shaking it. They didn't speak from then on.

Michael and Janice sat in silence until they could hear the moving noise again. It made Michael nervous, not sure if it would be a friend or an enemy. When the door opened, the outer room, this time well lit, was filled with friends and his father.

"We've got a problem, Son," Jacob said.

"Tell me about it," Michael agreed.

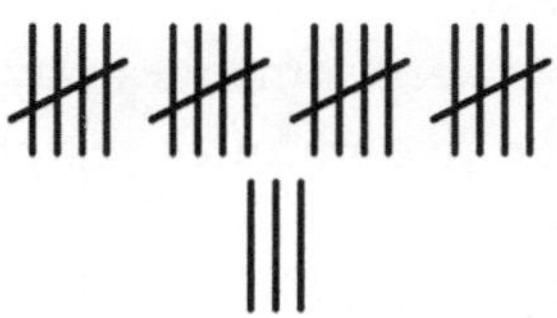

Neither SUV saw Michael pull into the shop. And no one saw either of them the rest of the day. When Roger Mills pulled surveillance videos, the two SUVs had sped past the shop, none the wiser Michael had turned into Mills Motors.

"They would've known where he was heading," Jacob said.

"Them speeding by could've been just a decoy. Knowing we would be reviewing the video," Roger said. "By now, you would think they would know we would be watching them as they watch us."

Jacob nodded. Then to Michael, "Where did you notice them following you, son?"

"I was up at the prison to see if I could see Rachel."

"Bad idea," Jacob said. "You know they won't allow that. It just places her in further harm."

"Says you, Dad. Things aren't like they were then."

"And they aren't bad now?" Jacob asked, his brows raised. "So, what happened?"

Michael sank lower into his chair and sipped his water. "They couldn't find her."

"*Hmmph*," Jacob said in a fatherly confirmation tone.

"What does that mean?" Roger asked.

"It means that the guards were told not to allow any visitors," Jacob answered.

"I don't know, Dad," Michael said, standing and pacing. "It seemed more than that. These guards didn't seem like they were purposely trying to keep me away. It looked like they were honestly searching for her. If they were acting, it was convincing."

"How so?" Jacob asked.

"If a guard were told to keep someone away, they would stonewall you. They wouldn't take five minutes searching their computers trying to locate a prisoner."

"He's got a point," Roger said.

"What are you suggesting?"

"I don't know," Michael said. "But I'm getting nervous. I was on my way to meet with Johnathan when I noticed my company. I tried to call him, but he didn't answer. I need to call him, but wouldn't they be able to track me if they are tracing his phone?"

Roger grinned. "Not when you're calling from here. We are under a dome that scrambles the signal; they can't trace your call. This location is a safe space for our team. I reinforced the garage when Pastor Eric was head of the church and upgraded when your father took over. If you didn't know, this is where we first began to meet."

"Yes, my dad has mentioned that. But he didn't mention the security measures. So, I can call Johnathan, and Edwards wouldn't know where I am?"

"Nope," Roger said. "The signal will bounce between the four towers in the area and make it seem like you are all over the place." Roger laughed. "They would run in circles like jackrabbits."

Michael laughed and excused himself, dialing Johnathan's number. After three rings, it went to voicemail again. "Johnathan, you need to call me. We have a problem with—" Michael's call waiting began to buzz. It was Johnathan.

Michael answered.

"Sorry, Michael, I have been on the phone all day. We have a serious problem. I've been meaning to call you, but between phone calls, I wanted to get my story straight before I got you worried for nothing."

"Okay. I have news for you, too, but I think we may have the same message. I think you are about to tell me Rachel is missing."

The line went silent for a moment, "How do you know that?"

"I went to the prison as you suggested to see Rachel, and they couldn't find her. Not even a record of her ever being in the prison."

"That's the issue with the court and why the trial's been delayed. After you left, I went by the courthouse to find out when we could expect to resume the hearing. I got the runaround, so I found my way into the judge's chambers."

"I bet that went over well."

"No, not at first," Johnathan said. "But I was lucky enough that she was alone. She told me when they called to bring her over from the prison that morning, the van returned empty. The driver said the jail couldn't find her; they had no record of her even being there."

"That's not possible. She was there," Michael said. "Wouldn't the guards know? Can't they interview them?"

"That's what I've been on the phone trying to do, but the prison won't give me access to them. No names, badge numbers, nothing. All I know is she was held in the non-violent offense wing. I don't know how many guards had access to her."

"What about the guard who brought her to us? The one who would snicker at us?"

"He was a courthouse guard. He took over from the transport wing in the basement. Nothing to do with the prison. He probably never even saw the prison guard. We could talk to the clerk who did the paperwork, but that's it. I'm on my way to the courthouse to do that now."

"What can I do?"

"Nothing right now," Johnathan said. "You aren't supposed to know any of this. We are still under the judge's gag order and everything she told me is under that order too."

"Watch your back. Officials are tailing me," Michael warned. "They followed me from the jail."

"Speaking of, where are you? I didn't pick up earlier because the phone did not ID the call as you."

"I'm—" Michael stopped himself. Just because the line was safe didn't mean they were not being listened to. "I'm in a safe place. Don't worry about me. Do what you need to. You said I can't do anything right now anyhow. I will just stay out of play. And since you are under a gag order, it would be best if we only spoke in person from here on. The phone is no longer safe."

"Agreed," Johnathan said. "I will talk to you when I talk to you. Can we meet at your house in the morning."

"Okay."

"And Michael."

"Yeah?"

"I'm sorry about Rachel. We will find her. The judge says we will find her. She is just as upset as we are."

"I understand. Thank you," Michael said and hit the *end call* button.

Michael returned to the office and confirmed with everyone what they all feared: Rachel was missing. They all expressed their condolences, and Michael accepted them but felt empty. His head was spinning, and he sat down.

"You okay, Son?" Jacob asked, sitting next to him.

"I don't know what to do," Michael said. "Johnathan said to stay put. But I feel I need to be doing something."

"Like what?"

"Out there looking for her. Something. Anything. Something more than sitting here on my ass."

"You just let Johnathan do what he needs to. He will uncover what is happening, and then we can go from there."

"I need to see the kids," Michael said.

"Take a break first." Jacob put his hand on his son's knee. "You can't see them in this state of mind. You will lose it, and they can't see you fall apart. You need to be strong. Yes, they know Mommy's in jail. And they have visions of her coming home. If you go home and begin to bawl your eyes out, they will know something is wrong. You can't put that on them. So pull yourself together, then we can go see them."

"You're right, Dad," Michael said, exhaling heavily. He stood, got a cup of water from the water cooler, and emptied it. "Where could they have taken her? This couldn't be Edwards, could it?"

Jacob sighed. "You want the truth?"

"Yes."

"It most likely is. I don't believe in coincidences. The timing is too perfect. Where Kendall has taken her is beyond me. For all we know, she is *still* in the prison; there is just no paperwork showing she is still there. That's the most logical answer."

"All of this because of his uncle?" Michael asked.

"I'm sorry, Son. But yes. This has to do with me, not you or Rachel. Kendall wants to avenge his uncle's death."

"You don't think—"

"Michael! No! Stop thinking that," Jacob said, standing.

"Why wouldn't he? You said Kendall wanted revenge."

"Michael, I said no such thing. Avenging and revenge are two different things. Revenge is cold-hearted. This is methodical. Kendall Edwards has a plan, and killing Rachel is not his style. He wants us to suffer. So, no, I don't believe for a second that Rachel is dead. And I don't want that thought in your head either."

"So, this was part of his plan?"

"If her missing is his doing, then this entire thing from the Plant to having her arrested to the hearing was his plan."

"Damn." Michael ran his fingers through his hair and faced the window.

"So, you can see what I mean when I say Rachel is not dead. It wouldn't make sense."

"Yeah, I guess it wouldn't," Michael said, sitting. "So, what is his plan?"

"I don't know. But give it time. I am sure Kendall will reveal it. Now that he has her hidden, it is only a matter of time before he lays his cards on the table."

"And then what?"

"Then we find out what he wants and determine the cost."

"What if it's too much?"

Jacob sat next to Michael and put his hand on his shoulder. "Let's cross that bridge when we come to it. God will show us what we need to do and provide a way out. He is always there for us. We just need to trust Him."

Michael was reminded of how spiritual his dad was. He had forgotten that when any situation turned tough, his dad turned to God. It was his go-to and always had been. It had been frustrating for Michael. It almost seemed like a cop-out from dealing with a situation. But even now he could see peace come over his father, and it was beginning to get to him. *How can he be so calm when my wife was missing, when it seemed like all hope is slipping away?*

Unable to restrain himself any further, the question burst from Michael's lips, "How can you remain so calm?"

"Michael, we don't have a choice. We have three options. We can get upset, and all that will do is distract us and cause us to do something rash. We can shut everything out, then we do nothing, and what help would that be to Rachel? Or we can give it to God and allow Him to comfort us. Then we can focus on what matters and trust in His guidance and timing."

"He's right, you know," Roger said, entering the room. "Sorry, didn't mean to intrude on a father-son moment. Patience is one virtue we need right now. Silence means everything is okay. Rest in that."

"It is eating me up, not knowing where she is. I'm supposed to be protecting her," Michael explained.

"You can do the next best thing and protect your kids. They are in good hands right now. Frank won't let anything happen to them. Nor will any of us. Will Jr. is heading over there now. He just left his shop, which is close to where he lives. He will call when he arrives. We have your back," Roger said.

"All is closed up, Pop," Josh said, entering the room. He was wiping his hands on a shop cloth.

"Thanks, Josh. Janice is in the other room with Mom, counting the till and doing paperwork."

"Okay," he said. "Good to see you again, Michael. Sorry, it's under these circumstances. Hope your wife is okay."

"Thanks, Josh," Michael said.

Josh smiled and disappeared into the other room.

"Nineteen and growing up too fast," Roger said. "He's made a mistake or two but owned up to it. But young love will do that. She is a great girl, and they are truly in love, and I wish them the best."

"How old is he?"

"Sorry?"

"The baby?" Michael asked. "That young and married. There must be a child involved."

Roger sighed and nodded. "Three months. Janice just turned twenty."

Michael raised his eyebrows.

Roger held out his hand. "Just turned twenty last week. Josh turns twenty next month."

Michael nodded.

"Still, they are babies having a baby. They said it was their plan to get married anyway, just not their plan to have children so soon."

Michael chuckled, "Guess they couldn't wait for the nuptials."

"No. And he knew we were not entirely happy, but to be honest with you, Jessica and I weren't exactly…"

"…pure?"

Roger laughed, "Right. You could put it that way. No, we weren't. I don't want to say it's okay. God calls us to remain pure until we enter marriage, but not many kids stick to it nowadays. It is still a sin. And we tried to teach Josh that. I guess we didn't do a good enough job of it. And our example wasn't the best teaching tool."

Michael snorted. "Rachel made me wait."

Roger laughed again, this time slapping his knee. "Well, of course, she would. She would have your father here to answer to. A twenty-year tenure pastor."

"So, you wouldn't have?" Jacob said, his voice rising an octave.

A female voice chimed in from the other room, "Be careful how you answer that, Michael."

All three men snickered.

"No, Dad. We actually discussed it. We chose to wait. I may have strayed from God, but I was not promiscuous. I dated, but it never went that far."

"Good boy," Jessica continued her chime in. "I can see our babysitting and Sunday School lessons paid off."

"Yes, Ms. Jessica," Michael said, jesting at her old church title. "You helped this boy turn into a respectable man."

"Okay," Jacob said with a relieved sigh. "Speaking of a respectable man. You've cooled off enough. Let's take you to see your kids."

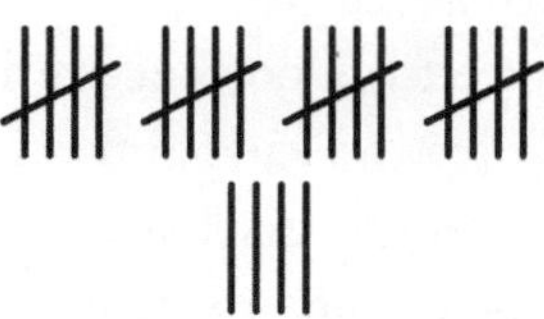

Michael poured his third cup of coffee and paced the kitchen floor. He walked to the door and peeked out the living room blinds, looking for Johnathan's car. He was late. The worst ran through his mind. Was it another Official encounter? He redialed his number, and after two rings, it went to voice mail. *Maybe he's on the other line,* he hoped.

Michael looked behind him and up the stairs. All was quiet with the kids. The previous night, after arriving home, they had yawned and were asleep even before he kissed their foreheads. He was relieved there were no questions. Millie said they had too much fun running around the farm and playing with the animals. But he was dreading the sound of footsteps in just a matter of hours, maybe minutes.

His thoughts were broken by the sound of an engine coming to a stop. Michael took a sip of his coffee, set it on an end table coaster, and made it to the door ahead of Johnathan's knock.

"Good morning, sunshine," Michael said, trying to lighten the tension.

Johnathan shook his head. "Clouds are rolling in, Michael. I wish I were the bearer of better news."

"Come on in. I have a fresh pot of coffee waiting."

Michael led him to the kitchen and poured him a cup. Johnathan sat, reaching into his briefcase. Micheal wondered if it was going to be another red folder.

"This isn't good, Michael. I don't know what to do. And that says something. I've exhausted every resource I have. Rachel is just missing. I can't find her. She's not in any database anywhere; at least none that I have access to."

Michael sat and sipped his coffee. He had prepared for this moment. After picking up the kids and bringing them home, he and his dad spent the evening discussing it. Jacob had explained what could happen. It was hard to hear, but building up to this moment was better than ripping off the bandage. His dad explained what Renae had been through regarding her experience of believing he was dead. He was prepared.

"My parents went through this," Michael began. "My father disappeared. Nathan Edwards had my mom believing he was dead. Now, I doubt Kendrick will be that foolish. It's just a matter of where he's moved her to. As Roger said, for all we know, she could still be at the prison; he just changed the paperwork."

"I doubt that. You can't just hide a person. Especially today." Johnathan said, sipping his coffee. "Although, it seems Kendrick knows enough to make one disappear. He may just be clever enough to make it seem like she was never there in the first place. But I doubt I could get close enough to speak to any guards to find out."

"What about a pseudonym?"

"It would still leave a trail. Especially this quickly. If he had time, that would be a possibility. But overnight?" Johnathan shook his head. "No, she's not at the prison. Erasing is easier than concealment."

"Can't we wait for a guard to get off shift and approach them?"

"Not a chance," Johnathan again shook his head. "They have an employee garage in the basement. The exit is at the rear of the building. It was constructed eight years ago after a case of witness tampering."

"Yeah. I noticed the parking lot was rather empty. There was only one vehicle that had police lights. Another that was official-looking. The others were civilian cars and trucks."

"We don't have enough information to know where they could've taken her. That's what I've been doing for the past twenty-four hours. I'm sorry, Michael," Johnathan said, defeat in his voice.

"I'm sorry, too," Michael said as the coffee pot sounded its timer shutting down. Time was running out on them too. It reminded him of something his father once said about the timing of the moment and how his experience led him to where he is now. That his experience in that cell was so far away from everyone and everything that…

"I know where she is," Michael said, jumping up, almost spilling their coffees. He picked up his phone and dialed.

"What? Where?" Johnathan said, picking up the knocked-over creamer container.

"C'mon, Dad, pick up," Michael said to his phone when he received his voicemail and dialed again.

Michael spun around when his father answered on his next attempt.

"Sorry, son, I was in the other room—"

"Dad! You once said you were not in the county jail when Edwards held you, right?"

"Yes?"

"And that place is here in town?"

"Michael, we've been over this. It's a car wash now, remember? You were upset with me because I allowed you to have your kids sit over it?"

"Yes, I know they demolished the offices, but did they get rid of what was below ground?"

The line stayed quiet for a moment. At last Jacob replied, "I don't know. I never gave it much thought. I suppose it would have taken too much effort to cement the whole place in."

"So the underground facility could still exist?" Michael said.

"I suppose so... Wait, you think that's where Kendrick took Rachel?"

"It would make sense. It *is* hidden, and no one but us would know about it."

"So it's a possibility," Michael and Johnathan say simultaneously.

"Sorry, I can hear him too," Johnathan said. "Where is the facility?"

"The Spik and Span Carwash on the edge of town," Michael answered Johnathan.

"And there is a prison underneath that place?" Johnathan asked.

"In a way," Michael said, then to his phone, "Dad, we need to check it out."

"No, Son, you need to stay away from that place. If she is there, chances are it is guarded. And Edwards is not one to underestimate. Nathan or Kendrick."

"Then we need a third party to scout the place, look for entrances, or see if any SUVs are around. Any of us would be spotted instantly, including Frank," Michael said. "Seems they are either oblivious to or ignoring Roger. They passed his shop when we were there. And with his vehicle access, he could easily take a car he is working on to have it washed."

"We can't ask him to place himself in that type of danger," Jacob responded.

"Of course not," Michael said. "But we could talk to him and see how he and Jessica feel about it. But we need to do this soon."

"Okay. I will talk to Roger about checking on the Spic and Span. Until then, *you* stay away. Don't get involved and jeopardize your safety. Think about your kids. Do something to occupy yourself. What about the hardware store? When was the last time you were there?" Jacob asked.

"Last week, I checked on Phillip. He seemed to have things under control. He and Becky understood the situation and told me to do what I needed to do. I haven't received any calls on the Bat Phone, so I assume the place is still standing."

"Okay. Let's check on them. It'll keep your mind occupied. We don't need your job to suffer. It's what you need to live on. You don't want to go through this and then have nothing for Rachel to return to."

"Alright. We can swing by there when you come get me. My car is still at Roger's shop."

Michael disconnected and thought about the last time he *was* in the store. It felt like it had been ages. He felt guilty about leaving Philip and Becky alone. They must be okay, or he would've heard something by now.

Michael dialed Phillip.

"Hey, boss. How's everything? I was about to send out the cavalry," the older gentleman greeted with a chuckle.

"Yeah, I'm sorry, Phil," Michael said. He wasn't sure how much to tell. Less was more, he figured. "Just been busy. I'm sure you probably already know about Rachel."

"Yes. I heard she'd been arrested. Sorry to hear about that. I'm sure it's a misunderstanding. She's a good person, wouldn't hurt a fly."

"We're working on it," Michael said. "Say, I'll be in later this morning to check on things. I feel I've neglected you and Becky."

"If you're busy, we're good. Everything's in order here, Michael."

"I know, but I'd feel better if I came in and just took a walk around. To tell you the truth, it may also help me focus. One less thing in the back of my mind."

"Sounds good," Phil said. "We'll look for you, then."

"Thanks, Phil," Michael said and swiped left.

"Everything looks great, Becky. I can't tell you how much I appreciate all you do," Michael said. "I know I've been MIA lately. I apologize for that."

"Sweetie, there's no need to explain yourself. You do what you need to do. Phil and I have things under control. Now get out of here. Go, before I have to call your mother," Becky said with a grin over her thick glasses.

"I'm going. My dad is out there gabbing with Phil, probably talking shop."

"Where are you two headed?"

"Just father-son stuff." Michael shrugged. His eyes looked to the floor, then out the office door, then back to her.

"There's more to that, dear," Becky said. "We've known each other since you ran around here in diapers. What's going on?"

Michael sighed.

"What do you know about the carwash on the corner," Michael said, nodding in its direction.

"The Spik and Span?"

"Yeah."

"It's been there for a couple of decades. They built it after…" Becky paused.

"Yeah," Michael said. "Don't worry. I know my dad spent some time there. I know everything."

"Maybe not everything."

"What do you mean?"

"Well, you know how Roger and Jessica own their shop and this place?"

"Yeah?"

"Guess what else they own?"

"You're kidding me," Michael said. "They own the Spik and Span?"

"You and your father aren't supposed to know," Becky began. "I only know because I do the books. But if you two go poking around over there, better you find out from me than find out on your own and go barging in on Roger yourselves."

"Why wouldn't they want us to know?"

"I can only imagine it's because of what happened there. With it sealed off; out of sight, out of mind."

"Sealed off? What do you mean? It's supposed to be gone."

"Well, the above-ground offices are gone. When the Mills' had them level the main office, it eliminated every other entrance."

"I see," Michael replied. "No other way in?"

"Well, there is *one* access point that takes you underground."

"How do you know this?"

The room was silent for a moment.

"Okay, you have me," she said, turning in her seat, blushing. "So, I'm a busybody. I am the file clerk. I've known for years. I read the job orders for all the work done. I just had to look when I saw the information because I knew what had happened there."

Michael thought for a moment. He pulled a chair next to Becky and sat. "Becky, let's say I wanted to get into that underground facility. Could I still get into it?"

"The door is only spot-welded shut. If you had the right tools, perhaps. It's within a storage room where they keep cleaning products. But why would you want to go down there? Your dad nearly lost his life getting out."

Michael looked back to the door.

"We have our reasons."

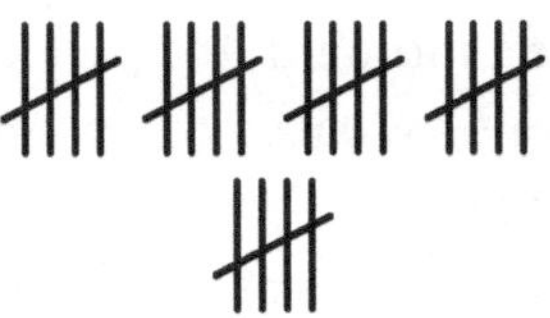

"I don't think this is a good idea, Michael," Jacob said as they pulled into a bay at the car wash.

"Dad, we've driven around the block for an hour now. We haven't seen any SUVs. If they were around, we would know it."

"Or they are camped out to where we can't see them," Jacob reminded.

Michael sighed. "I just want to take a look at that door."

Michael was driving a 2032 Ford Transporter, in the Mills' shop for a tune-up. The van was a shuttle for The Homestead, a local hotel that made trips from Carrelton to the San Antonio airport for those who chose to book in the town as a cheaper option to SA's rates. With frequent trips, the van using the car wash was a regular occurrence.

Michael found a Mills Motors polo shirt and Spurs cap behind a seat and put them on. He feigned washing while perusing the lot. There was only one structure that could house the door Becky spoke of. He had to admit Roger did an excellent job hiding it in plain sight when he built the facility.

It looked like a simple storage building. He had thought it would be hidden behind a crop of bushes in a back corner. But it fit right in with the business as storage for soaps, cleansers, and

180

other odds and ends for the facility, right up to the light over the door for night workers.

Michael tapped the side of the van with no reply. He rolled his eyes but remembered what his father went through not too far from where they were sitting. He almost lost his life. Two of his friends did lose theirs. *Maybe this wasn't such a good idea.* Michael released the spray wand trigger and went to the passenger's side of the van.

Michael opened the sliding door. "You okay?"

Jacob nodded.

"I'm sorry, Dad. I wasn't thinking."

"I'm fine. I just haven't been this close since..." his voice trailed off.

"I'm sorry."

"It's all right. I'm fine. What do you see?

"Just the storage shed—one door. Can't tell how it is locked up from here. But it is lit up. It most likely has surveillance."

"I'm sure this whole place does," Jacob said. "But if they have gained access to it without his knowledge, who knows who is watching right now? Watch your back."

Michael stepped back and gave a sweeping glance around the lot. It wasn't compelling. His father disapproved.

"Oh, good grief, Michael. At least use the wand when you are doing that."

Michael looked down at his hand, realizing his error. "Oh, right." He closed the door and resumed washing the van and scanning when possible. When he made another pass of the van's rear, he gave a final glance at the bunker. He wondered about the lighting.

If I were only able to turn that light off, I could get a better look when it was dark… Wait! Michael remembered that he had all the access he needed. He replaced the nozzle and got in the van.

"I have an idea," Michael said.

"Oh, brother," Jacob said. "Why don't I like the sound of that?"

"What?" Michael shrugged. He looked through the adjacent

lots before heading into traffic; all seemed clear. "We need to talk to Roger."

"Why Roger?"

Michael sighed, "There is something you need to know, but I don't want you to overreact when you find out."

"What does Roger have to do with it?"

"Roger owns the Spik and Span."

"What? No, that's not possible. I would have known about it. He would've told me."

"It's true. Becky told me. She's been paying the bills on it for more than twenty years. He bought it and was responsible for having it leveled. Then he had the car wash built. But the city would not allow him to cover the underground facility completely. That is why there is still the above-ground access point."

"So, Roger knows about what's going on down there?"

"I don't think so. From what Becky tells me, he has a manager overseeing the place. The manager cleans the facility, keeps the change running, and soaps flowing. If someone other than the manager frequents the place, it is under Roger's nose."

"We need to go see Roger," Jacob said.

"Now we are on the same page," Michael said. He turned the corner and was reminded of outrunning the two SUVs. He glanced in the rearview and double-checked for a tail. He followed the curve, but when he made the straight away was met with flashing lights.

"What is that?" Jacob pointed to the fire engine and EMS vehicle parked in front of Mill's Automotive.

Michael sped up and pulled into the lot, slamming on the brakes behind the fire engine. Both men approached the front door; Jessica and Josh were in the lobby. Jessica sat in a chair weeping uncontrollably; Josh had his hand on her shoulder, anger burning in his eyes.

"Josh, what happened? Where's Roger?"

At the mention of his name, Jessica screams into her arm. Josh leaned over and took her into his arms. He looks up at them and began to tear up himself.

"He's gone, Mr. Andrews," Josh said. "He's… gone."

"Who's gone?" Jacob said, then looked at Jessica. "Jessica, what is Josh talking about? What happened?"

"Mr. Andrews, she's too upset to talk about it. She's the one who found Dad. Let her be."

"He's… dead?" Michael asked.

Josh threw him an icy glare. Michael understood his faux pax. He mouthed an apology, realizing he didn't need to ask. Roger was dead, and it wasn't a natural death.

A law enforcement officer entered the room with an EMT crew member, "Pastor, what are you doing here?"

"The family called me," Jacob said without missing a beat. "They are parishioners. How are you, Jeffery?"

Jeffery locked eyes with Jacob, then gave a quick glance to the Mills, then back to the Pastor. "Can we step outside for a moment?"

"Sure," Jacob said. "Stay here, Michael, with Josh."

"Stick around, Mr. Andrews. I have a couple of questions for you as well."

"Yeah, no problem," Michael said.

Jacob and Jeffery left the waiting area. An EMT who introduced herself as Victoria offered Jessica assistance, which she refused twice. But after a third attempt, she gave in and extended her arm. Victoria left her name and instructions that if she were to experience any discomfort, to call her over, and she would be with the detective until everything was wrapped up.

"Thanks, Victoria. I'll let you know if I need anything," Jessica said.

"You've been with the Pastor all day?" Josh asked, his voice with a hint of doubt.

Michael looked to the office, then back to Josh, "Yes. Why do you ask? What's going on?"

Josh nodded to the office. "They're lookin' for you."

Michael looked back to the office, to Josh, then down to Jessica, who looked up at him.

"Now wait—"

"Oh, Michael," Jessica said. "We know it wasn't you. But they sure made it look like it was."

"Edwards?"

Jessica nodded.

Josh nodded to the shop, "They have fingerprints all over the place, Mr. Andrews. Of course, your car, but handles, knobs, and some tools. Blast how they did it."

Michael felt his stomach churn, wanting to vomit. He looked to the office, expecting that his dad was getting the same news or questioning where he had been for the last several hours."

"How long ago?" Michael asked.

"They say four hours," Jake said.

"I've been with Dad all day. We were at the hardware store this afternoon. They have video cam—"

"Michael. Stop it." Jessica sniffled. "We don't doubt you."

Michael sighed and sat, "I know. But will they." He gestured to the other office.

Both of his friends grunted in agreement.

"Maybe you should go," Jake said.

"Jake!" Jessica said.

"What?" Jake said. "If he stays here, he goes to prison for murder. And they have a solid case against him. If he leaves now, at least it would give us time to prove he didn't do it. If he goes to jail, Edwards wins."

Michael chewed on what Jake said. He had a point. Inside, he may disappear the way Rachel did. Outside, he would have a fighting chance to prove his innocence. But now would be the time. They only had one officer here, and it appeared there were no Officials around, yet.

Jessica's silence meant that she agreed as well. Their glance flowed between themselves, and no other words were said. Jessica looked at the office, stood, and walked toward it. She looked over her shoulder at Michael, nodded at the exit, then entered the office. "Jeffery, I have a couple of questions for you."

Michael looked at Jake, gave him a quick wave, and headed for the door, keys in hand. He went toward the van, and before he got there, Jake was behind him.

"Here," Jake handed him a set of keys to a Chevy Surveyor. "We just finished it this morning. There isn't an owner. We bought it as a fixer-upper from a junkyard. Doesn't even have a registration yet. So, they can't track it. Just don't get pulled over. Plates are still from the old vehicle."

"Thanks, Jake."

"No problem," Jake said, giving him a hug. "Now go find the bastards who did this to my dad."

"Do you know who this is?" the caller said.

"I think so," the answerer of the call responded.

"Good. I could go for a good cup of coffee," the caller replied, hoping he would take the hint.

"Yeah, coffee does sound good this morning."

"See you soon," the caller said and disconnected the line.

✝✝✝

"I thought you didn't like coffee," Johnathan jested.

"It grows on you," Michael said as he sat back and away from the window of the courthouse coffee shop.

"I'm just glad I remembered this place," Johnathan said, sitting.

"I figured it was the safest place right now. Everyone looking for me wouldn't consider I'd walk right into their hands."

"Gutsy. But I wouldn't play that hand for very long. It's a good thing there aren't any warrants out yet. I checked before I headed over. But that will change quickly. You're just a person of interest wanted for questioning."

"I didn't do it, Johnathan," Michael said, leaning forward on the table.

"I'm not saying you did. I'm just emphasizing that I'm able to have this conversation with you because if you were wanted, I would be under an obligation to turn you in. As a person of interest, I am required to suggest that you obtain counsel and turn yourself in."

Michael nodded. "Have you heard anything about Rachel?"

"No. But that bunker has a history, as I know you are fully aware."

"I know more about it now. But with that information, it only makes me seem more guilty. Roger Mills owned it."

"He was the one killed last night?"

"Yes. He was the owner of the car wash."

"That is what I was about to tell you," Johnathan said. "I found the owner's name online. It took some digging, but it was simply a business line-up between the three companies."

"Is that right?" Michael said flatly.

Johnathan said, "Sorry, you probably don't care about the ownership."

"I found out through my bookkeeper at the hardware store," Michael said. "She's been doing the books there since my dad owned the place."

"That links everything together."

"Yeah, and it looks bad for me," Michael snapped his head up from his cup. "Or my dad. He was the one who had caused trouble for Edwards. I need to call him."

Johnathan reached across and stopped Michael from dialing. "Let me do that. You need to be missing, remember?"

Johnathan dialed Jacob's number. He shook his head to Michael, showing there was no answer. "Hey, Jacob. It's Johnathan Clarke, Rachel's attorney. I'm trying to reach Michael. I was hoping you could give him a message for me. Give me a call at the number that's on your display. Thank you, sir." Johnathan ended the message.

"That seemed innocent enough," Michael said, rolling his eyes.

"Do you have a plan now that you are a fugitive? Well, figuratively. I couldn't legally condone your actions if you were, sir."

"Right, of course. I never thought that far. The family suggested that I just leave. They knew of my innocence, and with Rachel still missing, they didn't want all the family under Edwards' thumb. Not knowing where to go, I drove to the truck stops on 37 and camped there last night. Too many cars are passing through for one vehicle to be noticed."

"Smart thinking."

"Darkness helped too. I stayed in the middle and never made a trip inside. On the chance of the SUVs making rounds, I swapped between the three truck stops, just in case I would be noticed at one. All I needed to do was make it through one night."

"I see," Johnathan said.

"I need to find my dad. He knows about these things."

"What about your mother?"

"Nuh-uh. I can't get her involved. If Edwards is behind this, we need to keep her as far away from this as possible."

Johnathan jumped. His phone had started to buzz in his hands. He looked at the screen and showed it to Michael; it was his dad. "You want to take it?"

Michael nodded and took the phone, "Hey, Dad. Was beginning to wonder what happened to you."

"Well, well, well, Citizen," answered the voice on the line—it wasn't his father.

"Kendrick Edwards," Michael sneered.

"Hey! That's *Official* Edwards to you," Edwards snapped. "Or do I need to reprimand you for inappropriately addressing a federal officer?"

"Official Edwards. Where's my father? And where is my wife?"

"They are both in good hands, Citizen. *Tsk, tsk, tsk,* but I don't know for how much longer that can be said of either of them."

"You know you can't do this," Johnathan warned him.

"What other choice do I have?" Michael shrugged.

"He's right, Michael. We all know it's a trap," Jessica Mills said, then pointed to Johnathan and Frank, who were leaning against Dunham's kitchen counter. "At least let one of the guys go with you."

"He's expecting me alone. Who knows what he will do if he sees anyone else with me? I can't risk that. We already know he isn't above murder. If it means my life for theirs, so be it. Right now, he wants my father to suffer, and he wants me to witness it. Me going in keeps him alive. That gives me time to come up with a way to save him."

"How do you plan to do that?" Jessica asked.

"I don't know yet. I've always had a way with words. My dad has always gotten after me for having a smart mouth. Let's see if I can use it to our benefit."

"Just don't smart off too much, Son. Remember, mouths and Edwardses don't mix too well," Frank said. "You have the kiddos upstairs to think about."

"I know, Pop. I can control it. Believe it or not, I know how far to take things—most times," Michael said, eyebrows raised. "That is where my father and I differ."

"You do know, all it would take is a phone call to law enforcement, and he doesn't have to touch you. Local LEOs show up and arrest you. You are still a person of interest in Roger Mill's death," Johnathan said. "Sorry, Jessica."

"It's okay. It's true," Jessica said, trying to give assurance she was okay. "You need to think before you act, Michael. He could be baiting you just to *have* you arrested."

Michael thought about it, then shook his head. "No, that's not an *Official* way. They like to handle things on their own. They believe they are above local law enforcement. Dad said that was one thing that hasn't changed over the years. Letting local police take someone in would cause more problems than it would solve, even more so in Kendrick's case. It's too late now. I know the truth. I get arrested, and he knows I will expose what's happening at the shelter. No, this stays between us, here in Carrolton."

"Don't forget about the subservient dogs he sends to do his bidding," Frank said. "We haven't seen their faces, but we know they exist. There are at least two of them. And he isn't above using others, like he did your father's friend, Jesse."

"If that's the case, I wonder if Rachel was just a pawn to get to my father? And now that Edwards has my father, why is he going after me? Why not let Rachel go?"

"I don't know," Frank shook his head. "I wish I could answer that. To continue to punish your father, I suppose. Your dad took *his* uncle away. Maybe he wants to take your dad away from you?"

"Or worse," Johnathan said. "Sorry. He may want you to watch him take your father's life and put you in his current emotional state. Then he could call local law enforcement and have you arrested. Win-win for him."

"Watch your back," both Johnathan and Frank said in unison.

"You sure you don't want me to go with you?" Josh said.

"Your place is here with your mom. She needs you, Josh. I need to get going," Michael said and walked toward the door.

"Be careful," Jessica said.

Michael walked to Roger's pickup and looked up at it. It was larger than his truck and seemed even larger than their SUV. Josh said Roger had the same protection on his personal vehicle that was over the shop. While it wasn't lifted, he had to step up to get in. Nor was the engine souped, but it roared to life when he turned the key.

Michael looked at the dash. There were several types of radio knobs. He remembered his dad telling him about Roger having different radio band types and digital scanners. He wondered if it picked up police bands. He pushed a button, and the dash bleeped, and digital screens came to life. A welcome screen gave way to labels: 'Police,' 'Fire,' 'CB 19 Local', 'CB 45 OTR', "Air Traffic,' 'Official,' and "Home." Michael was impressed; he wondered how Roger had the truck wired to send and receive signals without seeing an antenna, but he had heard stories of his technical abilities. He selected the 'Official' channel and backed out of the spot.

✝✝✝

There was a sound in the distance. A sound that was all too familiar. An echo that Jacob had only heard in his dreams, or rather nightmares, for at well over the past two decades—the sound of a dripping faucet.

"Oh, God, no," Jacob muttered. He attempted to stand, but his aching body told him to remain on the cold concrete floor. He felt around when he realized he knew where he was. After all this time, the room hadn't changed. His hand found the leg of what felt like a cot. It was in the same place it was two decades ago. With the strength he had left, he dragged himself over to it and hoped they had at least cleaned the place before his return. When no dust entered his lungs, he was grateful—then the pain took him back into darkness.

✝✝✝

"Rise and shine, Citizen," Jacob heard with a slapping pat to his face.

Jacob opened his eyes, and the light from the open cell door cast a path to where they were. It lit up Kendrick Edwards' face. Half of it, at least. Jacob could now see the family resemblance in the evil grin of Nathan Edwards.

"Look familiar?" Edwards said, standing and swooping his arm around the room.

Jacob didn't reply.

"That is rude, Mr. Andrews. I even cleaned up the place for you. You would never believe how messy a place can get after two decades of just sitting here empty. Of course, Turner and Anderson did a fair job of cleaning up the cells down here."

"Cells?" Jacob said, leaning up on his elbow.

"Ahh, that got your attention, Citizen," Edwards laughed.

"Rachel," Jacob called out. "Rachel!"

"Dad?" Rachel replied. "Jacob, is that you?"

Jacob turned his head toward the wall vent, the one he had spoken to Eric through so many times.

"Yes, it's me. Are you okay? They haven't hurt you, have they?"

Kendrick didn't give her time to answer. "No, Mr. Andrews. We are not barbarians. We haven't touched the young lady. She hasn't given us the issues you and your son have. She is being held for her protection. We need to ensure that nothing happens to her."

"We both know that's a lie, Edwards. You created this whole thing. You are as much a fool as your uncle was," Jacob said.

"Hmm." Edwards scratched his chin. "I'm in a good mood. I will let that one slide, Mr. Andrews. The next time you accuse an Official without evidence, you *will* be punished." Edwards knelt next to Jacob again. "You fully know that outbursts like that are federal offenses now. In fact, your little debacle with my uncle helped that along."

"Your uncle was nothing but a murdering coward."

Kendrick sneered, and his eyes narrowed. He stood and backhanded Jacob across his already bruised cheek. Jacob could swear he saw every color in existence as he fell back into darkness.

†††

When Jacob woke again, the room was dark but for the light from the cell window. He had flashbacks and almost thought he had dreamt the last period of his life. He nearly called Eric's name until reality set in, and he sat up and looked around. He could make out his five-barred gates on the wall. Running his fingertip over them, he remembered the joy he felt, etching the last of them and thinking of getting to go home and the peace he felt because he was a new creation in Christ. He looked up and remembered it all.

This is the room where I met the Lord; this is where it all began for me.

He thought of second chances and Renae; then he remembered Rachel in the next cell.

"Rachel? Are you still there?"

"Yes," a weak voice said.

"I'm sorry," Jacob said. "Were you asleep?"

"Kinda. As much sleep as you can get in a place like this."

"Believe me, I know."

"Wait. Is this the place you were talking about?"

"Believe it or not, yes. This is the cell I was in in twenty-four years ago ago. You are where Pastor Eric was."

"Oh," Rachel said softly.

"Don't worry," Jacob said, thinking she may know his story. "That's not where he died."

Rachel chuckled. "That's not what I was thinking. It's just weird being here. You've always told the story about your history, and it was just a story. But being here and seeing all of this is just…"

"Surreal," Jacob said.

"Yeah. I guess that's a good word for it," Rachel said.

"You okay?"

"I'm fine. I just miss Michael and the kids."

"And they miss you. He has been worried sick about you. Wanting to do stupid things to try and find you. I can only imagine what he is thinking about doing right now to get in here. I hope he has good counsel."

Rachel laughed, "Yeah, that's him. Not thinking before acting. His heart's in the right place, but sometimes it can get him into trouble."

"Yours too, Rachel," Jacob said with a half chuckle.

"Yeah. I guess that's why I'm in here. I swear, though, I never knew that lady would do what she did."

"Well, if it is any consolation, she was instructed to contact you and to coerce you into doing what you did. They are called *plants*."

"Really? I never knew. Well, the thought crossed my mind. Why didn't Mr. Clarke say anything before what he did in court?"

"He couldn't," Jacob said. "They were watching him. You can't legally accuse people of things without evidence. Especially someone of Dr. Houston's status."

"Yeah, I know I was being watched. I had a liaison the entire time," Rachel said. "Mr. Clarke and I barely spoke after our initial meeting, now that I think about it."

"Now that you are missing, according to Mr. Clarke, the courts are at a loss. He spoke to the judge. Your case is pending until Monday. I don't know what they will do then."

There was silence for a moment. Jacob could hear Rachel's sniffles. He felt for her. He knew the feeling. His whole time in confinement, all he could think about was Michael. She had two children to think about, his grandkids. He looked around again. It felt as if he had come full circle. This time, he was the one with the strength of God. It was his turn to be the comforter. He needed to be her Eric.

Jacob took a breath. "God will see you through this, Rachel. I don't know how this will turn out, but He has a plan."

"I know," Rachel said softly.

"I apologize if I'm the cause of this. I don't want you hurt because of my past."

"You don't have to apologize, Dad. You aren't to blame."

"I don't think Edwards sees it that way."

"Regardless, I don't blame you," Rachel said. "Don't beat yourself up. All things happen for a reason. And we who are saved gladly bear our burdens for that purpose. God has a plan through it all."

"I'm grateful you see it that way. We just pray God reveals it to us," Jacob said.

"Maybe through all this, Michael will become closer to God. I know he's fallen away. He has spent more time away from the family, away from the church, and we've just seemed disconnected. Maybe through this, he will find God again and see He has His hand on us."

Jacob laughed, then coughed because of the pain.

"What?"

"Sorry. Even as a pastor, I sometimes find what God does a bit humorous and backward."

"How's that?" Jessica asked.

"We tell people to turn to the Lord and trust Him. This tends to paint a pretty picture that God will make things go smoothly for them. But look at us right now. You are on trial, now missing. I am here, beaten in a cell, and your husband is on the lam, accused of committing crimes that you don't need to know about right now. Some great God, huh?"

"What are you talking about? On the lam?"

"Rachel, trust me, it is best you don't know right now. My point is that God sure takes us down dark paths when people think it should be rainbows and sandy beaches."

"But we can manage it. While this is a tough situation, I know I'll make it. I don't understand why I must go through this, but I trust that God has a purpose," Rachel said.

"As do I," Jacob agreed. "And could this be for Michael's sake to draw him closer to the Lord? That is a considerable price. But I think both you and I would say we are happy to be sitting here right now if it meant that Michael would come to the Lord due to it. Just as I was sent here over twenty years ago, I met Pastor Eric, who helped me return to Christ. I wouldn't be close to God if it weren't for him. I needed to experience that. And for Michael, his experience will lead him back to God." Jacob grinned. "It's how God works with individuals. He uses the strong to reach the weak."

Rachel chuckled, "Are you calling my husband weak?"

Jacob laughed. "Not exactly, but God knows the heart. And He understands how much worldly pressure it takes to break someone. And He knows how much it takes to turn a heart back to Him. He uses that to reach us."

Rachel was silent for a moment, then asked, "I wonder where Michael is now?"

"I am sure he is on his way here now."

"What makes you say that?"

"Because he knows you're here."

The CB was silent as Michael approached town. Then, whether they could track the system or learn the vehicle, the radio came to life.

"Turner. What's your twenty?"

"Just across the tracks, Anderson."

"Let Official Edwards know the target is in sight. He's just coming into town from the North."

"10-4."

The radio went silent. Michael didn't see the vehicle that had noticed him. The tracks were to his right, and private ranch residents were to his left.

Passing the split in town where the first tail he had experienced occurred, he looked in his rearview mirror. No one approached him. It was still early; the sun had barely risen. The glows of oranges and yellows were beginning to fill the sky. A few headlights were headed his way, but they were just cars headed to San Antonio, locals or those who preferred the secondary road compared to Highway 37.

The outskirts of town were still quiet; no one was up this early on a Saturday. Michael could see the bright lights from the service station ahead. He remembered picking up his tail there the first time he went to Mill's Motors. He had to shake off the feeling of regret and fear. He couldn't let emotion get in the way. He needed a clear head to get through this. He owed it to his dad. He owed it to his wife. He owed it to their kids, who were oblivious to what was happening. All they knew was Mommy and Daddy were on vacation or having a sleepover at Pop and Mamaw's, taking care of the farm.

"Quarter mile," the radio squawked, making Michael jump.

"10-4."

Michael wondered how they could see him. He looked up and wondered if it was cameras on buildings or a drone. Through the window tint, he couldn't see anything in the air. He drove past the Spik and Span and into a service station, then parked along a wall facing the car wash.

"He's in the Stop and Shop across the road. You got him?" Turner said.

"I got eyes on him," Anderson replied.

Michael surveyed the area, but there were still no SUVs. It made him wonder if they had chosen another type of vehicle for surveillance. He looked to the sky again for a possible drone. Roger had once warned, *They could also be watching through city surveillance cameras.* He looked up. The gas station had plenty of those.

The car wash was still lit up; sunrise had yet to take full effect. Michael turned off the engine, then back to aux. The *pops* and *pings* from the engine filled the silence. Not sure what was next, Michael sat and waited.

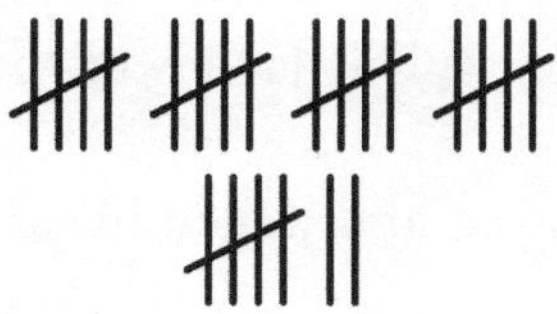

"Wake up," the voice shouted.

Jacob jumped. He must've dozed off. He hated doing that because it threw off his internal clock. Now, he was oblivious. He remembered the sick feeling of losing track of time during his first stay. Half the time, he wasn't sure if his etchings were accurate. If it hadn't been for Eric, he would probably still be in there thinking he was on his twelfth day.

The voice turned into a boot to his side.

"I'm awake," Jacob said, sitting up and squinting into the hallway light.

"You're being relocated. Get up."

Jacob's body ached, but he stood fast. He could tell the deputy meant business and was eager to dispense his authority.

"Where's Rachel?"

"Other inmate's whereabouts is not your concern, Citizen," came another voice. This one did not have the rough edge.

Edwards.

Jacob half wanted to continue questioning; the other half wanted to lunge at him and beat it out of him. "She better be okay, Official Edwards."

Edwards laughed. "Well, at least you have the Official part down."

Edwards nodded, and the first voice backhanded Jacob, knocking him back to the floor.

"Your daughter-in-law is fine. As I told you before, Mr. Andrews, I do not touch the ladies. If you, one the other hand, endure any consequences, it is on her behalf.

"Pick him up," Edwards said to the deputy. "Take him to the office on the sub-main level and wait for me there."

The muscular deputy pulled Jacob off the floor like a rag doll and onto his feet.

Jacob found his footing and jerked his arm back. "I can follow you just fine, Deputy."

It was a squinted hobble, but Jacob had no intention of giving anyone issues. He looked back to his etchings as he followed the deputy, hoping again that this would be the last time he'd see their scarring. He looked at the floor; Eric's memory flashed across his mind—him lying on the floor, dying in his arms. A wave of anger started to brew. He tried to suppress it. He had let that go a long time ago. But being this close brought it all back. Being this close to the kin of the man responsible. And Official Kendrick Edwards blaming him for the death of his uncle only added to the resentment.

Jacob took a deep breath and prayed. *God, why am I in this place again? I don't want to be here. I don't want to have these feelings. Please help me through this. Be with Rachel wherever she is. Protect her and see her through this as well. Guide Michael in whatever he is planning. Help him not to make any rash decisions. Show him the correct course of action to bring us through this. In your name, I pray.* "Amen."

"Did you say something?" the gruff deputy said as they ascended the second flight of stairs. This deputy was neither Anderson nor Turner, but in the same Official deputy uniform—*there were more of them.* Jacob noticed the stairwell had been recently repaired; not a speck of dust littered the area.

"Not a word," Jacob said, considering whether a witnessing attempt would be wise in this situation. *Was he like Jesse or hardened like the others?* His side ached, and he thought twice about it. His pain and the thought of a couple more boots or suddenly descending a flight of stairs was not a comforting thought.

They reached the landing, and the deputy opened the door. Jacob looked behind them and up the stairs to the darkened next flight. The stairs leading up were caution-taped off. Jacob wondered what the next level looked like. Had it been renovated like the lower levels? He wondered where and how it ended, knowing the surface had been plowed over and leveled. He must've taken too long in thought because his arm was nearly pulled out of its socket, and he received an expletive-filled reprimand.

Once through the door, Jacob observed his surroundings. He had not seen this level before. If he didn't know better, he would have sworn he was in an office building. Edwards really did go above and beyond with the cleaning job. The place was immaculate. The room was filled with large cubicles and short-style filing cabinets lining the side wall, and it smelled of new carpet and metal. None of the cubicles were occupied, but an office at the far end of the room had a light beaming from it.

Before he even came close to the lighted office, the smell hit him. The newness was replaced with a familiar scent that transported him into his past. If that wasn't bad enough, the room itself was a near replica of Nathan Edwards' office. How in the world those items survived a grenade blast and the ensuing fire was beyond him, but Kendrick had somehow recreated the office, from the leather chair down to the grenade collectibles on the shelves. The level of detail sent shivers up Jacob's spine.

The deputy laughed at Jacob's expression. "Impressive, isn't it? I've heard reverence from Anderson and Turner, but from your look, I can see they are spot on."

"It is like I've walked into my past if I'm being honest," Jacob said.

"The difference is none of those grenades are live, so don't get any cute ideas like you did the last time," the deputy said.

Jacob said nothing, not even attempting to explain. He was

sick of defending himself. He raised his hands in a defensive pose and pointed to one of the chairs in front of the desk. "May I at least sit?"

"Make yourself at home, but I have my eye on you. I have my sidearm. Try anything and you will be dead before you get out of the chair."

Jacob again raised his hands. "Gotcha, boss. You will have no issues with me. I just want to sit and rest."

"Then sit," the deputy said, pointing to the chair.

Even the chair held him in a familiar way. Jacob wanted to jump out of it but remained seated; he didn't want to startle his companion.

Silence held sway in the room for a long moment, the only sound was the ticking of a wall clock—it too was a replica; a ghost from Jacob's past.

Anything was better than quiet and listening to the countdown of his life. Small talk was his choice instead. "How long have you been with the force?" Jacob asked.

The deputy glared at him. He looked away and to the wall as if to ignore him, then shrugged. "Almost a year," he answered. "I'm from Austin but was called down last week. I was told there were… issues down here. I suppose they meant you." He looked Jacob up and down, "But you seem harmless enough. The lady, too."

"What's your name?" Jacob said, expecting neither an answer nor a sharp in-your-face response.

"Eric," the man said, then came to his senses. "But that's Deputy Granger to you. And don't forget it."

Jacob swallowed hard. *What were the chances?* He now thought about telling him they were being held against their will, but he wasn't sure where the deputy's allegiance lay. If Granger was a by-the-book deputy, he could get himself in deeper by speaking against his boss. The pain emanating from his side led Jacob to believe he was Official leaning. But his responses to his questions gave the impression he was just doing his job in front of the boss and had a human side. Jacob chose to throw caution to the wind and ask at least one more question.

"You've said yourself we are harmless, Deputy Granger. What does that tell you?"

Granger's eyes squinted. Jacob couldn't tell if he was getting through or if the deputy was mentally looking up the procedure number he had just violated. *I could could tell him,* Jacob mused. *I have the entire amendment and its subsections memorized.*

As much as he wanted to take the next step to push him over the edge, Granger needed to be the next one to speak. Accusing an Official without cause was a federal offense. He held the reason. So, whatever side he landed on would determine the course of action that would be taken. Jacob, for a moment, had hope. But as soon as the glimmer lit the man's eyes, darkness swam over them at the sound of a familiar voice.

"So Mr. Andrews. Do you like what I've done with the place?" Edwards laughed as he entered the room. "I tried to replicate the room from what I remembered as a kid growing up and from photos my uncle took. He did love that collection. Surprising enough, many of the pieces survived the fire." He nodded to the ledge with the guns and other ammunition. "I happen to know a manufacturer who was able to have them restored." He paced the room behind Jacob, admiring his collection. He picked up a grenade. "It was with one of these that you changed my family's life."

Jacob said, "Not quite how I remember it."

"Well, you were there. That's close enough for me," Edwards said. He sat at the desk and exhaled loudly. "Don't get the idea that you can do anything so miraculous again. None of those are live."

"Wouldn't think about it. And again, it wasn't me."

"Yeah. It was your buddy."

"He was *your* deputy," Jacob said. "If I were you, I would keep my eyes closer to home."

Edwards slammed his fist on the desk, "My deputies are above reproach. I am *nothing* like my uncle. I'm ten times the Official he was."

"Ah, so even you question who Nathan Edwards was?"

The younger Edwards was silent for a moment. Jacob thought he had caught him.

Edwards grunted, then smiled, "My uncle was a legend. Your buddy assassinated him with your help, and you got away with it. His fictitious video, which you probably helped him make, allowed you to walk away from that courtroom. And while I want you to pay for your crimes, sitting in prison for the rest of your life isn't enough, even in a facility such as this one.

"Now, your pretty daughter-in-law, that would've been another story. But your attorney was too damn good. That broad we hired? She was worthless. She was supposed to be the best. She put away so many up north, but she couldn't help convict a simple housewife. That judge was considering setting her free. So of course we had to take… other measures."

Jacob couldn't believe what he was hearing, a complete admission. He shook his head. "You are as bad as your uncle. When things don't go your way, you resort to violence."

Kendrick laughed. "Ah, but the difference is, I won't get caught— or blown up by a stupid underling with a tinker toy. I never allowed anyone close to you into my roost. That is where I am smarter than my flawed family member."

The phone on the Official's desk rang. Edwards grinned, exchanging glances between Jacob and the phone. "I wonder who that could be?" He picked up the phone and conversed with the caller.

"Is that right?" he said, laughed, and hung up.

The Official opened the top desk drawer and pulled out a cigar. He clipped and lit it. He took a long drag and puffed out the smoke. The replication of Nathan Edwards made Jacob cringe.

Edwards chuckled and sat back in his chair. "I've just been informed that we have a visitor upstairs."

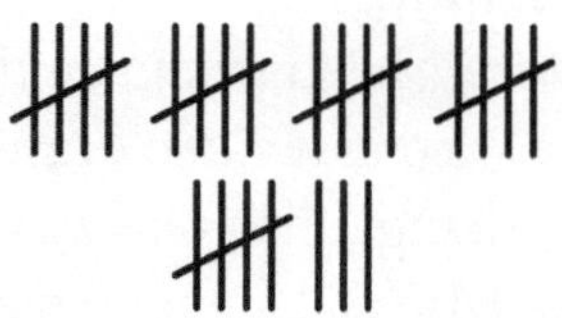

"Here goes nothing," Michael said.

Michael had chosen a direct approach. He remembered a verse his dad had taught him.

"Ask, and it will be given to you; seek and you will find; knock, and the door will be opened to you. For everyone who asks receives; the one who seeks finds; and to the one who knocks, the door will be opened."

Ask. Seek. Knock. It's about receiving blessings from God for those who are His. He laughed at the thought. He already knew they were watching him. There was only one way in.

Michael and Rachel had always teased that they would make sacrifices for the kids when it came down to it. One would have to live on for their sake. They needed a parent. But right now, his tunnel vision only led to her. He felt guilty for not thinking of the kids at the moment. He should have; that was their agreement. But knowing she was in there and that he could do something about it—he couldn't live with himself if he didn't do something. He would see any failure in his kids' faces for the rest of his life. And someday he would have to answer the question—why he didn't make that choice to save his wife.

Ask. Seek. Knock. It seems like a good prayer for this moment.

He needed the Lord more than anything. *Dad was right; the moment you need Him most is the time you realize your dependence upon Him.*

"I need you, God. I don't know what I'm about to get myself into. Guide me. Protect Rachel. Protect Dad. I ask that you expose what's going on here. Help us get through this ordeal and back home to our kids and family."

After Michael said *Amen*, he knocked on the steel door. An echo resounded through the shed as a video camera stared at him from the right side of the overhang. If anyone was down there, he would have been seen by now. Michael stepped back, and not sure what to do next, he looked up at the camera and waved.

A minute went by, and Michael knocked again. Another couple of minutes and still nothing. Two turned into five. Michael was starting to lose the courage that brought him there. Then it occurred to him that maybe that was the game. He closed his eyes, said another prayer, and took a deep breath. Just as he exhaled, the *click* of a lock made him jump.

The door creaked open, and an older gentleman in a deputy uniform stepped out. "Hello, Michael. I'm Senior Deputy Turner, and I'm a friend of your dad's. I'll be your escort to Official Edwards where you can discuss the terms of his release."

"Terms of his release?" Michael said.

"Of course. We don't intend to keep him here forever. We're not barbarians," Turner said with a rugged grin. He extended his hand toward the entrance. "Official Edwards is waiting for us. We don't want to keep him waiting."

"Of course," Michael said, entering through the door.

The room was larger than it seemed from the outside, and it did have supplies for the car wash, that was not a farce. He looked around for a staircase but did not see one. Turner locked the door behind them and walked to the opposite side of the room.

There was a keypad on the left side of a blank section of the wall. After the last number, the pad beeped three times, and a section of the wall slid open revealing descending staircase. Turner smiled and waved Michael on before leading the way down. "Watch yourself. The first time is always the trickiest."

Michael held onto the wall as he walked down the steps. Cracks lined the wall, and the smell of dirt and ash filled his nose.

"Don't worry about the smell," Turner said as if reading his mind. "We cleaned up on the service levels. It is only on the floors your buddy leveled that have that putrid odor."

"My buddy?"

"The mechanic. You know, the one who owns the lot. He leveled the place before building the car wash," Turner said matter-of-factly. Either he didn't know about Roger's death or didn't care. Either way, Michael didn't want to get into it with a man twice his size. He may have over twenty years on him, but he would still be a challenge.

Sure enough, after a couple of flights, the smell was gone, and the rusted iron was replaced by gleaming metal. They reached the next floor, Turner typed in another code, and they entered an office space. This area was in pristine condition. As the door shut behind them, Turner pointed to the light that was glowing from the only occupied office. Michael could hear voices coming from the room. Both were familiar to him—one very familiar.

"Dad?" Michael called when they came close enough.

"Yeah, son. I'm here," Jacob answered. "Relax. Be patient and cooperate. We'll be fine."

Michael entered the office and blinked to adjust his eyes to the bright lights. When his eyes adjusted, he wished they hadn't. He fell to his father's side and looked over his wounds, "What happened to you?"

"I'm fine. Don't worry about me," Jacob said.

Michael's face turned to Edwards, eyes burning.

"What have you done to him?"

"Nothing that won't heal."

Michael's eyes widened. *If Dad looks this way—*

"Where is Rachel? If you—"

"Relax! Why must I explain this to everyone over and over again? Your wife is unharmed. Not a scratch on her. Not even a broken nail since coming here."

"That is a load of crap, and you know it. She had bruises on her face when she appeared in court. Her attorney testified to that!"

"A simple mistake. I apologized, and we have been friends ever since."

"If she has one hair out of place..." Michael didn't raise his voice, but he got his point across. If Edwards was impressed, he didn't show it.

"Citizen, remember your place—and where you are," Edwards said, standing.

Jacob grabbed Michael's arm and pulled him down into a chair. "Not worth it, son. Definitely not worth it. Think of Rachel. Think of the kids. Let this play out; we're going to be fine."

Michael looked to his father, then Edwards, then back to Turner and Granger. Turner had his hand on his baton. He blew out a breath then turned his attention to Edwards. "I am sorry, Official. I lost my head for a moment. I'm afraid my wife's situation has been... stressful."

"That's better."

Edwards turned his attention to his deputies and said," That will be all, gentlemen. You may leave. I don't believe either of our guests will give me any more trouble."

Granger and Turner nodded and left the office.

"Now," Edwards said with a wicked grin, "we can talk about the matter at hand."

"And what is that?" Jacob said.

"Oh, that is between me and your son now, Jacob. You don't mind me calling you Jacob, as last names right now would be superfluous and confusing."

"Call me what you will. But leave my family out of this. It's me you have your beef with."

"On the contrary," Edwards said, standing. "Family is what *all* of this is about. You murdered my family—so, let's say, tit-for-tat, even-steven, quid pro quo. You owe me. Should it matter whose life is exchanged for the life that was taken from me?"

"Edwards… Sorry, Official Edwards, that was a long time ago," Michael said. "I was two."

"Should life have a time stamp, Michael?" Edwards said. He took a breath, sat on the corner of his desk, and leaned over. "If you are so concerned about age, perhaps I should bring one of your twins in here?"

"You know I would give my life for theirs," Michael said.

"Good. Then it's settled." Edwards slapped his knees and began to pace again. He walked around to his desk and sat. He opened his drawer, pulled out a leather holster that held a silver pistol, and placed it on the desk.

Michael saw Jacob swallow hard at the sight of it.

"I can see you recognize this, Citizen," Edwards said. "This gun has only been fired twice. I usually keep it in a case in my home as a homage to my uncle. A reminder of that day he was murdered."

"What is that, Dad?" Michael asked.

"It's the pistol Nathan Edwards used to murder Eric Lassiter, son."

"Wrong!" Edwards said, "He used it to defend himself against an unruly prisoner."

"Who told you that bunk?"

"Eyewitness accounts," Edwards said.

"Interesting," Jacob said. "The only people in that cell were me, Eric, and your uncle. Jesse wasn't there. He came in after the shot. He came in *because* of that shot."

"Doesn't matter. Accounts exist, and I know about them. Anderson and Turner were deputies for my uncle that day. They know what happened. And an Official's testimony is above reproach."

"How did they avoid prison? From what I remember, they were responsible for the fire up in New Braunfels."

"Always placing blame where it isn't warranted, Citizen. That evidence was inconclusive. They were released, as they should've been, and were transferred to Orlando. I recalled them because I needed someone familiar with the facility to manage this situation better.

"Regardless, we are here now, and so is my uncle's pistol. Amazing how high of a temperature in which silver can survive. They found it under the desk. Everything here was willed to my father, and he willed it to me. I never understood how important it was to my uncle until I read their correspondence. They sent so many emails back and forth. They talked a great deal about this place and his struggle with the audacity of one Eric Lassiter and a short-term prisoner named Jacob Andrews. His final correspondence was about him expecting to receive a special order. This gun. Now I own it."

"And you plan to use it to murder two more civilians," Michael stated.

"Murder? No, I wouldn't go that far. But one of you gets to die. Call it a *sacrifice*. You Christians should understand sacrifice. Isn't it a tenet of your cult? C'mon, Pastor. Isn't that what you call yourself, Jacob? You teach your parishioners to sacrifice their lives as their beloved Jesus did. *Heh,* rubbish."

"It's not quite like that, Official. Yes, follow Christ who led a sacrificial life, but *living* a sacrificial life has little to do with *dying*."

"You Christians are such hypocrites."

"On the contrary. Living a sacrificial life involves putting another's needs and comfort above your own. The Bible teaches us that when we share in sufferings, we will share in the comfort He gives us. It can, in some cases, involve death, but that's not the norm. Yet, if it does come to that, as it did in our Savior's case, a Christian will be rewarded because of their sacrifice."

"How many actually follow through with that, though?" Edwards challenged.

Jacob sighed. "I couldn't tell you. I don't know many who have been faced with that extreme."

"Again, hypocrites," Edwards snickered. "The lot of you."

"I know of one," Michael spoke up.

"I wasn't talking to you," Edwards snapped.

"You wanted an example? I can give you one." Michael stood and placed his hand on his father's shoulder. "He's in this room. My father. He stood up for the faith and to your uncle. I've heard the story. He stood up with a gun pointed at him. A bullet was shot past his head, yet he still stood his ground for Christ.

"He stood his ground when your uncle threatened him with violence, and the only thing that coward, your uncle, could do was shoot an unarmed man to death. So if you won't accept my father as an example of a hero of the faith, Eric Lassiter, the man your uncle shot, was."

"Sit your ass down, Citizen, and hold your tongue," Edwards said, pointing the revolver barrel at Michael.

Michael complied.

"If *he* is the hero," Edwards pointed the barrel at Jacob, "how do you feel about dear ol' dad being the one to die for you? Just like your example, Christ?" He exchanged glances between the two of them. "Wait a minute. I'm sorry. I have it mixed up, don't I? The *father* sent the *son* to die, am I right?" Edwards switched his aim to Michael—and grinned.

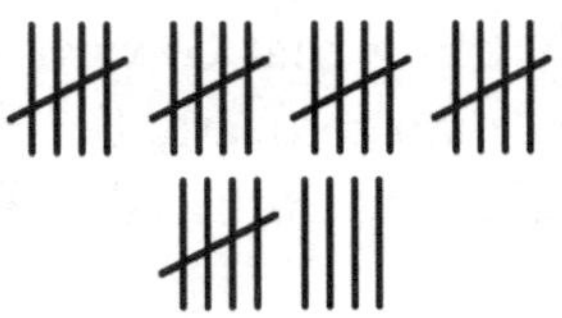

"Tell me something."

The voice startled Rachel from her daze. She looked up to the window and saw a dark figure through the cell opening.

"What is that?" She didn't know what to expect. *Another test?*

"Why are you in here?" the figure asked.

"What kind of question is that? Aren't you my captor? Aren't you an Official who is supposed to know these things?"

"No, I'm a deputy. Deputy Granger." Granger unlocked the door and entered the cell. He knelt beside her. "Don't worry. I'm not going to hurt you. I am new here. I was just told to guard this place. I don't even know what this is. It isn't like any facility I've ever seen. Doesn't even look sanctioned. So I have questions. But I cannot ask an Official. I know better than that. The man who was in the next cell, they worked him over pretty good. That also appears to be unsanctioned. We don't harm citizens. Do you know him?"

Rachel wasn't sure how to answer. *Is this a test?* Being her only hope, she had to take a chance, "Yes. He is my father-in-law."

"It seems he and the Official have a history."

"I've only spoken to Kendrick Edwards a couple of times, but I believe he's a relative of the Official who arrested my father-in-law more than twenty years ago. And you are not far off about

210

this place; it was an unsanctioned prison he used. To make a long story short, the first Official Edwards was after another man, a pastor, and my father-in-law got in the way. In the middle of it, the original Edwards was killed. Now *our* Official Edwards blames my father-in-law for his uncle's death and is using me to get back at our family."

"I see," Granger said. "But why you?"

"I don't know. Perhaps he's trying to hurt him through his grand-kids and son."

"Son?"

"Yeah? Why? What?" She could see the panic on Granger's face.

"Oh, no," Granger said. He looked back toward the door.

"Tell me."

"Your husband is here. He is with Official Edwards and your father-in-law right now."

"He's here? I told him to stay away."

"Well he's upstairs," Granger said. "When I left, they were all in the office, and Edwards had a gun on both of them."

"What?!?"

"He wouldn't shoot two unarmed men. A man in his position would have too much to lose, and he's not psychotic."

"Isn't he? Look around you, Deputy."

Deputy Granger took in his surroundings and then looked at Rachel. It must've hit him that they were in a damp basement cell that only a handful of people knew about, not a federal prison cell. "You okay?"

Rachel nodded.

"I'm coming back for you. I will get this straightened out. He shouldn't have you down here. I will go over his head and take it up to Austin or D.C. if I have to. Just sit tight, okay?"

Rachel half grinned. "Okay," she said softly.

Granger stood and exited the cell, locking the door behind him. "Don't worry, Mrs. Andrews. We will get this straightened out soon." The light reentered through the window, and Rachel laid back down, a bit of hope returned, but she wasn't willing to giving into it just yet. Johnathan had said not to give up hope. But he said that before, and then the lights went out, and she ended up in this room. She had learned not to give in to hope so easily.

✝✝✝

Deputy Granger felt he was in a unique position. He had never disobeyed a direct order before; he never needed to. Every Official he had served under was reputable and acted in accordance with the law. He had never witnessed one on a personal vendetta. He felt from the get-go that something was off about this assignment. At first, he wondered if it was a training op where he had to act, no questions asked. He had faced those before. One question, and you were reprimanded. He didn't need that at this point in his career. So, *act and don't ask.*

But wasn't a training exercise. This was real and innocents were in harm's way. The game had changed. The whole reason he was doing what he was doing was being tarnished. Even if this Official carried heavy brass, his conscience could not bear the weight of harming those he was supposed to protect. Now was the time to act. He just needed a plan.

It was his understanding that the two other deputies on the case were former residents and were brought on because of their familiarity with this facility. That meant they could not be trusted. He was alone. He didn't know anyone connected to the men in the room. But what about the lady, Mrs. Andrews? It was her husband and father-in-law up there. She surely knew someone.

Granger raced back down the stairs and to the window. "Mrs. Andrews. Is there anyone I can contact on the outside who could get a message to someone of value?"

"What good would that do?"

"Calling the cavalry, I suppose. Do you have your attorney's number?"

"I don't know it by heart."

"Family?"

"My grandfather."

"Give me his number. I'll contact him. Let him know you are alright and of our situation. Maybe he can contact someone with some clout."

Rachel gave him the number. "I don't know how he can help. All he knows is a few retired cops. And if they were to call around, they would get the run-around, especially on the whims of an old man who has been calling them the last two weeks seeing phantom SUVs."

"It's still worth a try. He's our only hope. Maybe he can reach your attorney. I will leave that in my message."

"Message?"

"Yes, I'm not going to attempt to call. I can't risk being pulled into a lengthy conversation and being overheard. I will text him."

"I understand. Thank you, Deputy, for helping us."

"The name's Eric."

"We know that name well," Rachel said, standing and walking to the window.

"Jacob reacted to that name as well. I don't understand."

"It was my parents' pastor's name. The one who sacrificed himself for them."

"Understood. If I get caught doing this, you may have another Eric to add to that list."

"You will be fine, Eric. Thank you," Rachel said, putting her hand up to the window. Eric put his hand up to hers.

"God bless," he said.

"You as well."

Deputy Eric Granger turned and headed back through the hallway and up the stairs. He stopped at the end of the landing and, pulling out his phone, entered the number he had been given and typed a message.

```
Mr.  Dunham.  Jacob,  Michael,  and
Rachel are okay. Need assistance. Spik
```

and Span car wash. Passcode: 032775.
Please hurry.

He hit send, and once he was confident it was sent, he deleted the conversation and muted his phone. He took a breath and headed upstairs in a slow, official manner as if it were routine.

"Where have you been?" Turner asked when Granger reached the landing. He was sitting at a desk scribbling on his paperwork. "We need to ensure these documents are official looking enough to make this operation legitimate."

"I heard some screaming down there. I had to go shut the lady up. If you know what I mean."

Anderson grabbed his arm. "Just as long as you didn't lay a hand on her. You know the rules."

"Get your hand off me," Granger said, shaking his arm free. "I wrote half of those rules, you fool." He didn't, but it sounded good, and it would at least keep the guy from messing with him again.

Granger paced the room and looked toward the stairs. "He still up with them?"

"What's it to you?" Turner asked.

"It's my job to know, and I can't do my job if I am out of the loop. I may be the youngest deputy here, but he has known me the longest. You two are only here because you know the facility. So if things go sideways, who do you think he will he believe when he asks for an explanation?"

Turner was silent for a moment, then with a calm voice, "They are upstairs in the office. Situation unchanged."

"Thank you, sir. I appreciate your assistance," Granger exhaled and headed toward the stairs.

"They don't want—" Turner started.

Granger turned to him with a stern eye. No words were needed.

"Never mind. It's your funeral," Turner returned to his paperwork.

Granger headed up the stairs. *Maybe more than you know, Turner.*

The next-floor landing was cold and dark. It had been lit up on his last visit. There was a switch on the wall, but he dared not turn it on and alert anyone to his presence. A stealth approach was better, but what was he hiding? No one could've known what he had done or what he was up to. Perhaps a direct approach was the better choice. It could get him closer to his target. However, Official Edwards was acting irrationally. Who knew what would happen if just walked through the door? The only other entrance was the opposite door, accessible through another stairwell on the far side of the facility. He didn't know if he had that much time.

Granger sidled against the wall and slowly peered through the door's window. The room was dark except for Edwards' office at the end of the room. With the lack of office furniture, he wondered if the key panel's touch tones would be loud enough to be heard in the office. If they were, his stealth approach would be off the playlist. He figured that would determine his game plan. If Edwards heard the keypad, he would behave as if he were supposed to be there and make an excuse for his appearance.

He stared at the keypad, for a moment, his mind was blank. He couldn't remember the combination. Granger sat back, took a deep breath, and reminded himself he was here to do a job. *Protect and serve.* He closed his eyes and saw the keypad in his mind; he saw his fingers hitting it. *032775. That's it.* He released his breath and peeked through the window with each key press and soft beep it gave. More likely, the tone was for him, but with the empty office, the echo could have sounded like a rock concert. But there was no reaction from the office. Even when the door gave its familiar click that it was safe to enter, no head peeked out of the halogen-lit room.

Granger turned the handle and slowly pulled on the door, careful not to give the door a chance to bellow a creak or moan. When there was just enough room for his built body to shimmy its way through the opening, he grabbed the handle on the opposite side and repeated the process. When the door shut, it gave the loudest *click* imaginable. His heart pounded, and he soft rolled into a nearby cubicle, not even looking to see if the tone drew a reaction.

He thought he could hear the trotting of footsteps on carpet, but it was only the thumping of his heart in his chest—*Safe so far*. He had to kick himself. All that backwoods shooting and sniper fire training, and a simple door shutting had sent him diving for cover.

Now, on his hands and knees, he peered around the corner. The room had not changed. He figured if someone had been alerted to his presence, the room would've lit up.

Getting from where he was to the office was a matter of taking a position and advancing in short hops. This part was easy because he was out of view. As long as he stayed quiet, he could remain hidden. The only issue was the lack of cover. The room was relatively empty, and just a few locations were beneficial for advancement. He mentally made his moves and counter moves until he would be at the cubicle twenty feet from the office. Once satisfied, he sat back silent and listened.

He did not hear any movement or voices nor see any activity through the doorway. He was clear. The deputy low crawled to his first cover location and waited.

Still no voices.

He began to wonder if they were even in the room. *What if they had left the premises?* He thought. He waited a moment longer with his eyes closed, listening. Then came what sounded like a throat clearing in the distance. *Bingo!*

The Deputy looked to the next cover and made his way to it. Then to the next with no issues. His final location would be the most difficult to reach. It would take him almost to the door to Edwards office. In his current position, he could hear mumbling but could make out few words. Something about *'placing blame where it is warranted'* and *'emails from his uncle.'*

He knew he heard, *"Murder two more civilians"* and *"one of you gets to die."* Granger leaned up from where he was, but he still couldn't see into the room. *Does Edwards have a weapon? They did say murder.* It was one thing that he hated about his job. Deputies only carried batons. No service weapons. It wasn't warranted as their position carried the weight needed. Their presence was their weapon. Most often, their size and club instilled fear. That kept law and order. But Edwards had stepped over the line, and he needed to do something about it. Those he swore to protect and serve depended on it.

He heard someone, the younger one, he believed, Michael, Rachel's husband, *say, "So, if my father was not a hero of the faith, the man your uncle shot, Eric Lassiter, was."*

He remembered the stories of Eric Lassiter. The laws on the books were now created because of Eric Lassiter. And an Official named Nathan Edwards. *Was it because of what happened here?* He looked around and suddenly felt ill. It hit him; he was in the place where it all happened.

"Wait a minute. We have it mixed up, don't we...."

Granger took a breath and stood. He had no weapon other than the baton at his side. It was no match for a revolver, but he had to do something.

"… The father sent the son to die, am I right?"

Granger stepped into the room. "I don't think that would be wise, sir."

"Just what do you think you are doing interrupting my interrogation, deputy?"

"Interrogation? Looks more like a double homicide to me, with all due respect."

"Well, your interpretation of the situation is inaccurate, son. Now turn your ass around and get out of here. Pretend you were never here, or you will be reprimanded so hard you will be lucky to get a security job at the community college. You got me?"

"I'm not sure you understand, Official Edwards. My job is to protect your image. And you are in danger of tarnishing that image at this moment," Granger hoped to appeal to his ego.

"My image is above approach, Deputy. I appreciate your concern. Now, get out."

Granger took a deep breath. Insubordination was not in his blood. He looked to the two men and back to Edwards, holding the silver pistol in his grip. "With all due respect, sir. I cannot do that."

"Oh, hell," Edwards said. He raised the weapon and fired it into Granger's chest. Granger fell to the ground and didn't move.

"Now, see what you made me do?" Edwards said, waving his weapon. "This is on your heads." Edwards began to pace the room, "What is it with you Andrews clan? What mojo do you have over our Deputies that you turn them against me? There would be far less bloodshed if you just left it all alone. Well, this one didn't get quite as far." Edwards grinned. "This proves that I am the smartest of the family. I even outwitted my uncle. Now, where were we before we were so rudely interrupted, gentlemen?"

Jacob and Michael didn't say a word. Jacob reached out, and Michael accepted his hand.

Edwards looked at the pistol in his hand. "Of course—we were discussing which of you is going to die." Edwards paced the room, walking behind them towards the office door. He looked down at Granger's body.

"You know, it's sad. I kinda liked the kid. It also makes me think. With this new puzzle piece. I can't have any witnesses. So, the question now becomes which of you I trust to not sing like a canary once I release you. Who do I trust more? The old man with a church he wants to keep hidden from the authorities, or the young fool with two kids he would give his life to protect?" Edwards laughed to himself. "Decisions, decisions."

"And it is a decision you will not have to make." Boomed a voice through the darkened room, "Now drop the weapon, Official. That's an order."

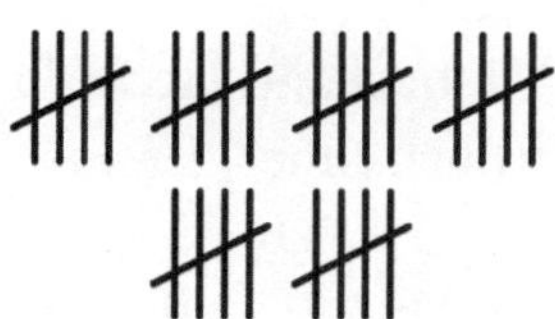

Official Edwards spun around, weapon in hand, waving it at air.

"Don't think that's a good idea, Official," the voice barked. "Drop it—final warning. You have three weapons trained on you, Edwards. Expert marksmen, and they do not miss. Take two steps back, set the weapon on the desk, raise your hands above your head, and interlock your fingers, and an officer will come to you. Make the slightest move toward the weapon, and Joe here will put a bullet in your head. If you cough, sneeze, scratch your head, or even pick your nose, you'll have another hole in you to worry about. Understood, Official Edwards?"

Edwards did not answer, but he did move. With fear in his eyes, he complied with the orders given him.

"Very good. Now, remain still as my officer approaches you. His name is Daniels. He will inform you of your rights and take you into custody. This is for everyone's safety. We will straighten all of this out in a more appropriate facility. Is that understood?"

Edwards again did not answer. He slowly turned as Daniels approached him. The tall, thin officer holstered his weapon when he was close enough.

The voice said to Jacob and Michael, "You two, alright?"

"Yes, sir," Jacob answered.

"You?" the voice addressed Michael.

"Yeah, I'm okay."

"We will get you out of here as soon as we clear the scene. Shouldn't be long now."

Daniels took Edwards' arm and cuffed it. Not fighting, Edwards lowered his other arm, allowing Daniels to cuff him. "Please come with me, Official Edwards."

Edwards looked at Michael and Jacob. "This isn't over. You two cannot get away with your crimes. I am a Federal Official. I am *above reproach*."

"You killed a man in cold blood," Michael said. "We will see how that holds with your above reproach."

"*Heh*. His blood is on your hands. Two words and all of this is accounted to your transgressions. My actions here will be rewarded as the defense of a fellow serviceman. Your days are numbered, Citizens." Edwards began to laugh as he was escorted out of the office.

Another officer entered the office and examined the room. "All clear." he called back to the darkened room, which lit up seconds later. "Medics are on their way down. Sit tight, gentlemen."

"We will need three," Jacob said.

"What?!" the officer and Michael said in unison.

"You okay, Granger?"

Granger moaned for a minute, then rolled over and coughed, "You have no idea how long I've been holding that in. And I'm about as good as I can be for getting shot point-blank into a vest. So, yeah, I will take that medic now."

"How did you know, Dad?"

"How could you not?"

Michael shrugged.

"Blood, son." Jacob pointed to the floor. "I can't believe that even Edwards missed it. There was no blood when Edwards shot him. When he still didn't move, I figured he was either unconscious or waiting for the right time to make his move."

"I'm glad someone noticed. Would've needed the help when I finally advance my position."

"You were covered, deputy."

"So, why did you help us?"

"I met your wife downstairs. She explained everything, and it upset me. I am an upstanding deputy. That lowlife brought tarnish to the badge, and I needed to act to protect all of you, even if it meant my life. You, your wife—"

"Rachel!" Michael said. "Where is she?"

"Downstairs," Granger said. He rubbed his chest and stood. "Follow me."

Granger led the two Andrews men down the two flights of stairs to the lower floor. He entered his code, and the door screeched as he pushed it open.

"Rachel!?" Michael called to the cell doors.

"Michael? Rachel answered, surprise in her voice.

"Yes, it's me. I'm here."

Granger turned the key. The door *clicked* and *clanked*, and he pulled the door open; Michael forced past Granger. He apologized as he nearly pushed him over.

Michael took his wife in his arms, and she fell into his embrace. They melted into each other, forgot about where they were, forgot about time, and just enjoyed the moment of being reunited. He kissed her, and she kissed him. She really kissed him. He remembered how much he loved her and how much he had neglected their passion; he vowed never to let it go that far again. Their embrace broke, and she looked into his eyes and smiled.

He smiled back, "So, did you remember to pick up trash bags?"

Epilogue

Six Months Later

"When do you leave, Dad?" Michael asked.

"A little after we eat," Jacob said. "My meeting with the DA is at one-thirty."

"Are you sure you don't want me to go with you? They say support is always best in numbers."

"I'm fine, son. You need to be here with your family. If things go south up there, I will need your help to continue what we've started here. You know what to do, right?

"Yes. Keep the gym open at whatever cost. But make the adjustments we talked about." Michael swallowed his coffee—a beverage he had grown to enjoy every morning now. He wouldn't have been caught dead even sipping it a year ago. "I'm just not sure I can do this."

"Of course, you can. It's what we have been training you to do for the past few months. You are out of danger now. You saw the news. Edwards was indicted and will be held accountable for his crimes. He lost his position and is in federal prison as we speak. As far as we know, no more little Edwards are running around to come back to haunt us. We are free now."

"Free," Michael snickered.

"You know what I mean," Jacob said.

"Everything could change after your hearing, Dad." Michael sighed. "I don't see why you can't just give them what they are asking for?"

"I cannot give them my sermons *before* they are preached, Michael. That would give them control over everything I say from the pulpit. They could easily redact anything or worse, give me words to say. Nuh-uh. I'm sorry. I just can't do that."

"What about—"

"Michael, we've had this conversation. I won't give a false sermon. That is lying."

Michael sighed. He knew his father was right. He had learned firsthand that his father would stick to his guns and that God would honor his faith through that. His recent experience taught him that. His wife had shown him how faith can get you through anything, and learning about his father's past revealed to him who he was and that he was here because of a stand his father had taken more than twenty years before and had retaken just six months ago.

"So, are we good?" Jacob asked.

"Yeah, we're good," Michael said. He raised his coffee cup. His father met it.

"Will the munchkins be up soon?"

Michael looked at the clock. It told him he should be hearing the pattering of footsteps any moment.

"I hope so. They've been asking for you."

"I would like to get a hug before I head out," Jacob smiled. He looked up to the ceiling, willing them awake.

As if they felt his pleas, two pairs of feet could be heard thumping around and heading for the stairwell.

"Grandpa!" They called in unison, as he saw them entering the kitchen.

Jacob pushed his chair back and held out his arms, "Come here, you two." He pulled them into a hug. Holding on longer than usual. "I'm heading out of town. I'll be back later. I will miss you."

"Aww, you can't stay?" Aiden said.

"No, buddy. I can't. Not today."

He hugged Angela again. "I'll see you two next time. Okay, Princess?"

"Okay, Grandpa," Angela said.

Michael looked his father in the eye as he stood; he was on the verge of tears. He knew something they didn't. When the kids headed back upstairs to get dressed, he addressed the issue.

"What aren't you telling me?"

"Nothing. Everything's fine," Jacob said.

"Then what's with the tears," Michael said. He put his hand on his dad's shoulder. "You can talk to me about anything."

"I know. And I would if there was anything to tell. It's just been a crazy year, and seeing you and the kids where I have always prayed you would be gets me. That's all."

Michael nodded. He didn't believe him but accepted his explanation. "I love you, Dad."

"Love you too, son."

Michael walked him to the door and watched him climb into his car. Rachel sidled up to him and they waved as Jacob pulled away..

"Everything okay, love?"

"I don't know. Dad just seems off. He hugged the kids as if he would never see them again."

"What are you thinking?"

"I don't know. But I really think I should go up to Austin with him."

"Then why don't you?"

"He said he was fine. He said he has parishioners up there for support."

"And you left it at that?"

Michael shrugged.

"After all that you two have been through the last year, you're letting him leave alone?"

"You and the kids need me here."

"*Hah*. We can handle it. There is no one here to bother us. We can't be afraid of what happened anymore. The judge dismissed the case with prejudice. It's over, Michael. We are free."

"I know. But I am wondering what Dad is so afraid of," Michael said, nodding toward the empty driveway.

"Maybe you should follow him and find out."

"Maybe I will."

Acknowledgements

First about the novel. I had always thought *The Five Barred Gate* would be stand-alone. But as time moved on, I felt led that Jacob's story was not complete. I had toyed with ideas and even spent some time freewriting a story about his son who was two years old at the time of the incident. I thought about what life would be like for him as a grown-up. Then realizing that the world could've only gotten worse, because that is just how life is. So, I sat on the idea. But then the writing bug hit me, and a few ideas and news headlines hit me. Then the words flowed.

I want to thank the *Five Barred Gate* fans who once I mentioned the thought of a sequel, encouraged me to keep going. You were excited about it, and it fueled this writer's flame. I can't wait to hear what you think.

Thank you, Mike Parker, for allowing me the chance to delve back into this world and publish again for Wordcrafts Press. You have been a blessing to me throughout my career and I pray for its success for the both of us.

Thanks to all the Writing Community and followers on Twitter (X) who continue to push me on when I am empty. Words of encouragement are appreciated, and I continue to pray for your success as well.

I again want to thank Pastor Duane Mayberry of First Baptist Church Charlotte. While Jacob Andrews does not preach much in this novel, his tenacity continues, and I still pull from what I pick up from what I learned in the first book and what I see in one of my mentors. God bless you, Pastor.

And what would a book be if I did not thank the woman who is my life and my inspiration? This past year we celebrated our 25th wedding anniversary. By the time this book hits shelves, it will be 26. Again, you are amazing. Thank you for allowing me and pushing me to pursue the dream and calling God has given me. Here's to the next 25!

Finally, thank you again, dear reader. I pray you enjoy this installment. Yes, Lord willing, there should be a third, you will see what I mean. I should have that written by the time you read this. We will see what time has in store for Jacob, Michael, and our newest characters.

In His Exciting Service,
Jeff S. Bray

About the Author

Jeff S. Bray lives with his wife, Carolyn, and the last of their five children who has yet to fly from the nest, in a small town in South Central Texas.

His professional writing adventure began in 2008 with the launch of his personal blog "Moments for the Heart," which led to paid writing assignments, including an article about fatherhood for *The Lookout* magazine in 2017. That opened the door to larger writing gigs and then to regular freelance work. In 2018, he began writing a series of Children's books titled *Elissa the Curious Snail*.

Jeff also writes adult novels in a variety of genres, but always with a strong faith element. He has an immense passion to serve Christ and prays his words touch hearts and lives and give people hope and the desire to pursue their own relationship with our loving Savior.

Connect with Jeff online at:

jeffsbrayauthor.com